TUNGEE'S GOLD

TUNGEE'S GOLD

THE LEGEND OF EBO LANDING

TOM BARNES

iUniverse, Inc.
New York   Bloomington

Tungee's Gold
The Legend of Ebo Landing

iUniverse books may be ordered through booksellers or by contacting:

iUniverse
1663 Liberty Drive
Bloomington, IN 47403
www.iuniverse.com
1-800-Authors (1-800-288-4677)

ISBN: 978-1-4401-9646-1 (pbk)
ISBN: 978-1-4401-9648-5 (cloth)
ISBN: 978-1-4401-9647-8 (ebook)

Printed in the United States of America

iUniverse rev. date: 1/4/10

— ACKNOWLEDGMENTS —

The following people, places, museums and libraries were of tremendous help to me during my research and writing:

Ship's of the Sea Museum, Savannah, Georgia.

Saint Simons Island, Georgia and the people that led me to the small reed covered cove where the legend had its beginning.

The Carnegie Library in Atlanta, Georgia and its staff for digging out the best material on Clipper Ships and their sailing characteristics.

The County of Los Angeles Library System and the Los Angeles Public Library staff for their help in the California Gold Rush era .

Ellen Roberts (Where Books Begin) editor for your story and editorial skills.

Patty Foltz at Way2Kool Designs for the book cover design.

— ONE —

Late August 1851
Road between Marysville and San Francisco

The Cahill brothers broke camp early and were on the road at sunrise. Tungee sat on the left side of the two-horse rig with Davy to his right as he clucked to Dolly and Big Sam to pick up the pace.

Young Davy was in a foul mood and mumbled something under his breath.

"What are you grousing about, Davy?" Tungee quipped.

"I said you never forgave him."

Knowing full well what was coming, "Forgave who?"

"Papa," Davy said adamantly.

Tungee looked at his brother. "It's not the point of forgiving Papa. I forgave him, but I'll never forget what he did to Mama."

"Shit, T you always did put Mama up on a pedestal,"

Davy remembered their old man as a hero who fought on the side of the Creek Indians and was killed for his efforts. Tungee didn't discount his father's hero status, but he found it impossible to forgive his hard drinking and whoring around. But after a long moment of reflection Tungee rubbed his beard and said, "Aw, hell, Davy you never saw Papa up close like I did. You never had to go down and haul him out of a saloon or a whorehouse dead drunk and then have to drag him back home and explain to Mama."

Davy stared straight ahead and said innocently, "I didn't know that, T."

"Bullshit, Davy, you just don't want to admit it."

And that's the way it always was. Davy would retreat into a kind of sullen silence never admitting any of Papa's faults. But on the other hand Tungee reasoned, maybe I've been too tough on our old man. He held a firm grip on the reins and scanned the area, fully aware of the dry season. The landscape was a light bleached tan and only a few sparse grasses, some brush and a scrub oak here and there had managed to survive the summer sun.

Davy was silent for more than an hour before he came alive, stretched and yawned. He glanced at Tungee and enthused, "Be good to get back to Belle Mundy's place." Then he giggled. "Them whores in Sacramento and Marysville are the pits."

"Good God, Davy. Is that the way you plan to spend the rest of your life, jumping from one whore to another and judging their performance?"

"I don't know, but I do know this," Davy said with a serious tone," I never found a woman yet I wanted to spend the rest of my life with."

"The chances are you've been looking in the wrong places. If you ever expect to find someone to marry, you probably ought to look somewhere outside of a whorehouse."

"Oh, I don't know. I hear Belle Mundy was the mistress to a prince."

"What the hell has that got to do with anything."

Davy cocked his head and grinned. "It means she's got good taste."

Tungee looked at his brother disgustedly and flicked the reins. "Come on, Dolly. Let's go, Big Sam."

An hour later the team slowed and the wagon creaked and groaned as they dipped down into the dry wash.

"Look out, Tungee!" Davy yelled.

All Hell broke loose. A half dozen men jumped out of the brush firing weapons and screaming like banshees. Tungee's stomach leapt into his throat as he popped the reins and bellowed at the team. Davy got off a shot at the man lunging for Dolly's bridle and hit his mark. Blood gushed from the bandit's head as his body bounced off the side of the wagon and dropped into the dry riverbed. The team responded to Tungee's signal and bolted out of the gulch so fast that the bushwhackers lost their chance for an ambush.

Dolly and Big Sam may have run the fastest mile of their lives. And it was not until they began to tire and slow to a middling pace that Tungee looked around for his brother and realized Davy had fallen over the seat and was laid out on the goods in the back of the wagon. Tungee turned and called, "Davy!" Then he squinted back along the road and could clearly see the bushwhackers flailing their arms and shaking their fists. He determined from their actions that they had no saddle horses.

He called to his brother a half dozen times but got no answer. Finally Tungee pulled the team up, jumped over the seat, kneeled down and shook Davy. But there was no response. He lifted him out of the wagon and laid him in the dry grass beside the road. Tungee felt Davy's wrist and neck, searching for a pulse, but couldn't find any. Then he saw a blood stain on his brother's vest. And when he pealed the leather back he could see a clean bullet hole in the left side of his chest. Not conceding the worst, he dug among their belongings and found a bottle of whiskey took the cork out and poured some of the liquor over Davy's lips, but he still felt no pulse.

Tungee finally sat down beside the body and crossed his legs. He stayed in that position for several minutes numbed by the experience and rejecting the reality of the moment. He repeated his efforts, trying to revive his brother, but nothing worked and he had to face a fact. Davy was dead. He took a long moment and then gently lifted his brother's body into the wagon and covered it with a blanket. Then he stepped forward and put his boot on the hub of the wheel and was about to haul his body into the seat when he became weak and could hardly breathe, as he felt overwhelmed by a kind of suffocating silence. There wasn't a whisper of a breeze and the horses stood like statues, not moving a muscle.

Tungee eventually began to breathe heavily as he looked back along the road. The bandits could be following on foot. The thought brought his body to life and he jumped into the seat and flicked the reins. The team pressed into their harness and with the squeak of leather and grinding wheels, they moved out in a westerly direction along the road to San Francisco.

Tungee sat watching the high scudding clouds as a knot formed in the pit of his stomach and suddenly he was overcome by a sense of guilt. Had it been his fault? Davy wanted to leave the mine back in the spring to get some rest. But I had stubbornly insisted that we go ahead and work that rich vein at Lost Mountain until November and celebrate Thanksgiving in San Francisco. We had spent a hard year and a half in the California gold fields and Davy said we had earned a rest. And he was probably right, but I didn't think so at the time. I badgered and cajoled him along until August. Then suddenly one morning, he threw down his pick and declared, 'Dammit, T I quit. I'm dog-tired.' Well, I couldn't come up with a good argument so I agreed with him and we went to work securing our gold. Not many folks trusted the local banks, so we took two large stashes into the mountains and buried them. Then back at the mine we sealed off the rich vein, covered the entrance, blended it into the terrain and headed back to civilization.

The team kept up a quick pace for the rest of the afternoon and they made good time except for a water stop. While the horses drank from the stream, Tungee filled two canteens and topped off the water barrel that hung on the side of the wagon.

The sun was just nesting on the horizon when he spotted a grove of trees and veered off the road in their direction. The horses pulled themselves up as the dry limbs and leaves at the edge of the grove began to crackle beneath their hooves.

He jumped down from his seat and took a few minutes surveying the area. Then he grabbed Dolly's bridle and led the team into the dull shadows beneath the tree limbs. After removing their harness and gear he picketed them on a patch of grass where they immediately began their evening feed.

His mind was on security and the possibility that the road bandits might follow on foot. So he took out his long knife, cut a branch off a scrub oak and used it as a rake-broom to scratch out the wagon tracks between the road and the wood.

Once he got back to the wagon he retrieved extra weapons and loaded them. Then he spotted each one in a different location. Not wise to make a fire, he thought, so he dug amongst the provisions and retrieved a piece of dried beef and a hard biscuit.

As he chewed on his meager rations he walked the grounds and worked out a strategy in case he was found and attacked before dawn. His hands trembled and he couldn't seem to shake off that feeling of guilt that began to overshadow reason. Was it his fault? Was he somehow responsible for the ambush and Davy's death?

He finally settled down on a large mossy area and took the best part of an hour sorting things out. He tossed and turned on his forest bed as night sounds became prominent and apprehension began to distort reason. The crack of a limb, the sound of a cricket, or the hoot of an owl would add to his fear. Then as he began to relax a picture of their house on the hill came to mind. That was his boyhood home and it overlooked the waters of the Ocmulgee River in Central Georgia, Creek Indian country. Papa Cahill was Scots, kilt and all, and Mama Sue a full blood Creek Indian. The schoolyard bullies called him "half-breed." Those hateful words and taunting slurs caused most of his boyhood fights. Looking back, he knew that many of those encounters could have been avoided had he chosen to use his first name, Robert, rather than Tungee. But that was not his way. He was proud of his Creek name and wore it like a badge out of respect for his mother. And although thoughts of those early years kept intruding on his conscious mind, his tired body finally relaxed and he fell into a deep sleep.

The sun woke him with a start. "Good Lord, I've overslept." He sat up and rubbed his eyes. "Get a move on, Tungee," he muttered. Pick up the weapons and put them aboard the wagon. Then he literally threw the harness on the team. I've got to get cracking. Get to a San Francisco bank before they close for the day and if I'm not in time, figure a place to stash the gold, check into a hotel, take care of Davy's body and find a livery for the horses. Maybe not in that order, but it's all got to be done.

Dolly and Big Sam eagerly responded to his quick actions and pulled the wagon back to the main road. Tungee sat on the high seat holding the reins and began to think about the future without Davy. He pondered the subject, as the sole survivor of our mining interests; will my life be filled with punishment or reward?

They must have been two hundred yards down the road when he

saw the oncoming wagon. He pulled off to the side to let them pass. Another set of bright eyed folks heading out for what they hope will begin their rise to riches.

The man hailed. "Howdy, mister. How was your luck?"

"Like most things, I reckon, some good and some bad."

"There's gold, ain't there?"

"Yep, but it takes time, lots of hard work and a bit of luck won't hurt either."

"About what we expected."

"Stay alert to road bandits," Tungee warned. "And I might add, I'm telling you that from first hand experience ... load your weapons and keep 'em handy."

The man held up his rifle and said, "Thanks, neighbor."

Tungee gave them a high sign as they passed by. Then he clucked the signal for Dolly and Big Sam to move out.

The team might have felt it first, a sudden tinge of excitement in the air. Then as they topped a gentle knoll, Tungee felt a quickening of pace and an added jauntiness in the horses' stride. Perhaps it was imagined, but he believed he smelled the salt air of the Pacific as it came into view. He breathed deeply and gazed toward the distant horizon and looked at the blue-diamond brilliance of the ocean. Enthused by the sight he stood up in the wagon, stretched and scanned the area from Point Bonita past the Golden Gate and San Francisco Bay. Then he slowly shook his head and frowned as he looked down at the grotesque mass of tall ships that cluttered the shoreline. Many of those ships had been run aground and abandoned, left behind as captains and crews joined with dreamers, drifters and prospectors debarking the vessel and making a headlong dash for the gold fields.

— TWO —

Tungee shook the reins and the team picked up the pace as they moved through the outskirts of San Francisco and onto Third Street. They were passing through a sparsely developed area, which showed no damage from the great fires reported back in the spring. Well, he figured the newspapers might have exaggerated their stories and that gave him second thoughts about something else he had read. That had to do with the growth of San Francisco and the article had pointed out that the city was growing like a giant mushroom and was moving in two different directions. One part of the city was attracting commerce and industry and was gaining a certain amount of respectability. But on the other side of San Francisco a roaring boom-town was growing up with a gaudy red light district known as the Barbary Coast.

Tungee glanced up at the sun and automatically took out his pocket watch to confirm the time. Five minutes past four, too late for the banks. Next best thing would be the Wells Fargo freight office on Montgomery Street.

As they neared Third and Market, he tried to recall, now is Montgomery to the right or to the left? He called out to a produce vendor. "Yo there. I'm looking for the Wells Fargo office."

The old gentleman, wearing a derby hat, shouted back. "Take a right here and go on past Geary, now that's a long block, but at the end you'll see where Post and Montgomery come together at Market. When you get that far along look up to your left, you'll see their sign."

"I'm much obliged to you."

When he turned into Market Street and looked off toward Russian Hill, he could see what the papers had reported, one large section of that area had been completely gutted. As they moved along the street he was struck by the bustled of activity and fire or no, it looked to him like the folks of San Francisco just shook off the tragedy and were going about their business.

Old derby hat was right, for just as he turned into Montgomery Street he saw that familiar Wells Fargo sign. He pulled the team up to the front door and jumped down to the ground, stood for a moment and stretched. Then he walked to the back of the wagon and opened the tailgate.

The Wells Fargo freight agent came out and said, "Howdy. Freight?"

"Yep." Then Tungee picked up the first box, walked it into the office and set it down in a corner where the agent was pointing.

The Wells Fargo man held his pencil poised to write and asked, "Where to?"

"Don't know yet, could we just call it overnight storage for now."

The agent hesitated for a moment. "I reckon that'll do."

Tungee nodded and continued carrying the boxes into his corner of the office. When he finished stacking them he gave an affable smile toward the agent. "Would you just give me a receipt for fifteen boxes and we'll get to the particulars in the morning?"

"That'll work for me," the agent said as he picked up a bill and began to write. "What's your name?"

"Tungee. Tungee Cahill," and as he said his name, he was going over in his mind what to say if the question of contents came up... It never did and he didn't volunteer.

The agent finished writing the receipt and handed a copy to his customer.

"See you in the morning," Tungee said as he strode out of the office and boarded the wagon.

The agent came out the front door and called, "Where you stayin' tonight?"

"The Kinsey House, if it's still standing and they have a room."

"It didn't burn, can't say if they've got a room or not."

8

"Thanks," then he shook the reins and the team moved out into traffic. The horses held their heads high as they trotted along Montgomery in the direction of Telegraph Hill.

He pulled the team to a halt in front of the Kinsey House, tied the reins around the hand brake, jumped down and walked quickly into the lobby. The clerk apparently didn't recognize him, but with his normal hotel diplomacy said, "Good afternoon, sir. May I help you?"

"You can if you've got a room."

The clerk turned the register around and said, "We certainly do, sir. Sign here please."

Tungee signed where he was told and then turned it back to the clerk.

"Tungee Cahill? Hum. You've stayed with us before, I believe. I'm sure I should recognize you." He stared and then laughed. "Why it's the beard. You didn't have a beard before."

"Pay it no mind. It gives me a start now and then when I see my reflection."

The clerk chuckled. "They do make a difference."

"I'm in kind of a hurry. If I bring some of my things into the lobby, would you mind getting them up to the room."

"Of course, we'll be glad to take care of it. Good to have you back, Mr. Cahill."

Tungee trekked back and forth to the wagon several times before he got all of his personal belongings, clothing, books and weapons into the lobby. When he finished, he removed several pouches of gold from a saddlebag and put them on the desk. "I'd like to store these in your safe."

The clerk smiled and put the pouches on a small scale, made out a receipt and handed it across the desk along with the door key. "There you are, Mr. Cahill. Your room is number 309."

Tungee said, "Thanks," walked back to the wagon and climbed into his seat. The day was getting away fast so he urged the horses to move out. He turned into Broadway and was making his way toward Battery when he spotted a livery which seemed to be a good location to stable the team and park the wagon. He had no more than turned into the wharf area when he saw a familiar face. Charlie Boone was standing on

9

the dock next to his boat, the Molly B. Charlie, Tungee and Davy had made the rounds, drinking in some of San Francisco's finest as well as some of its raunchiest saloons.

He moved the wagon close to the boat and called out, "Charlie Boone!"

Charlie looked up and slowly scratched his head. Then after a long moment, he said, "Tungee! Tungee Cahill! Gosh, it's been a coon's age."

Tungee jumped down from the seat and grabbed the skipper's hand.

"Where's your brother?" Charlie asked.

Tungee pointed to the wagon and explained the ambush. Then he said sadly, "Davy always wanted to be buried at sea." Then he hesitated. "Now I know this is asking a lot, but could you lend me a hand, Charlie?"

Without hesitation the skipper said, "Let me stoke up the fire, she's just about smoldered down to an ember."

Tungee had no idea what that crusty old charter captain's answer was going to be, but his response sure did make him feel good.

As soon as Charlie got the fire going, he came up to the wagon and they carried Davy's blanket covered body to the boat. After they lowered the body onto the deck Tungee remembered something he needed to do and looked back toward the team. "Charlie, do you mind if I take time to stable the horses?"

"Not at all, it's gonna be a spell before I can build up a head of steam."

"I just saw a livery around the corner, think it'll do?"

"Aw, heck yes, they'll do you right."

Tungee took Dolly's bridle and as he walked the horses toward the livery he heard the sound of gunfire in the distance. That jarred his memory and a clear picture began to form in his mind. It was almost a year after they buried their father. Tungee and Davy were riding home from the mill with burlap bags filled with cornmeal strapped to the back of their saddles. When the sound of gunfire rang out in the distance.

"Bet somebody just bagged a turkey or maybe a deer," Davy shouted.

Tungee hoped his brother was right, but something deep inside told him otherwise.

They pulled their mounts up near the kitchen and quickly poured the meal into a clean bin.

Davy, in almost a whisper, said, "Tungee?"

"What."

"Something ain't right."

"I know."

They called, "Mama," a dozen times, but all they got in return was a piece of an echo. The place was still and it seemed the only thing in the world that moved was the river at the bottom of the hill as its muddy waters flowed past the boat dock.

The boys ran through the house and kept calling and opening doors and the doors didn't even make their proper sound. A muffled quiet was all they heard.

Davy said excitedly, "She must be down at the bee-hives."

They ran out the front door, jumped the porch rail, just missing Mama's flowers, and landed on the run. Tungee and Davy both called out as they crossed the sandy yard and raced for the brush covered trail that led to the hives.

They stopped short of the wood. Horrified at what they saw. Their mother's lifeless body was sprawled near the trees. She must have died instantly from a single gunshot wound to the head. Her protective bee clothing was still in tact. Her left hand clutched the smoker and her right lay lifeless beside a two-gallon pail of honey.

Davy grabbed one hand and Tungee took the other as they knelt down and called to their mother -- unsure about what to do.

A horseman could be heard thrashing through the brush. The youngsters froze in place, too scared to move. When the rider came into the clear they relaxed. It was their cousin, Ray, one of Mama's kin.

As soon a he saw the boys he put his finger to his lips, signaling them to be quiet. Riding his sorrel bareback, Ray leaned over the mane nudged his mount closer and whispered, "Tungee, you and Davy clear out. Run away. Hide yourself, don't stay here and don't take a boat. They're watchin' the river."

"What'll you do?" Tungee asked.

"I'm goin' West to join Menawa. He's gonna try and make a stand."

"Why can't we go with you?"

"Because I say you can't."

Ray wheeled his horse and kicked him into a trot. Then he called over his shoulder, "Now bury your ma and git."

Tungee had no idea how long he had been standing in front of the livery. But he finally became aware of an old wrangler with a bushy white mustache and a wide grin patiently waiting. "Are you in charge?" Tungee asked.

"You got that right, young fellow. What can I do for you?"

"I need to park this rig, stable and feed the horses."

"You betcha, be glad to take care of 'em."

"I don't have any spending money on me, but I do have some dust, will that be all right?"

"Be just fine, but it ain't necessary, tomorrow'll do."

They swapped names and Tungee told him what he called the two blacks, not that he needed to, but the old wrangler seemed delighted and tipped his hat in a friendly gesture as Tungee turned to leave. He took his time walking back to the boat trying not to think at all, but that didn't work, he couldn't get the tragedy of the day before off his mind.

Charlie Boone called out. "Steam's up, Tungee, get a move on."

Charlie went to work on the forward line and Tungee cast off the aft. And in a matter of minutes they pushed away from the dock and got under way. Charlie steered a course straight toward the middle of the Golden Gate.

"You best get to work and tie down and ballast Davy's body," Charlie ordered, as he pointed to a piece of canvas that could be made into a shroud and a rope to secure it with.

Tungee's concentration was not on the work at hand, but his seaman's skills took over and he automatically began the process of sewing and tying the canvas that secured Davy's body inside.

Charlie called over the sounds of the engine, "You've done a first class job on that shroud, sailor."

A dubious honor, Tungee thought as he shook his head and gave a faint smile to acknowledge the compliment.

They were just breaking outside the Golden Gate when Tungee looked up and began to appreciate the beauty of that night. The light of the stars and moon striking the white caps made quite a setting. And that beauty just seemed to point out his own inadequacy at performing any kind of burial service for Davy. Not only that, he didn't know what would be fitting? "Charlie do you have a Bible on board?"

The skipper shook his head. "No."

"Do you know the right words for a sea burial?" Tungee asked reluctantly.

"I wish I could help, but I just don't know any."

Tungee frowned and took hold of the rail for a minute. Then it suddenly came to him. "The valley of the shadow of death." Part of a verse from the Twenty Third Psalm. His mother had recited it to him many times when he was a boy and he could still recall the sound of her voice.

They kept to a westerly heading for almost an hour before Charlie shut down the engine. Then it was quiet except for a little steam hissing out of the boiler and the light Pacific chop slapping at the side of the boat.

Tungee felt a little shy about saying a prayer out loud and he was hesitant and pensive at first, but once he got going the words came out strong.

"The Lord is my shepherd; I shall not want.

He maketh me to lie down in green pastures: he leadeth me beside the still waters.

He restoreth my soul: he leadeth me in the paths of righteousness for his name's sake.

Yea, though I walk through the valley of the shadow of death, I will fear no evil: for thou art with me; thy rod and thy staff they comfort me.

Thou preparest a table before me in the presence of mine enemies: thou anointest my head with oil; my cup runneth over.

Surely goodness and mercy shall follow me all the days of my life: and I will dwell in the house of the Lord forever... Amen"

Then he said plaintively, "I'm going to miss you, little brother."

Charlie added a somber, "Amen." And after a long moment of

silence they took hold of opposite ends of the shroud and lowered the body over the side.

*　　*　　*

Back at the dock, Charlie secured the boat and Tungee handed him a small pouch of gold and the skipper said it wasn't necessary, but Tungee insisted.

Charlie finally took the gold, stuffed it into his pocket and they walked off into the San Francisco night.

— THREE —

The early morning sun played on his face and Tungee turned over with half a notion of going back to sleep. But that didn't work, he was wide awake. He rubbed his eyes and looked around half expecting to see the leaves and trees with his horses standing in the background. Then he mused as he stretched and yawned, no that was yesterday. Now, I'm in bed, in my hotel room. Well, sort of in bed. He had slept on top of the covers, fully clothed. Too embarrassed to put his dirt and sweat stained body between the clean sheets. He was still covered with two days of accumulated road dust. The last bath was a plunge into the Sacramento River just before they broke camp for the last time.

He rolled over and put his feet on the floor. Every muscle and bone in his body ached and he was stiff. A vivid reminder of that hard wagon seat he had occupied since the day they left the mine.

Then he glanced in the mirror that hung above the bureau. What a mess, something's got to be done about that bushy beard and mop of hair. But on closer inspection he figured it was nothing a good barber couldn't fix.

He soaked in his tub for half an hour, one of the simple pleasures in life. He took his time lathering soap all over his body and as he relaxed he thought about Davy and some of their recent conversations. They talked about the gold and what it could mean. Commercial investments in San Francisco and possibly some land they had seen in the Sacramento area. Of course Davy was more interested in champagne, women and travel. Fact is, he was always more of a hell raiser than I am, Tungee thought. Maybe there's a lesson there, why not try and be a little more outgoing. He splashed soapy water on his face and then he was struck by a funny thought, what about a house on Nob Hill? A half-breed living on Nob Hill. I suppose it could work if I used Robert instead of Tungee. I'll give it some thought. Another thing, I need some decent clothes.

Feeling good after his bath, he went back to the room and put on clean dungarees, polished boots, a white cotton shirt, brown leather vest and a wide brimmed felt hat.

Then he went down to the hotel restaurant and ordered coffee, scrambled eggs, bacon and biscuits. He finished his meal, tipped the waiter and walked out to the street. He figured he'd walk the kinks out of his body and at the same time get reacquainted with the city. The fog had rolled in and blotted out the sun that had given him his wake-up call earlier in the morning. He walked along at a brisk pace observing his surroundings. The residence and business buildings were mostly one and two story clapboard with gabled roofs. Some were painted white and others weathered wood. All of a sudden he got a grim reminder of the fire that swept through large portions of the city back in the spring. The strong smell of charred wood hung heavily in the air. As he strode along Montgomery Street he saw a number of burned out buildings. There was a bright side, however, everywhere he looked there were stacks of lumber and the sounds of hammers and saws working. He also noticed that some of the new buildings were using stone, brick and mortar in their construction. Looks like in spite of the fires, some folks think San Francisco is here to stay. He spotted the Wells Fargo sign just ahead and stopped and took out his watch. The morning was slipping away it was almost ten o'clock. He hurried back to the hotel and went directly to the front desk where he removed two of the five gold pouches from the safe. His next stop would be The Merchants and Mining Bank of San Francisco located just a few blocks from the hotel.

He entered the front door and stepped up to the teller's cage. A young bespectacled man moved forward and Tungee asked, "Can I open an account with some gold dust?"

The teller said the gold would be all right, but he needed several pieces of routine information, name and address and the like. Following that brief inquiry, the young man turned a form around for a signature.

"How much do you wish to deposit, Mr. Cahill?"

Tungee put two pouches on the counter. "Will this do?"

The gold was poured into a small metal dish that rested on top of the scales. The teller smiled. "That'll be just fine." Then he wrote down the weight and said, "Do you need any cash?"

"I suppose two hundred will do for now."

Following the transaction, Tungee thanked the teller and walked back to the street. He noticed the fog was beginning to clear as he hustled along the busy sidewalk en route to the livery.

The old wrangler greeted him. "Howdy."

"Good morning, Mack," Tungee said, "I need to know your long term livery rates."

Mack was no push over when it came to haggling about prices. But Tungee felt generous and they reached a quick agreement and settled on terms for a full year.

"I need to take the rig for an hour or so."

Mack grinned. "Come and go as you like, Mr. Cahill."

Tungee walked into the stable area and found Dolly and Big Sam making themselves right at home in their stalls near the back of the barn. But they seemed eager to get into harness and go to work.

The Wells Fargo Freight office was his first stop. The agent took the news in stride when told the stored boxes were not leaving town. The man simply collected the storage fee and helped Tungee load the wagon.

He left the freight office, drove up Montgomery, turned down an alley and parked behind the bank. He jumped down from the seat, strode to the back door and knocked. Someone inside opened the green shade. Two men stood behind the window armed with shotguns. He laughed and carefully held his deposit slip up to the window for their inspection. One of the men finally cracked the door and Tungee said, "We need a set of scales capable of weighing a large amount of gold dust."

After a long wary look at the boxes on the wagon another fellow came to the back door and introduced himself as Simon Estes, head teller. Estes was a soft looking man in his forties.

Mr. Estes gestured and one of the guards put his shotgun down, rolled up his sleeves and helped Tungee bring the gold into the bank.

The weighing process was almost finished when Simon Estes left the room and returned with a robust gentleman wearing a dark broadcloth business suit. He had a square face and wide set, dull gray eyes.

"Mr. Cahill," Simon Estes said genially, "this is our bank president, Mr. Mason Albreght."

Tungee reached out and shook the rigid hand of the bank president. "Pleased to meet you, Mr. Albreght."

Mason Albreght seemed much more interested in the gold, as he gave Tungee a cursory look and mumbled, "Mr. Cahill." Tungee noticed the bank president's eyes brighten as he watched the brilliant metal flow onto the scale and listened to the tally. When the final weight was marked on the chalkboard, the figure read nine hundred and seventy three pounds. One of the assistants cleared his throat and announced, "Gentlemen, we have a total of fifteen thousand five hundred and sixty eight ounces."

Tungee did a rough calculation in his head and figured that even at the lowest exchange rate that batch alone was worth some where in the neighborhood of a third of a million dollars. Not a bad neighborhood, he thought.

The bank president wrung his hands, pursed his lips and muttered something under his breath.

Tungee gave a little whistle and began to add up in his own mind the two stashes and what was left in the mine. A rough calculation came to just over a million and a half-dollars. Funny thing though, he didn't feel much like a millionaire. More like a working stiff that had just put in a solid half-day's work.

Mason Albreght's manner was cordial in the extreme. Tungee was ushered into the president's plush office. An assistant ran in and out with papers needing both their signatures.

Simon Estes joined the group as Mason Albreght said, "These papers indicate that you are the sole owner, Mr. Cahill."

"That's right, it's all mine."

"Are you a native Californian, Mr. Cahill?"

"No. I wouldn't say that I am."

"Then you're from the states."

"I started out in Georgia ... But about half of my life has been spent at sea."

"You have relatives out here, Mr. Cahill?" the president asked.

"Not that I know of."

Then Mr. Albreght carted out what sounded like his standard, more than a hundred thousand and less than a million-dollar deposit speech. "Let me say on behalf of the bank, it's employees and the board of directors that we are honored to have you as a valued customer, Mr. Cahill."

He then offered Tungee a cigar from a well-appointed humidor. Tungee's first impulse was to decline, but he changed his mind and took it. Mason Albreght struck a match to light the cigar but Tungee waved him off. "Think I'll smoke it later, if you don't mind."

The bank president grinned. "Not at all."

Tungee took another look at the papers he'd been handed, then wrapped them around the stogie and put them in his pocket.

"I need some cash for spending money."

Simon Estes asked, "How much do you need, Mr. Cahill?"

"Make it a thousand dollars, if you don't mind." Tungee signed for the cash then he was introduced to every person in the bank. Eventually it became a little embarrassing to him. All he wanted to do was get out of the place, which he finally did leaving the same way he came in, through the back door.

Tungee dropped the horses and rig off at the livery, paid the balance he owed on the rental agreement and walked to a neighborhood barbershop. He found a barber named Sam who ushered him into a barber chair. Sam was in his mid thirties, balding and jovial. He put the apron on his customer and said, "What would you like me to do?"

Tungee grinned at what he saw in the mirror and said, "Go ahead and use your own judgment and let's see what happens."

Sam picked up his comb and scissors and opened the conversation. "Been here long?"

"You mean San Francisco?"

"Uh huh."

"Just got back last evening."

"Bet you were in the gold fields."

"Yep."

"You've been here before though."

"Many times, in and out. The last time was about a year and a half ago when we struck out for the gold."

"Things have changed since then. The fire back in the spring caused a lot of grief," then the barber took several deliberate snips with his scissors, "but we may have a problem now that's worse than the fire."

"What's that?" Tungee asked.

"The Sydney Ducks."

"What is a Sydney Duck?"

"You really have been out of town," Sam said affably as he brushed the excess hair off his customer's shoulders. "They're a gang of thugs that came here from Australia and hang out around the Barbary Coast."

"What makes them so bad?"

"Well, they are thieves and scoundrels, the lot of them." Sam's voice took on a ominous tone. "They'd as soon shoot you dead for a dollar as for a thousand."

"Sounds bad."

"Tis bad," Sam declared. Then the barber returned to his task. He clipped, combed and hummed. Suddenly he stopped and stood back. "You better take a look in the mirror and see if I'm on the right track."

Tungee looked into the big glass for several seconds before saying anything. "You know something, Sam. I don't like the beard, why don't you just take it off and leave the mustache."

Sam went back to work with his shears and trimmed the face whiskers. Then he mixed up a warm foamy lather, pushed the chair back, brushed the foam into the stubble and put on the hot towel to soften the whiskers. Tungee relaxed and almost went to sleep while the barber worked on his beard.

When Sam was all through, he brought the chair back to an upright position, Tungee looked into the mirror and nodded his approval. Then he was struck with an idea. "I need some advice, Sam."

"Be glad to help if I can."

"I'm thinking of buying some good clothes. Thought maybe I'd go to a tailor. Do you know of a good one that's also reasonable?"

Sam scratched his head and drawled, "The best one I know is also quite reasonable."

"That sounds promising."

"I cut his hair and some of my customers go to him and say they like him. He's German and talks with a heavy accent. His name is Wilhelm Hurtz, but folks just call him Willy."

"Willy." Tungee rubbed his smooth shaved face and said, "Interesting. Where do I find him."

"He's on California Street just above Polk Gulch."

Tungee joined the pace of the crowd in the streets as he walked toward the tailor shop. He noticed that businessmen dressed in broadcloth suits derby hats or trilby's. Most of the carpenters and other working people wore cotton trousers and shirts or overalls and cloth caps. He laughed as he compared the real folks with the fancy dressed up dummies in the store windows. Most of the models in the windows were dressed in clothing that was a bit too fancy to suit him. Maybe Willy will have some ideas. He located the tailor shop and Sam was right, the tailor was German, short, chubby and balding. Tungee thought he looked like a German version of Ben Franklin.

Willy was an efficient and affable fellow. He took out a style book that was filled with gentlemen's suits and coats.

Tungee selected three suit styles and the colors he wanted. He took the tailors advice regarding weight of the wool cloth. Then he smiled as a new idea popped into his mind. I need a dress suit, something I can wear to the theater. Then he chuckled at his own thought, I've never been to a theater or opera in my life, but there's always a first time I suppose.

Willy was a whiz with the measuring tape, he measured, took notes and talked while holding a dozen pins between his lips and he did it with alacrity. He kept up a constant chatter and was jovial until he touched on one of the same subjects the barber had talked about.

"Dem Sydney Ducks is bad for business."

"I've heard that, Willy."

Suddenly a wry grin came over the tailor's face and he said with good humor and thick accent. "San Francisco needs a few goot laughs."

Tungee grinned. "What have you got in mind, Willy?"

"Hang dem ducks in every store window. Ja, San Francisco needs a few goot laughs, don't you tink, Mr. Cahill?"

Tungee walked away from the shop chuckling at Willy's dark humor solution to the Duck's problem. When he got back to the hotel he strode directly to the desk. Bob Sloan was on duty and Tungee asked for and got a business sized envelope, which he addressed to himself at the Kinsey House.

He took the bank papers out of his pocket and separated them from the cigar. Then he removed the earlier bank receipt from another pocket, put it along with the other papers into the envelope and handed it to the clerk. "I'd appreciate it if you would put this in the safe."

"Be glad to, Mr. Cahill," Bob Sloan said affably.

Tungee tipped his hat and turned toward the stairs. As he climbed to the third floor, he made the decision to dash off a couple of letters.

His first letter was written to Morgan Stern, a lawyer friend of his in Baltimore. Tungee sat and mused about their first meeting. He had wandered into Bloody Buckets all over the world and had been in his share of barroom brawls. On that particular evening he had had just enough bourbon to dull his senses. One of the rowdies took offence to his name and called him a half-breed son-of-a-bitch. Tungee answered with a swift right cross that knocked the bigot to his knees. But just moments later he realized he was in trouble when the bigot's pals took up the fight. Fortunately a large man that had heard the slur came to Tungee's aid and they eventually fought their way out of the place. Once they got to the street they introduced themselves and located another saloon. Within the next two or three drinks Tungee found that his new friend, Morgan Stern, was also a half-breed -- Jewish and Cherokee Indian. And that night was the beginning of their friendship.

The other letter was to his Uncle Mitchell Cahill in Augusta,

Georgia. In both messages he told briefly about the death of Davy and that he planned to stay a while in San Francisco.

When he finished his correspondence Tungee moved to an easy chair and tried to relax. But he couldn't. He was thinking about the mail and for some reason he got a desperate urge to post the letters.

— FOUR —

The late afternoon sun cut dark shadows across the San Francisco landscape. Tungee hustled along Montgomery Street in the direction of the post office. His thoughts were about the evening, a good meal, a few drinks and a toast to Davy.

He arrived at the post office just as the clerk was about to shut the window. The gentleman was kind enough to take the letters and toss them into the outgoing mailbag. "Thanks, I appreciate your time," Tungee said.

"Think nothing of it."

Tungee turned and walked back toward the Kinsey House. He was less than a block from the hotel when he shuddered as a sudden chill ran up his spine. The air was balmy, not cold. Maybe it was anxiety of some kind, he thought, but what? He took a deep breath and tried to rationalize the problem. San Francisco was known to be a tough town. What the hell is it, fear? Maybe some of Sam's and Willy's talk about the Sydney Ducks had made more of an impression than he had thought at the time. He reached underneath the flap of his jacket and felt reassured by the cold steel as his fingers wrapped around his Navy Colt 44.

Once inside the hotel he looked around, then quickly crossed the empty lobby and attacked the stairs with a vengeance. When he got to his room he began to consider what additional weaponry he could carry without looking like a walking arsenal. He searched for and quickly found his tiny double shot over and under palm gun. And just for good measure he added a long knife. He laid the weapons out on top of the bed cover, picked them up individually to get the feel and balance. Open the guns check the safety, then snap and load.

He spent the next half-hour at the washbasin, cleaning up and then rummaging among his bags to find suitable clothes to wear that evening. He didn't have a dark suit, but found a clean shirt he would wear with an open collar, dark jacket and a pair of gray trousers.

Then he splashed on some lilac water, which the hotel had provided. Maybe it was that sweet smell that sparked his enthusiasm to get out of the room and enjoy his night out on the town. Thoughts about where to spend the evening had been running through his mind. One thing was sure; it wouldn't be in the area of the Barbary Coast. Then he looked into the mirror and smiled, the answer was obvious, Ernie Maxwell's Saloon was just a few blocks west of his hotel near Nob Hill.

The night air was crisp and he felt good as he made his way along the darkened street. Fog had rolled in again and as he neared the saloon he realized just how dark it was. The only bright spots were close to the street lamps; otherwise it was almost pitch black.

Ernie Maxwell's establishment was located near Nob Hill on Clay Street. The place was fancy, some even called it pretentious, but it had about all the elements you could want for a night out. The restaurant served good food and some of San Francisco's finest occasionally dined there. Tungee walked straight through the bar and into the gaming room, just to check out the action. It was a noisy, crowded, smoke filled room and it felt like a party was in progress. He spotted Ernie Maxwell in the middle of the room and when he got to a little less than shouting distance, they made eye contact and walked toward one another. Ernie stuck his arm out, squeezed Tungee's hand and pulled him into a bear hug.

Now Ernie Maxwell was not simply a self-serving greeter. He was a large man who dressed in the latest styles and wore diamond rings, tie clips and cuff links, but he was a man you would feel comfortable with. He allowed no hot games in his place, in fact, if he caught any of his dealers cheating the public; they were fired on the spot. Ernie was a rare breed, especially in his business and thought of by people who knew him to be an honest man.

"Tungee, you old devil, how are you? Where have you been?"

"Up in the gold fields with the rest of the fools."

"How'd you make out?"

"Not bad, Ernie. Not bad, and from the crowd I see here tonight, you're not exactly on hard times."

"No we're doing all right, I guess."

Tungee gestured toward the restaurant. "Supper ready?"

"You bet, just follow me, I'll get you a table."

The table turned out to be the best booth in the house. Ernie summoned a waiter and left with the standard, "Enjoy your meal."

Tungee looked around and saw a number of familiar faces in the room, but no one he really knew.

The waiter came right over and handed him a large sized menu and asked if he needed anything to drink?

"No, thank you, not just now."

The waiter moved a discreet distance away to give his customer a little time with the menu. Tungee was busy looking over the large card and paid no attention to the person making his way to his table. And as a consequence, the first impression he got was from that booming voice. There was only one like it and it belonged to, Captain Jack "Thunder" Parker.

"Tungee, you old sea pirate, how be ya?"

Tungee stood up and shoved his hand toward Thunder's and they sawed the air with a generous handshake. "How do you do, Captain Parker? Have a seat."

The captain accepted and moved his rather substantial frame into the booth. Parker's mischievous eyes were set in under bushy eyebrows and belied his thunderous voice.

"Where you been?" Parker asked jovially, "I ain't seen you in month of Sunday's."

"Gold country."

"Well now, tell me, mate. Did you strike it rich or did you strike out?"

"I managed to pan a few ounces." Then Tungee grinned and

directed the conversation away from himself. "Have you tried your luck up there?"

Parker slowly shook his head. "The way things been goin', I might better have been there."

"What do you mean, Skipper?"

"Well, hell's fire and damnation, you cain't put a crew together to save your soul. My ship is settin' out there in the harbor right now with a load of grain. She's been loaded for more than a month. I'm suppose to be at sea and headin' for Liverpool, but we cain't put enough men together at one time to make up a sailin' crew."

"Yeah, the bay does seem a bit crowded, but I hadn't given the crew problem any thought."

"This dang gold fever is just half the trouble. These here recent fires in town have taken all the skilled men off the sea goin' jobs. They get more money right here in San Francisco puttin' up buildings than we can pay for a voyage."

"Once you get out of here, maybe you'd better steer clear of San Francisco for a year or so."

"The way it looks now, I might be here that long."

"It'll work itself out, Captain Parker. Just last month up in Sacramento I talked to several fellows and they all seemed about ready go back to sea."

"Gold fever coolin' down some."

"From what I can tell, it is."

Thunder Parker looked around the room and shook his head. "I know half the captain's and mate's in this room and we're all in the same fix. What about you, Tungee, you ever sail with any of these folks?"

Tungee looked and gestured in the direction of a man that had just entered the room. "Gideon Foster. Don't you remember, Captain. I'd just finished a tour with him as second mate when I signed on with you as first kicker."

"Ah sure, I remember that." Parker squinted toward Foster for a long moment and then quietly said, "He's a nasty one ain't he, Tungee?"

"He's tough and sometimes disagreeable I suppose, but all in all I found him to be fair."

"I just heard he was a bad one."

"I heard some of it too." Then Tungee looked straight at Parker. "Come to think of it, Skipper, I heard some of that same kind of stuff about you."

Parker's eyes lit up and he gave his unique clap of laughter, drawing the attention of everyone in the room. "Well I spect there be a little truth in what you say. If the whole crew liked the captain, chances are he ain't tough as he ought to be."

Tungee nodded and smiled agreeably.

They had finished their meal and were having coffee when Thunder Parker said, "Why don't you give some thought about throwin' in with me. Help me to get this here load of grain to Liverpool."

Tungee didn't want to give him an answer he had too many things to do in San Francisco. "I'll give it some thought, Captain Parker. It may be the best way to get back to the states unless I decide to use the overland route."

"Aw, Tungee. You don't want to do nothin' like that. Them Western Indian fellers might not recognize you as a brother. And I hear tell that some of 'em are down right ornery when it comes to folks crossin' their lands."

Tungee chuckled. "You might have something there, Captain Parker."

Thunder Parker headed for the street exit. Tungee wanted to say hello to Gideon Foster and started toward his table, but he noticed he was in deep conversation with two men. So he decided to wait, he would likely see him later in the other room.

Tungee stood just inside the entrance to the gaming room and from the looks of things, the craps table was getting most of the action. He strolled over and squeezed into a spot next to a French sea captain that was on a roll.

From what they said at the table, the man with the dice had made seven straight passes.

Tungee tossed a small pouch of dust on the come line just as the dice went cold. He chuckled at his dumb move; guess I should have watched for a while. He backed off after that first quick loss, but stayed in the game for the next hour. He had given himself a five hundred-dollar loss limit and figured at worst that amount would carry him until midnight. It didn't. The five hundred lasted less than an hour and when it was gone he eased away from the table. Then he turned and walked back toward the bar, grinned and thought of an old slogan, winning may not be everything, but losing is absolutely nothing.

Ernie Maxwell caught up to Tungee, slapped him on the back and declared, "There will be better days."

"That's all well and good, Ernie. But I'm stuck with this one."

"Tell you what I can do, I'll buy you a drink."

"Well, I'm looking for a hundred and eighty degree turn-around," Tungee said jovially. "But I'll be happy to accept a point or two in the right direction."

They moved to the bar and both ordered whiskeys. Tungee turned to Ernie and in a serious tone said, "You obviously have a good idea about the business climate in San Francisco. I'm thinking about investments, do you have any good ideas in that area?"

Ernie hesitated, and then took a sip of his drink. "You know something, Tungee, if you'd asked me that three or four months ago, I would have said, sure, I've got a half dozen good ideas." He pursed his lips. "But things have changed."

"What do you mean?"

"This gang of cut throats called the Sydney Ducks is raising hell in the business community. And scaring off investors."

"I've heard about them and I was told they operate out of the Barbary Coast. But I had an idea that whole thing was a little overblown."

"No. Not at all, it's damned serious. One of my regulars was murdered in broad daylight not three blocks from here."

"Did they catch the killer?"

"Some of the folks on the Vigilance Committee traced it to one of the Ducks, but they never got much out of him." Ernie paused and said worriedly, "He was small fry and he never said he was innocent. The committeemen never quit. They questioned him all the way to the gallows and he never gave them a name."

"Maybe he didn't know any," Tungee suggested.

"Nobody believes that. What they do believe is that the big fish is a shark and that any one of the Ducks would rather hang than rat on him."

One of Ernie's dealers rushed up and said, "Excuse me, boss, but we've got a doozie in Arnie's game."

"What's he doing?"

"You name it. He seems very resourceful and hard to spot. But it looks to me like he can do it all."

The saloon owner threw up his hands and said, "See you later, Tungee." And followed the dealer into the gaming room.

The bar was quiet, as Tungee tasted the last sip of whiskey in his glass. He looked around the room and saw Charlie Boone sitting at the other end of the bar. He went over and slid onto the stool next to him. Charlie signaled and the bartender brought another glass. Tungee picked it up and Charlie filled it from his bottle of bourbon.

"I saw you over talking to the boss, decided not to butt in."

"Yeah. He bought me a drink. You know something, Charlie, I had one of those nights, at the craps table, that when you wake up in the morning you just hope it was all a bad dream. Then after checking your wallet, you know it wasn't."

Charlie laughed. "I've had more of them than I can count."

Tungee took a sip of his drink and then said glumly, "I came out tonight with the idea of some kind of celebration, but it's difficult. We bury my brother one night and the next we sit here talking about nothing. He doesn't even rate a mention."

"Aw, damn, Tungee. I didn't mean to be disrespectful. I just figured you might not want to talk about it."

"No. It won't bother me to talk about Davy." Then Tungee looked up and smiled. "In fact I'd just as soon include him in the party."

"They do that at Irish Wakes, you know," Charlie said as he poured new drinks.

Tungee touched Charlie's glass and then raised his own toward the ceiling. "This one's for you, Davy. And from here to eternity, may you be blessed with a quartering wind and the storms always on the other side of the horizon."

They clicked their glasses and downed the bourbon. Then Charlie chuckled. "You're soundin' more like a drunken sailor every minute."

"You could be right, but I don't feel drunk." Then Tungee said soberly, "You know something, Charlie, Davy was not only my brother, he was my best pal."

"He was easy to be around and always full of piss and vinegar."

Tungee brightened. "Remember that infectious giggle he had."

"Yeah. And you could never tell if he was laughing with you or at you."

Tungee stood up, took a deep breath and stretched. "Just had another thought. Knowing Davy like I do, maybe I should save the big toast for Belle Mundy's place. She didn't get burned out, did she?"

"No, the fire missed her. She's got a couple of new spitfires though." Charlie grinned and winked. "They're real lookers too."

"Now that's more to Davy's liking anyway." Then he turned toward the door, "Still foggy out?"

"Yep. You can hardly make out the light, one lamp to the next."

Tungee turned the collar up on his jacket, looked at his friend and said, "Night, Charlie." Then he walked directly out the front door.

The damp fog hit him in the face and he shuddered. There was a chill in the air that went right through to the bone. He stumbled along the plank sidewalk, squinting hard, trying to make out the next street lamp. Suddenly he sensed something, or someone, following close. He opened his jacket and whipped out the forty-four and wheeled around to confront his suspicion. Out of the corner of his eye he saw an object falling toward his head and ducked. The club stung his shoulder just as he fired into the attacker's belly. Suddenly a gun butt slammed hard behind his right ear. And in those seconds it took him to fall to the sidewalk he heard a few words muttered in, what he made out to be, a broad cockney accent. Tungee's head exploded like a bright comet streaking across the sky, then it slowly dimmed and faded into the night.

— FIVE —

"All sail, hoist the mains and brace for close haul on the starboard tack," a strident voice called out to an unknown crew.

Tungee's eyes popped open and all he could see was the fuzzy outline of a room. He pulled himself into a sitting position and through a blur he began to see bunks, bulkheads and a washstand. I'm in a cabin and that's a fact. But who's cabin and on what ship, he wondered? His head throbbed and a hand went up to nurse the hurt behind his right ear. "Get to your feet, Tungee," he moaned. And with a desperate effort he scrambled and clawed his way up to the porthole and slowly scanned the surface of a moving sea. Cobwebs cleared just enough for him to make out the little tug Juniper bobbing her way toward the Golden Gate. She was heading home, but God only knows where I'm going.

His new found world of yesterday circled and crashed as he slammed his fist into an unforgiving bulkhead. Tungee winced and cradled his bloodied hand as he gazed out the porthole and saw his freedom vanishing over the horizon. His stomach was tied in knots and he couldn't breathe, but he heard something and turned toward the noise. Then he blinked and looked past his own misery and saw two others on the floor. One man stirred and emitted a familiar guttural report. If I had the energy I'd laugh he thought, as he looked into the eyes of his last night's supper companion.

"Well now, Tungee. Looks to be we've got ourselves a proper

problem," Thunder Parker announced as he grinned and rose up on his elbow. "That thar bulkhead didn't give much, did she?"

Tungee spat on his right fist and wrapped it with his handkerchief.

The third member of their party, a dark skinned man, began to stir and pulled himself into a sitting position and blinked. "Who are you fellows?"

"Well, it won't make no never mind the way things are shapin' up, but mine's Jack Parker and the Injun over there is Tungee Cahill."

"What about yours?" Tungee asked.

The third man said with a touch of humor, "Randolph, Jeff Randolph, I think."

They all had questions what, where and how did they get on board? But no one uttered the obvious word -- shanghaied.

The sounds of a ship coming to life were clear. Timbers creaked and groaned while the wind filled sails tugged her forward and toward the high seas. There was an active crew on deck and in the rigging, manning bowlines, halyards and braces. Someone belched a continual stream of orders. "Man the royals, fore, main and mizzen. Get a move on, shake a leg up there, you top-men."

Thunder Parker turned to the others. "How do you think we ought to play this thing?"

Tungee laughed at the outrageous remark. As if they had any choice, "My guess is we'd better spend some time listening."

Thunder Parker wore the same broadcloth suit he had on the evening before and sat on one end of the forward bunk. Jeff was built like a runner, wore a gray flannel shirt, denim pants and high leather shoes. He rested easily on a sea chest.

Tungee paced the cabin like a caged lion, and suddenly felt a pain in the arch of his right foot and he began to limp. He sat on the end of Thunder's bunk, pulled off his boot and massaged his foot. When he reached down into the boot he felt something. Then a big smile spread over his face as he pulled out the small weapon and showed it to the others.

"Not much," he said, "but better than nothing." Then Tungee asked, "Have either of you been shanghaied before?"

Parker thought for a moment. "Back in the twenties I was hangin' out in a little bar in Rio and before I knew what for, I was on my way to Canton, China." Then he shook his head and smiled lightly, "But it didn't turn out too bad cause we sailed right back to my home port, Boston."

Tungee, Thunder and Jeff paced, sat, squirmed and speculated about their fate and destination.

Thunder Parker said, "I be of the opinion this skipper got pretty strict orders to do what he done."

"What do you mean?" Jeff asked.

"Well, the laws bein' what they be, I can't see no skipper takin' this kind of chance, unless there was a whole heap at stake." Then Thunder reasoned, "Unless somebody had him nailed to a board."

Parker's theory was sound. San Francisco bay was filled with ships and most of their captain's were unwilling to break the law and go the shanghai route. But for some reason this skipper ignored all that and put to sea.

Jeff said thoughtfully, "How many others came on like us?"

Thunder pursed his lips. "No way of knowin', leastwise not while we be locked up."

The ship was apparently trim and gliding through the short-capped waves. She must have found a course, because the scurrying around the deck had settled down. A three masted square-rigger was Tungee's guess and probably an American Clipper. That had to be a plus. They could have just as easily been slugged aboard an old sea-going scow.

Several hours passed, conversation ebbed and a kind of helpless quiet took over. Tungee began to wonder about his actions the night before. *I ignored my own basic instincts and walked right into the trap. That feeling I had as I walked from the post office to the hotel should have been a red flag, but I ignored it.*

Keys rattled just outside the door and everyone directed his attention toward the sound. A key was inserted in the lock and suddenly the door popped open. And a gust of fresh air rushed in.

The man standing in front of them was of average height, broad shoulders and had a brown trimmed beard and mustache. His first words might just as well have come from a purser greeting his paying passengers. "Good afternoon gentlemen. Welcome aboard the Marcus F. Childs. I'm the first mate and my name is Fritz Cheny. If you people keep your noses clean we won't have no trouble. Follow me, the captain wants to see you."

Tungee, Jeff and Thunder looked at each other and resignedly fell in behind the first mate and walked aft down the companionway. Tungee wondered why the first mate's words had been so downright pleasant. But, I guess they could afford to use the velvet glove approach. However, the absurdity of the situation was almost funny.

Fritz Cheny stopped in front of the aft cabin, rapped on the door and a voice from inside called, "Come on in."

Cheny opened the door and ushered the three inside. Bright sunlight flooded the large cabin by way of four portholes, two on port side and two aft. The cabin apparently served as both office and living quarters, there was a bunk forward in the same vicinity of a bureau and washstand. A large chart table occupied the center of the room.

"Come right in gentlemen," a voice called out from the aft part of the cabin.

The three turned and saw the man sitting behind a substantial oak desk smoking a thin black cigar. They knew him all right, at least Thunder and Tungee did. Gideon Foster was a compact man with fair hair, dark restless eyes and a waxed mustache. He wore a blue serge suit cut in a military style with brass buttons. Captain Foster grinned as he gestured the others to take a seat. There were ample canvas chairs setup and facing the captain.

Tungee, Jeff and Thunder accepted his offer and sat down. Cheny remained standing near the door. The three sat in silence, all glaring at the captain. But even as they showed their irritation, all seemed content to use Tungee's suggestion and listen for a while.

Captain Foster puffed a time or two on his cigar then he put it down in a copper ashtray before speaking. He took his time and cleared his throat. "I expect I know what you folks are thinking, and you may be right, that I'm an S.O.B., but I won't hold that against you." Then he laughed heartily and looked up at the three. "I'd probably feel the same if the shoe was on the other foot. And I suppose I owe you an apology. I know it's going to be an inconvenience for all of you. But I needed a crew and you three are now a part of it." He flicked the ashes off his cigar. "Now, there are several ways to play this game, but only one will work. Accept your present situation and do as you're told we can get along. If, on the other hand, you choose another course it will be a mistake.' Then he gave a benevolent smile. "You'll get your wages at the other end."

Tungee moved uncomfortably in his chair and finally said, "I have a question, Captain."

"What is it, Cahill?"

"Did you know about this last night, at the time we saw you in the restaurant?"

"No I didn't." Foster said, as he looked straight into Tungee's eyes. "Now, you may not believe this, but the first time I was aware that you and Parker were onboard was this morning when I was making the rounds and sizing up my crew."

He stopped and relit his cigar. "At the time, I was both pleased and perplexed. Damn good men, I thought, maybe too good. I wrestled with and put off final decision up to the minute we cut loose from the tug."

"Looks to me you would have sent us back. How come you didn't?" Thunder Parker grumbled.

"I need you, it's as simple as that."

"It ain't right, Gideon ain't lawful neither."

"I was hoping you fellows would look at this thing from my side," a slight grin played across his face, "and maybe even treat it with a touch of humor."

Cheny looked at the somber faces of the three and chuckled. Then he began to laugh and there must have been something infectious about his laughter because Thunder let go with one of his familiar guffaws. And almost like the tide rolling in, everyone in the room picked up on the insanity. The merriment made no sense, but it did give some momentary relief to their predicament.

When the laughter subsided, Gideon Foster said, "Well, welcome aboard, gentlemen. I hope you won't be too offended by what I'm about to say, but you fellows will remain under lock and key for the next day or two."

"Why, Captain?"

"Well now, Cahill, if I were in your shoes, I'd likely ask the same question. I'd also be asking myself -- how do I get off this ship?" Gideon Foster put down his cigar and clasped his hands together and rested them on the desk. Then his face went from humor to thoughtful resignation.

Tungee had seen that look before. The captain was troubled and seemed to be working something out in his head.

Then just as it appeared that he was about to speak, what ever it was he had on his mind, he decided to keep it to himself. Foster took a deep breath and after a long moment, looked toward Cheny. "Take them back to their quarters and arrange for their chow."

Captain Foster gazed at the three as Chaney made his exit and closed the door behind him. Foster drummed his fingers on the desk and had mixed feelings about his decision to keep Thunder and Tungee on-board. But that ambivalence about person to person decisions didn't begin with the shanghai business. It was something that had dogged him all of his life.

Gideon Foster grew up on a farm in Pennsylvania and put in long hard days on the family farm. But that was never enough, at least not enough to please his father. His old man was a combination tyrant, religious zealot and only once in a while was he a loving father. Fortunately his mother was always a buffer between young Gideon and the hard side of his father. The boy was intelligent and during his formative years became a student of the Bible. And that study eventually led to the Philadelphia Seminary College to study for the ministry.

While at college Gideon fell in love with the daughter of one of his professors and during their relationship she became pregnant. He was perfectly willing to marry the girl, but he couldn't face his father with an out of wedlock wife and child and as a consequence he turned away from both and went to sea.

He worked himself up through the ranks and had no trouble passing his master's examination and getting his license. But something he was never quite sure of, was it fear of his father or was he just afraid of taking on the responsibilities of a husband? Those were questions that always tormented Gideon Foster.

The key had no more than turned in the lock when Tungee, Thunder and Jeff all began forming questions relating to their just finished talk with Captain Foster. For their part, they had handled the meeting as well as could be expected. There was one large exception however; they had failed to ask the most basic question -- what port are we bound for?

Thunder Parker growled, "He be a worried man. And if I don't miss my guess, somebody is holdin' a gun to Gideon Foster's head."

Tungee was of the same mind, but didn't have a clue as to who it was or why.

Thunder went to the porthole and looked out for two or three minutes before he turned back to the others. "This here ship's name, the Marcus F. Childs."

"What about it?" Tungee asked.

"Aw, you must have heard the story."

"Don't think so."

"Well, it was back in the early forties. Somethin' happened to a ship called by the name of Marcus F. Childs. It was mid Atlantic, thought to be latitude thirty-five and longitude double zero, or there about." He paced the room trying to recall the story. "Strange thing happened to her. She sprung a leak and there wasn't a thing they could do to stop the sea comin' in. They was pumpin' and pumpin' fer three or four hours and water was still inchin' up the bulkhead. Sea was calm, wind too."

"Couldn't they patch the leak?" Jeff asked.

"Seems they couldn't. Anyhow the captain, I think his name was Bonnett or Bonner, told them to take to the boats and that they did. They pulled out a ways and got clear of the ship. Then all of a sudden, the wind picked up and commenced to fill the sails. Well that dang ship started to steer a course to the southwest."

"She didn't sink?" Jeff exploded.

"Don't know that for sure. She just sailed over the horizon and that was the last they seen of her. The men lucked out and were picked up a day or two later. I hope I may die, if that ain't the honest to God's truth. Leastwise that's the yarn they was tellin' around Boston."

"Jack, that was Alvin Bonner," Tungee recalled. "I shipped with him sometime after that incident. He had fallen out of favor with the owners of that lost ship and had been demoted to first mate. The only reason he was pulling duty at all was to work off a contract he'd signed with Lindsay Arthur Griffin. From what Bonner told me, nobody walks away from a contract with Griffin."

"How long were you with him?" Thunder asked.

"The better part of a year, I guess. The thing that strikes me is that Gideon Foster was the skipper on that voyage."

"Where did you sail to?" Jeff asked.

"China. We hit Canton and Shanghai. Then back to New York. The only other port we made was St. Katharine Island. That's just off the coast of South America. We took on provisions and water there going and coming." Tungee stopped for a moment and then said, "Something else about that trip. We took one passenger to that island on the way out and picked him up on the way back. Oscar L. Hooper was his name. A little squint eyed fellow that wore thick glasses."

"Were he a company man?"

"Of course he was. My understanding is that he's Griffin's right arm."

Tungee was troubled by the name change of the ship and suspected it could cause problems down the line. His thoughts centered on the disappearance of the old ship by the same name. The present situation likely has something to do with insurance. "What's your guess as to our destination, Thunder?"

"I'm of two minds on that. Our heading is westerly and iffen we keep to that, it's likely to be China."

"China?" Jeff asked incredulously.

"Well now, that there is one mind, but there's another that makes just as much sense." The wily old captain paced the floor and then turned to the others. "I got an idea that Foster's doin' what I'd do were I the skipper and wantin' to head east."

"But you just said we're heading west," Jeff reminded Thunder with more than a hint of frustration in his voice.

"That be just what I did say, Jeff. Ta fetch the best winds, I'd keep her bow pointed west ta southwest, maybe a day or a day and a half before bendin' around and takin' my shot at the Horn."

Thunder Parker's speech would win him no scholastic awards, but his knowledge and skills in the field of navigation would. Tungee rated Parker on a scale by himself when it came to plotting a course from port to port. And the man had the best natural instinct of anyone he knew in finding the quickest winds. Thunder took his time, pursed his lips and said thoughtfully, "I 'spect it to be the Horn."

— SIX —

Gideon Foster and Fritz Cheny stood beside the chart table in the captain's cabin studying a large map of the Western Hemisphere. Foster moved his finger from a point near their present position, a little more than a hundred miles west southwest of San Francisco, directly to and around Cape Horn. Then up the East Coast of South America to a small island in the Atlantic just east of Rio de Janerio. He tapped his finger emphatically on the black print that read St. Katharine Island.

"Well, I guess we should expect that, it's getting to be a second home port," Cheny said with a touch of cynicism.

"Orders call for it." Then Foster frowned. "From there, it says Liverpool. But there is no consignee for the cargo."

"Well, it's mostly grain and that usually means Liverpool," Cheny said.

"That's logical Fritz, but don't count on logic when dealing with this outfit."

"Gideon, I know you pretty good and I've got a feeling something's bothering you. Is it the name change, is that it?"

Foster slowly shook his head. "That's part of it, but those three inch guns we found in the hold are not listed on the manifest. What do you make of that, Fritz?"

"I don't know, Captain, but we've got to find out."

Foster walked around the chart table and puffed on his cigar. Then he leaned over his desk and picked up an envelope. "This was handed to me sealed just before I boarded. It's marked, for your eyes-only, to be opened at sea and burn contents after reading. It's just a note and all it says is to change the nameplate from Orient Leaf to Marcus F. Childs."

"That's all it says?"

"That's it."

Changing the name of a commercial vessel while on the high seas would make any captain question the order. Foster didn't even want to speculate. He suspected something was rotten, but he didn't want to discuss it with Cheny, not yet anyway. He figured they'd find out at St. Katharine Island.

Raindrops began to spatter against the portholes and Cheny looked out to check conditions. "Captain, the sea's turning and we're getting a light rain. Could be a squall working, I'd better go topside and take a look."

The captain grabbed a rain slicker off the hook and said, "I suggest we both turn to."

Cheny jogged along the companionway and shinnied up the ladder with Foster right on his heels. They arrived on deck only to find the rain had stopped and high boiling clouds were tumbling over the northeast horizon.

Captain Foster checked with the helm and found that the barometer was holding steady and that the rain shower had caused little change in wind direction or velocity. So he turned around and went below decks just as Hank Jensen hustled out of the forecastle and made his way toward the quarterdeck. He was a hard wiry little man that drank too much; smart enough to have become a master, but had no self-discipline. Jensen had been first mate on several occasions, only to be set down because of his drinking and gambling habits.

Cheny called. "Mr. Jensen!"

The two met just outside the on-deck chart room.

"You might as well go ahead and make out your full watch list." Cheny said.

"Do I get the other three?"

"Which ones are you talking about?"

"Them in cabin C, Parker, Cahill and the Nigger."

"The captain said he'd turn them out tomorrow morning."

"Then they can begin with the 1200 watch."

"No, put them into the rotation beginning with the dog watch," Cheny said alertly.

Jensen bristled. "What's so damned special about that bunch?"

"Nothing that I know of, but I just gave you an order, Mr. Jensen." Cheny glared at the second mate. "Put them on the first dog watch."

"All right, Fritz, all right."

"Mr. Cheny!"

Jensen was livid, but sucked it up. "Aye, Mr. Cheny. Does the Nigger go to the galley?"

"If they need him there."

Captain Foster returned to the quarterdeck.

Jensen said smartly, "Good afternoon, Captain."

Fritz Cheny touched his cap. "Captain."

"Gentlemen." Foster looked toward the second mate. "Do you have the watch rotation in order, Mr. Jensen?"

"Just about, Captain."

Cheny said, "He just needs to add Cahill, Parker and Randolph. You didn't say exactly when they would be available."

"You can count on them beginning at noon tomorrow."

A distasteful grin crossed Jensen's face as he glanced at Cheny. "Very well, Captain, thank you, sir."

"Mr. Cheny, I need to see you in my cabin. Come on down as soon as you and Jensen work out the watch rotation. And bring me a copy."

The forecastle was the main crew living quarters and it was usually smoke filled and stuffy. Bunks hung on both port and starboard sides of the ship in two and three tier setups. Hammocks were slung in the forward most part of the ship, where the hull narrowed into the bows, to augment the bunks.

A poker game was almost always in progress at the large table located in the middle of the living quarters. Four players sat on benches next to the table and one man kibitzed from the sidelines.

Sitting at the table was Everett Dobbs who was of average height, medium build and likeable. Oliver Simms was smaller, but carried a bit of fat. Dan Thurston was slim and had a tough look. Will Farmer had an average build and wasn't the brightest person in the world, but was loyal to Captain Foster. Farmer was a regular signed on crew member, a rare commodity on all counts aboard the MFC. All the players at the table were Australians, with the exception of Farmer. Alf Talbot, a bull-necked Aussie with a hard menacing face, stood on the sidelines. The penny ante game was played for recreation only and money was of little consequence.

The talkative Dobbs said, "I've me a little inside straight, mates, which I do believe takes this here pot."

The other players threw their cards into the middle of the table. Dealers' choice was the game Dobbs picked up the cards and handed them to Simms for a new deal.

Alf Talbot glared at Farmer. "What have you got agin money?"

"Nothing, I just don't want to get it that way."

Simms shuffled and asked, "How else do you plan to get your share then, mate?" Then he said pointedly. "It ain't gonna be paid to you workin' these here ships or in a penny ante card game."

"Maybe I won't get my share."

"You one of them Holier than Thou bastards," Talbot demanded. The big Aussie was an intimidating figure, but Farmer didn't back off. He turned his head and glared at Talbot.

Dobbs said lightly, "Knock it off fellows, and let's get on with the game."

"Any wild cards this time?" Thurston asked.

"Not while I'm dealin', mate." Simms smiled, "They'll play just like they read."

"I think you're one of 'em, Farmer," Alf Talbot snarled in a raspy voice.

Farmer stiffened. "That's just about enough, Mr. Talbot."

"Tell me how you plan to back that up, little man?"

"Well. I don't want to fight if that's what you're getting around to."

"Folks that can't fight had best keep a tight lip."

Will Farmer bristled. "I didn't say I couldn't fight, I said I don't want to."

"Comes down to the same thing don't it." Alf Talbot belched as he moved menacingly close and shoved Farmer hard against the table.

Farmer leapt out of his seat with a roundhouse haymaker that landed on Talbot's jaw. The punch didn't have much sting, but there was enough of a jolt to get the big Aussie's attention.

Thurston yelled, "Hey, you guys are screwing up a good game."

"We really do need this kind of shit," Simms bellowed.

Ignoring the card players, Alf charged at Farmer, but the little man dodged and planted a right to the bully's gut.

Alf Talbot doubled over and groaned, but stood up quickly and backhanded Farmer with a wicked blow.

Farmer came back with a left jab to Alf's mouth and blood spattered. The blow cut both Alf's lip and Farmer's knuckles.

Alf blinked several times and backed off. Then he charged in with a roundhouse left to Farmer's right ear. The small man was hurt, but rallied and came up with a hard right that caught Alf flat footed, it stung the big man and he kicked at Farmer's groin, but missed.

Farmer booted Alf Talbot in the knee and the Aussie screamed in pain wobbled, sagged and backed away. Then he steadied himself, reached inside his jacket and pulled a long knife. Then with taunting gestures, Alf Talbot began to play the game he knew so well. Farmer lunged for the weapon and missed.

Talbot took a wide swing and ripped the blade down Farmer's front, spattering blood and opening flesh from his shoulder to the lower abdomen.

Dobbs and Thurston grabbed the muscular Talbot and Simms pulled the blood soaked Farmer away.

The bull was in a rage and the physical restraint was barely enough to keep the fighters apart.

Simms held onto Farmer and called, "Somebody go get the sawbones this bloke is cut bad."

Talk in Cabin C had turned away from speculation about their fate to general conversation.

Tungee turned to Jeff. "Then you got part of your name from Thomas Jefferson."

"Sure did," Jeff said proudly. "I was born just two farms over from Monticello."

Thunder grinned. "You grew up in tall cotton."

"I remember Mr. Tom use to ride by our cabin most every afternoon."

"Did you ever talk with him?" Tungee asked.

"Nothing more than, 'Hi, Mr. Tom.' Papa talked to him, though. They even talked about slavery and Mr. Jefferson said it wasn't right, but it was going to take time to undo a system that had been around for so long."

"How did you get out of it," Tungee asked cautiously, "slavery that is?"

Jeff answered directly. "The Randolph's signed some papers and they told me I was free."

"Did you feel different when you got your freedom?" Tungee asked.

"I'm not sure," Jeff gave a mirthless chuckle, "when you've been a slave all of your life, I expect it might be like a caged bird that's never know it's freedom or maybe one that's forgot. But when the doors open and you are free to go, you don't hardly know what to do."

"What do you mean?" Thunder asked.

"I mean I didn't know where to go or what to do." Then he smiled. "But I ran -- I just kept on running and I never looked back."

Thunder slowly shook his head. "I 'spect if you was of a mind to you might say we're in that same fix. But," he looked up and smiled, "we got no place to run."

A half-breed, a black and a sea captain were tossed together in Cabin C and by all rights Thunder Parker should have felt superior to the others, but he didn't. He had felt inadequate all of his life, brought up in an orphanage and according to rumor, was the bastard son of a prostitute.

He left the orphanage at the age of fifteen and spent two years in the Buffalo, New York area working cargo vessels on Lake Erie. When he had had enough of that he went to the New York City waterfront and signed onto a Clipper ship as common seaman. From that day forward he made the high seas his home. Thunder Parker was always tough enough to hold his own and he worked up through the ranks to boatswains mate. He held that rank for almost a decade before he was promoted to second mate. His reading and writing skills were barely adequate, but he pursued and studied for his master's exam, but was not successful. Eventually though, several old time skippers knowing Thunder Parker's abilities stood up for him and arranged an oral examination, which he passed with flying colors. But even with the rank of captain Jack Parker never quite felt legitimate.

Captain Foster and Fritz Cheny were more than a little concerned about the Farmer-Talbot fight. It was the first instance of any kind of crew problem, and that alone was enough to send up the red flag.

Gideon Foster paced his cabin and puffed on a stogie. "It doesn't seem quite natural to me for men that have been shanghaied to be so damned quiet about it."

Fritz Cheny sat in a canvas chair near the desk and scratched his head, but made no comment.

"Think about it, Fritz, the shanghaied folks up there in the forecastle ought to be setting up a howl that could be heard back in Frisco. But up to now there's been one incident that we know about." The captain sidled around the chart table and finally came to rest on the edge of his desk. He blew a half dozen smoke rings before he said, "Just one fight. Come on, Fritz, that doesn't seem realistic."

"Maybe you're worrying about something that don't exist, Skipper."

"Bull! You don't believe that, Fritz." Foster took a paper from his desk. "Is this watch list complete?"

"As far as I can tell it is," the first mate said.

"Then we start right here, Fritz, by taking a hard look at the two watch lists."

"Ok" but what are we looking for?"

"Don't know that yet," Foster grumbled as he studied the roster. "Take a look at this starboard watch, Fritz and tell me how many of those men you know."

"Well, I know the man in sick bay, Farmer." Then he squinted hard at the list and said, "Here's a bunch I don't know, Whitaker, Baker, Simms, Talbot and McCoy."

"Does that look at all funny to you?"

"Can't say it does. Why?"

"Who made out the watch list?"

"Jensen put the most of it together, but I OK'd it. Why, what's wrong?"

"Maybe nothing. But are you sure there's enough experience on this starboard watch?"

"Well, I just took Jensen's word for that."

"All right, Fritz. Do this. Sit down and make two new watch lists. But this time, mix them up. Use half the people you know on one side and half on the other."

"Ok." Fritz said reluctantly. Then he looked at the captain and said, "What if we do that and there is something funny going on. Won't that tip our hand?"

"Don't think so. Tell Jensen that you are concerned about the balance of experience. Seems that should answer any questions."

"All right, Skipper."

"You got some doubt?"

"Yes I do, Captain. I think we ought to hold off a while." Then Fritz grinned, "Give me a little more time to nose around."

Foster took a long drag on his cigar and said, "You've got twenty four hours and in the meantime, get the new lists ready."

Thunder and Jeff were propped up in their bunks while Tungee looked forlornly out the porthole.

Thunder Parker fixed Tungee with a look and said, "You seem like a man that would druther be off someplace else."

Tungee nodded. "An understatement, my friend."

"I'm bettin' it's got somethin' to do with gold," Thunder muttered softly. "Tell me, Cahill, how much didja come back with?"

"What are you talking about?"

"You know dang well what I'm talkin' of," Thunder said in a low gentle growl, "The gold, Tungee, the gold. How much didja come back with?"

"You didn't believe what I told you the other night at Ernie's, did you."

"Naw, now come on, what didja git?"

Tungee took as much time as he could before answering. How

47

much should he tell these men? One fact he had to consider none of his California resources would be worth a nickel if he couldn't get back there and take charge of it. How much of an asset would these two be? It might be sticky, he thought, but what the hell. "A lot."

"What do you mean by, a lot? Ain't you weighed it out?" Thunder asked.

"Not all of it."

"What about the part you did weigh?" Jeff said anxiously.

"A little over fifteen thousand ounces."

Jeff gave a subtle laugh while Thunder's eyes danced. "Why you dad gummed oyster."

Then Jeff and Thunder began to shake with laughter until Jeff touched on the irony of it. "The Million dollar slave."

"Now I understand that dang fist bustin' the first day," Thunder said dryly. Jeff chuckled. "How does it feel being rich, Tungee?"

Tungee gave a dull chuckle and looked out the porthole.

Keys rattled in the companionway and seconds later Gideon Foster entered Cabin C. He looked around the room and announced. "Gentleman, you're free to move about the ship as you like. But I would suggest you not spend a great deal of time in the forecastle. We had a disturbance up there last night and one of our regular crew got a knife in the belly." The captain had a distressed look on his face as he turned to leave, but stopped at the door and looked back. "Randolph, you'll report to Brett Herman in the galley. Parker, you and Cahill check in with Fritz Cheny. The three of you will continue to use these quarters," Foster grinned and said, "I don't see any bruises. Think I'll leave you where you are."

Then the captain turned and walked down the companionway toward his quarters while Tungee and the others stood in place, staring at the open door.

— SEVEN —

The sky was almost clear and the ship was running before the wind with a full set of lightweight canvas. And there was just enough fine spray kicking off the bows to make you feel alive. Tungee stood for a moment, amused at his own thoughts. He was a prisoner, but that didn't seem to matter, he felt the same excitement every sailor feels when working a tall ship. He scanned the horizon and then looked about the rigging and confirmed his suspicions. She was an American Clipper carrying three squares and a spanker rigged to the fore and main skysail with a mizzen's upper top royal.

Fritz Cheny assigned Tungee to the port watch and Thunder to starboard, beginning that evening with the dogwatch.

Tungee was anxious to get aloft and the first thing he did was to climb up to the crow's nest. He spent a half-hour up there reorienting to the sights, sounds and feel of a square-rigger. Then when he got back on deck, he confirmed something he had thought all along the ship was solid all right and with good reason, she had been designed and built by John McKay, one of America's top shipbuilders.

For the balance of the afternoon he walked the deck trying to get his sea legs back and thinking about his predicament. He was well aware that all of his gold was absolutely worthless under present circumstances. Could the skipper be bought? How much would it take for Captain Foster to turn around and go back to San Francisco, a better question might be, would he believe I have the money? Put yourself in his shoes and say you went for the deal. Couldn't some other member of the crew press shanghai charges once you got back to port? Nope. It would take a naive man to go that route and Gideon Foster is not naive.

By the time Tungee checked in for his first watch he had decided, at least for the present, to go ahead and work the ship. In his way of thinking, that was the way to survive the voyage. He was convinced they were on board a solid vessel, but what about the crew? Are they capable of handling the ship in those treacherous waters around Cape Horn?

The wind had moved around a quarter and they were sailing a broad reach on a twenty-degree port tack. In the middle of his first watch, Tungee walked toward the helm and was greeted by an affable fellow. "Hello, mate. Mine's Everett Dobbs, what's yours?"

Tungee was stopped by the accent. The accent he had taken a dislike to just before he blacked out on shanghai night. His answer was abrupt and cutting. "Tustungee Cahill."

"You don't sound like the most friendly bloke."

Tungee bristled. "So what?"

"Tell me, mate, how was it you came to sign on this here scenic voyage?" Dobbs asked lightly.

The fun seemed to be at Tungee's expense, but he decided to go along with it. "Well, you see, I had a personal engraved invitation, landed hard just back of my right ear."

"You know what I believe, mate. I believe they sent them invites out in mass. And early on I was feeling so honored that mine was special."

"Mr. Cahill," Fritz Cheny called, "You're wanted on the quarterdeck."

Dobbs drifted off toward the bow and Tungee jogged back to the quarterdeck and joined the first mate.

During that first two-hour watch Tungee was introduced to several men, including the second mate, Hank Jensen and watch mate in charge of the mainmast, Gabe Toombs. But most of his time was spent with Fritz Cheny who passed along several orders from the captain. Tungee was made watch mate in charge of the foremast. He was also given the task of bending the novice sailors into shape. He considered that last order to be his most formidable task.

A gangling young bespectacled fellow with a shock of black hair curling over his forehead called out, "Mr. Cahill?"

"You've found him, but Tungee, will do just fine."

"I'm Eugene Blakely. Mr. Cheny told me to see you."

"Are you on my watch?"

"Yes, sir. And Mr. Cheny said that you could teach me something about the rigging."

Tungee said laughingly, "Is that what he said, teach you?"

"Yes, sir. That's what he said."

"That'll work, I suppose. Now here's where we start, you call me Tungee and if it's all right, I'll call you Gene."

"That's fine with me." The young man said.

"What about your spectacles? Could you get along if you lost them up there?"

The boy smiled. "I'd miss them, but I could manage."

"All right, but remember, you could get hurt up there if you couldn't see." Then Tungee gestured toward the rigging.

"Been up there yet?"

"Yes and it's frightening."

"Heights scare you?"

"No."

"Then what's the problem?"

"Well, I just don't know what I'm doing up there."

Tungee thought for a moment. There was sure to be others in need of training and he had to get himself back in shape, so why not take the kid along. "I want to tell you something right up front, you won't learn it all in one day or even one week. But if you'll pay attention and put the stuff I tell you into practice, you will get the hang of it in short order. Come on, follow me."

Tungee explained masts, sails, yardarms, ropes and ties. He couldn't have ordered a better test case the kid was bright and bubbling over with enthusiasm. Gene Blakely listened and followed his instructor up the foremast and back to the deck twice. Then on the third climb, Tungee decided it was time for a breather and a talk. They positioned themselves atop the yardarm of the fore upper topsail and sat for a while just feeling the breeze and taking in the beauty of the sea and cloud formation.

They talked a while and young Blakely told about his family coming to California from New York on an old bark. Funny thing was that he had been shanghaied on his seventeenth birthday. But that didn't seem to bother him, in fact the youngster appeared to be excited about being on board the ship.

Tungee chuckled at the lad's spirit and he got the impression that young Gene Blakely would have cheered the unfurling of the "Jolly Roger."

"Why would they wait till they got to sea to change the name plate on the ship?" the boy asked in a serious tone.

"I don't know. What are you talking about?"

"We sailed out of San Francisco Bay as the Orient Leaf, then overnight that name was painted out and the next morning it read Marcus F. Childs."

"Are you sure of that?" Tungee asked unbelieving.

"Yeah. And I'm not the only one that noticed it. Nobody seems to know why."

What is that all about, Tungee wondered? Then he recalled that first meeting in the captain's cabin. Gideon Foster was troubled about something he didn't want to talk about. Could the name change have something to do with his strange demeanor?

Following his conversation with Gene Blakely, Tungee began recording dates, names and events in a journal. If his suspicions were right about the odd circumstances surrounding the voyage and later on legal problems cropped up, then maybe the notes would come in handy.

Within a few days he determined that his journal would prove invaluable. Names and numbers began to pile up as to just who had signed on and others, like himself, that had come onboard the hard way. By the middle of September he had determined that approximately forty five men were on board the ship and he had some limited information on twenty one of that number. Out of that list, eleven had been shanghaied.

Tungee and Everett Dobbs were still in the rigging after completing a routine tack change. Dobbs was grousing about how difficult it was learning the sailor's routine and his general displeasure about being on board. "I suppose I was in the wrong place at the wrong time." Then he looked at Tungee and laughed. "Speared on my own petard."

"What's that suppose to mean?" Tungee asked.

"I reckon you were locked away too long to hear the regular scuttlebutt."

"Could be."

"The fact is, mate," Dobbs said as a slow grin crossed his face, "Back in San Francisco, I was working for the ones what put this thing together."

"You mean you worked for the crimp?"

"That's about it. But if I was you, I wouldn't call him no crimp."

"Are you saying that bastard is on board?"

"That's exactly what I'm sayin', mate."

"Who is it?" Tungee asked cautiously.

Dobbs shook his head. "You mean you don't even know that?"

"You said it yourself. I've been locked up in Cabin C."

"I guess you're right, mate," Dobbs sputtered.

Tungee expected the Aussie to continue, but he suddenly clammed up. Tungee took his time and repeated the question, "Who is the crimp?"

Dobbs gave an embarrassed look. "I'm afraid I just stuck my foot in my mouth and if you don't mind, mate, all things considered, I think I'll just leave it there."

Three of the trainees had just climbed to the top of the foresail yard. Tungee stood on deck pointing out the standard way of holding a sail at a given angle, "The technique is called bracing."

Fritz Cheny tapped him on the shoulder and said, "How are they doing?"

"So far so good. It'll take a while, but they're trying and that's all you can ask."

"Tungee, the captain wants to talk to you. He's back at the chart house."

"Sure thing, Fritz." Then he gestured up the mast. "They're working on their bracing, give 'em some pointers."

Gideon Foster held the chart house door open and motioned Tungee to come inside.

"Mr. Cheny said you wanted to see me, Captain."

Foster took his time and lit one of his small cigars. "I don't know for certain, but my gut tells me we've got a problem."

Tungee looked square into the captain's eyes, but said nothing.

"It's gonna bust wide open. And damned if I know what shape it's going to take."

"Mutiny?" Tungee asked.

"Maybe." Then Foster gave a worried look and said, "When you pull as many men off the streets as we had to, there are bound to be problems."

"I didn't exactly sign on," Tungee said bluntly.

"I know that and I'll make it up to you somehow," Foster said apologetically.

Tungee projected a hard fixed smile that gave the captain no comfort.

"You're one of the few people onboard this ship I feel I can trust." The captain flicked his cigar ashes into the copper tray. "And I expect I'm going to need your help."

"Cheny sold me on the idea of shaping up some of the new men. I'll do the best I can with them."

"I appreciate that, Tungee, but what I've got in mind is likely to be far more important than that."

Tungee thought about the whole mess and he knew the skipper was about to press him for a big favor. But he wasn't quite sure he wanted to cut him that much slack, the same man that had just paid to have him shanghaied.

Foster began to pace and chew on his cigar, "I want you to move in with the crew, up in the forecastle."

"You're asking me to be your spy?"

"I guess you could call it that. Fact is, we've got to find out what's going on up there."

Tungee frowned and squinted at Foster. "I don't know that I owe you that kind of loyalty, Captain."

Gideon Foster held his palms out. "I guess I stepped into that one. And I can't blame you for feeling that way. But, Tungee, we've got a real problem that could involve the safety of every man on this ship. If it was to get out of hand we'd all suffer."

Tungee's Indian blood boiled as he looked out the porthole, considering the whole situation, but he didn't say anything.

"I'd like to ask you as a friend, Tungee." Foster said gently, "Move into the forecastle and lets try and root this thing out."

The captain could be on to something, but he didn't want to move in with that crowd until he had a chance to work it out in his own mind. And another thing, he wasn't about to give Foster the satisfaction of a quick answer. "I'll think about it Captain, but if I decide to do it, it'll be in my own way and in my own time."

"That's all right with me," Foster said, "but I have a strong feeling that time is not on our side."

During the night the fair winds diminished to a flat calm. The waters were almost still and the timbers of the ship creaked out a lonely groan. It was the quiet that Tungee awoke to. He rolled out of his bunk and looked out the porthole and saw fog hugging a calm sea. His watch time was almost an hour away, but he was fully awake and decided to go on deck.

Standing amidships looking forward he could barely make out the flying jib hanging lazily over the bowsprit. The running lanterns were not much more than light specs in the distance.

Thunder Parker walked out of the shadows whispered in Tungee's ear and took him by the sleeve, urging him forward. The old man spoke in a raspy whisper. "Same time as the wind played out, I was in the rigging makin' a mite of a change in the mizzen topgallant yard. And as I eased down the pole I heard Alf Talbot talkin' to somebody. Couldn't tell who it was. The spanker was tween them and me. They knowed my presence, you can bank on that. Now listen ta what Alf said. 'Iffen we kill the captain and the first mate, it'll make it easier fer to take charge.' I came on down to the deck and they walked off toward the stern."

"Is that all you herd?"

"I 'spect they wanted me to hear that and no more."

Tungee figured they could be sounding Thunder out, just to see where he stands. After all, if they take control, they'll need a skipper.

It's very likely a mutiny is in the works. But the question is who and how many are involved and when would the takeover begin?

"What do you think about a mutiny, Thunder?"

"From a skipper's point of view, can't say much fer it. I was up again, one myself. Had some stores go bad and I had to cut way back on the chow rations. We'd come out of Valparaiso, Chili caught some nasty weather roundin' the Horn. Cold wind damned near pushed us to the limit. It was a killin' cold comin' offen Antarctica. We lost some canvas and some days, but no lives."

"I've heard of men freezing and dying in the kind of cold you're talking about, Thunder."

"It's an awful thing to see. Anyhow, things turned around fer us; we caught a three quarter wind that was shovin' us a dozen knots ahead toward Liverpool. Well, them lost days made fer shorter rations and that was enough to fire up an already nasty bunch. Madeira Island was a hundred miles east of my course and they wanted to put in there and resupply. But the way I saw it, with the wind holdin', we could be in Liverpool quicker than gettin' off course to Madeira."

"Make for Liverpool," Tungee said emphatically.

"That's what I done," he slowly shook his head, "but in less than twenty four hours, the winds quit and we laid into a dead' calm."

"Bad luck."

"That sure is a fact. Things got real nasty. I was lookin', down a gun barrel when my first mate throwed a marlin spike that laid the gun totin' leader low." Thunder's eyes opened wide and he said, "I talked like a Dutch uncle, Tungee. I must have been pretty convincin', for they calmed down. But in them few minutes I was thinkin' I wouldn't be onboard when we got to port. I stood my ground, but there was a knot in my gut bigger than two fists. Thank God the winds picked up."

"What happened when you got to port?"

"Nothin'. For by the time we got there, the ringleader was dead and the rest were more scared than I'd been. They came to me and said they wuz wrong. That was all there was to it." Thunder pursed his lips and said, "No, mutiny scares hell out of me, Tungee."

Pieces of the puzzle were floating around, but they didn't seem to be in any kind of order. Tungee was feeling more and more uncomfortable about the Aussies on board and their connections to the Sydney Ducks in San Francisco.

Things Dobbs and the kid had said left little doubt about who rounded up the crew. And Dobbs said that there was trouble in their own ranks. Something about a last minute surprise. Just before sailing time a call went out for two more men. The person in charge of the roundup took the easy way and shanghaied two of their own. Tungee began to wonder if there was any connection between the ship's name change and the possible mutiny. Another thought occurred to him. Are there two separate conspiracies at work? One thing for sure, he had to figure out his own options, line up the odds and decide which way to jump when things begin to heat up. Hell of a thing -- lots of questions and still no answers.

— EIGHT —

Tungee's conversation with Thunder Parker reinforced his own thoughts about Cape Horn. Prepare as best you can for the bone chilling wind and cold, expect the worst and maybe you'll get fooled the other way around. The ship was carrying lightweight canvas and none of the novice crew members had any experience in changing a sail. All that lightweight canvas had to be changed to heavy before they hit foul weather. Tungee surveyed the thirteen pieces of cloth he was in charge of and he determined that the fore upper topsail was showing the most wear. And as a practical matter it would be good experience for the new men to go ahead and make the change. He called Blakely and Dobbs to work with two regulars on that piece of worn canvas that was located half way up the mast. In normal practice, eight men would be used to make the change, but four could manage. That way the new people would be forced to pull their own weight and if they couldn't, better to find out in fair weather rather than foul.

Tungee explained his idea to Cheny and the first mate enthused, "Go ahead. Go down to the sail locker and tell the old man what you need."

Following Cheny's suggestion, Tungee put the men to work removing the worn sail. Then he went aft and located the sail locker. A small man sat in the back part of the room sewing a piece of canvas.

Tungee called out, "Are you the sail maker?"

"Yeah." Walter Greenleaf was an elf of a man, clean-shaven, wrinkled and balding.

The two exchanged names and Tungee explained the problem and what he needed.

As soon as they finished the business at hand, Walter Greenleaf said, "I understand I just missed sailing with you a few years back."

"That's news to me," Tungee told him.

"Yeah. The captain and I talked about it a day or two ago. I believe it was your first cruise with Gideon."

"Why didn't you make the voyage?"

Walter Greenleaf chuckled and continued to talk as he searched the shelves of the locker for the needed piece of canvas. "I live in Vermont and we had a terrible snow storm. I got snowed in. When I finally dug myself out and got to Boston, you fellows had already sailed."

"Sorry we missed each other."

The old man smiled. "I've got the heavy canvas you need, just have your men bring the worn cloth down and we'll make the exchange."

"Right," Tungee said as he hustled back toward the foremast. The men had the old sail off the yard and neatly folded into a bundle on the deck.

He instructed them to take the old canvas down to the locker. Tungee followed along and once the exchange was made he hung around as he got the impression that Greenleaf had something on his mind.

As soon as the men left, the sailmaker said in a matter-of-fact way, "I gather we don't have a happy crew on board."

"That may be an understatement, Mr. Greenleaf."

The sprightly little man opened a small hatch at the back of the sail locker. Then he looked around furtively and gestured to Tungee. "Go on through, the captain needs to see you."

The companionway was on the other side of the hatch and Captain Foster stood near the door to his cabin. He nodded. "Go on inside and have a seat."

Tungee followed his instructions and took a chair between the desk and the chart table.

Captain Foster walked around the cabin, puffing on one of his black cigars. He finally settled down on the edge of his desk and looked at Tungee. "This has to do with the talk we had the other day. Now, I have it on pretty good authority that there is a group of men onboard that plan to wrest command of this ship from me."

"Any scuttlebutt as to why, Captain?" Tungee asked.

"No. But Brett Herman, in the galley, heard a couple of things. It was between the Aussies. Alf Talbot said that after they got control they'd move into a position just off Panama."

"Is that all he heard?"

"At that time, yes. But a week or so ago we found two three inch guns in the hold that were not listed on the cargo manifest."

"Three inch guns, huh. Maybe they plan to pirate for gold shipments that are heading for the states."

"That's my thinking," Foster said.

"Captain, I just got wind of the name change business. Now, you've got to know what that's about."

"Damn it, Tungee. The name change is as much a mystery to me as it is to you. The change was given to me by way of sealed orders, not to be opened until we got to sea."

"What reason did they give?"

"None. They didn't tell me a thing, other than to paint out the name of the Orient Leaf and make the new lettering Marcus F. Childs. Then to proceed to St. Katharine Island and thence to Liverpool."

"You know what it sounds like to me, Captain. Insurance fraud."

Foster was bewildered. "I guess anything's possible. But Alf Talbot and his gang are the immediate problem. If it's a mutiny, there's going to be some killing."

"Yeah, and from what I hear, you and Fritz Cheny are at the top of that list." Tungee took a deep breath. "About Talbot, Skipper, can't you just arrest him and slap him in irons."

"It's not that simple, Tungee. Too many men involved now including some of our own. Trouble is I don't know which ones. We also don't know if they are using money or intimidation to lure them over to their side."

"It would be simple enough if it's just force. If we could get to them, they'd come back in a minute."

The captain squirmed a little. "I'm hoping you're about ready to move in with the forecastle crowd."

Tungee's stomach knotted up, but he said calmly, "Well, I guess there's no time like the present. I have a question though, how do we make it look like something other than a plant?"

"Do it any way you want to."

"Can we trust Brett Herman."

Foster nodded. "I can vouch for him."

"Then I'll pick a fight with him in the chow hall."

Tungee screwed up his nerve and frowned. "Pass the word to Herman to expect it at the next meal."

"Done," Foster said approvingly.

On his walk back to Cabin C, Tungee shuddered at the thought of a confrontation with the burly Brett Herman. But he was in the game now and if they were to survive this voyage they'd have to find some answers. And his moving into the forecastle might be the only way to get them. Jeff Randolph was alone in the cabin when Tungee arrived.

"You look like you've just seen a ghost, Tungee."

"Might be better if I had."

"What do you mean?"

Tungee turned, locked the door, pulled the small pistol from his boot and handed it to Jeff. "You take charge of this little beauty, for now."

"I hope there's more to the story than this."

"There is. Now, I consider you a friend, Jeff. And I hope the feeling is mutual."

Jeff didn't say anything, but gave an agreeable smile and a positive nod.

"In less than an hour I'm going to be slugged and thrown into the forecastle."

"How do you know that?"

"It's a plan that involves your boss, Brett Herman and me. There will be a fight and I'll wind up in the forecastle."

"I hope you know what you're doing," Jeff remarked.

"You and me both." And Tungee said seriously, "Now there may be times in the next few days that things don't make sense. I may call you Nigger, or worse. It'll be part of the sham. I don't know what any of these people are up to, the captain and his regulars or Talbot and his gang. Something is terribly wrong on this ship and I aim to find out what it is. I guess what I'm saying is that I need your help, Jeff. So I want you to listen for anything, any tidbit of information that we can use."

"I don't know what you mean," Jeff grumbled.

"To tell you the truth, I'm not sure either. But I do know there's a possible mutiny in the works."

"Should we talk to Thunder about it?"

"No. Not right now anyway. I like that old man, but there are too many unanswered questions."

"Ok. But be careful of Brett Herman, he can be as mean as a snake."

"Thanks, Jeff, that's reassuring as hell."

Tungee screwed up his nerves as he entered the mess and took a seat near the end of the port side table. He didn't have to wait long for the moment he turned toward the galley, he saw Brett Herman lumbering in his direction with a pot of stew. That wasn't a part of the cook's normal routine. Show time, Tungee thought.

Herman sat the pot down and Tungee took his cue. "What are you feeding us today, rat soup or bilge bouillon?"

The big man turned and his blue eyes glared out of a fleshy boyish face. Tungee thought about Jeff's warning when he saw rage in the cook's eyes.

Brett Herman moved into position and tipped the pot of hot stew into Tungee's lap. The victim kicked back and turned the bench over sending all hands sprawling to the floor.

Herman punched Tungee in the face and that along with the hot stew that seared his belly almost took the fight out of him. But knowing he had to make it look good, he came up punching and kicking his oversized opponent.

Herman lifted Tungee like a wet mop and threw him into the bulkhead. But the Indian bounced back and kneed Herman in the groin. The big cook doubled over in pain and by that time every man in the chow hall had joined the fray.

Jeff made an untimely entrance and received a stiff right to the jaw. He went down for the count.

Brett Herman recovered from the kick to his groin and swung at Tungee's jaw, but missed.

"Knock it off!" Cheny yelled as he entered the chow hall.

Better late than never, Tungee thought.

The first mate scanned the room. "Who started this fight?"

Brett Herman grabbed Tungee by the nape of the neck and replied, "This one."

Then without another word, the cook and first mate made like a couple of barroom bouncers and hustled Tungee up to the main deck and then forward to the forecastle. They kept up the show as the cook booted Tungee through the door, catapulting him to the deck below. The victim landed hard on the floor of the forecastle crew quarters.

Fritz Cheny cupped his hands and snarled, "You're home, Mr. Cahill," all for the benefit of the gathering crowd.

Tungee lay in a heap at the foot of the ladder, his body riddled with cuts and bruises and his belly was on fire from the hot stew. Men from his watch slowly descended the ladder and while they didn't talk very much, he sensed a kind of tentative acceptance.

Dobbs said jovially, "Welcome to our humble home, mate."

Gene Blakely found some turpentine and dabbed it on Tungee's wounds. There was no empty bunk, so he slung a hammock forward. Not much in the way of comfort, but all things considered, it might be good for the image he needed to cultivate.

His first few days in the forecastle were spent in passive observation. Better to stay neutral for the time being and save the questions for later. He did try to cultivate a speaking relationship with Alf Talbot and while the big Aussie hadn't shown total antagonism toward him, he hadn't noticed anything that would indicate acceptance either. Talbot was an intimidating figure and from what Tungee had observed, Farmer was the only man in the crew to ever cross him. Of course Dobbs had managed to cross the line from time to time, but it was always in a humorous and jesting way.

A light mid afternoon shower accompanied by gusting winds had caused Fritz Cheny to call out the crew to effect a massive sail change. After an hour's hard work, most of the top men had returned to the deck. Tungee told Dobbs to stay in the rigging. They needed to talk.

"How did you get to know Alf Talbot?" Tungee asked.

"I've known the bloke for more than a year back in San Francisco."

"Then you didn't come from Australia with him?"

"No. I never laid eyes on Alf down home. But he was the one that got me into the Ducks."

"Do you like him, Alf I mean?"

"I'd soon as not make no pronouncements about that, mate."

Well, it's a beginning Tungee mused, one question answered. Intimidation is apparently a big part of the Ducks recruiting and enforcement policy.

"Dobbs, if it came down to a fight between Captain Foster and a bunch bent on mutiny, which side would you take?"

"I ain't got a clue about that, mate." He hesitated and then added, "I'll just wait and play this here thing one day at a time."

"Do you think Talbot will do the same?"

"Not on your life, mate, not Alf. He's got it all worked out in his head. He had plans worked out before we got on this bloomin' ship."

"What are you talking about, Dobbs? I thought you two were shanghaied, same as me."

"I was brought aboard like you was, mate, but Alf didn't come that way."

"You mean he signed on?"

"No." Dobbs laughed, "he ain't signed on and he didn't get brung on neither. Alfie walked on board as straight up as you please." Then he added in a conspiratorial tone. "Now the skipper thinks he was brung on the same as you and me, but it ain't so."

"Tell me something, why did they shanghai some of their own men?"

"There was only two of us Ducks what came aboard that way. And I'm among that small group of unfortunates." Dobbs shrugged. "I was told it was because I was good with a long gun and my pal, Oliver Simms just happened to be with me at the time. Now I ask you, mate ain't that the pits?"

"If they can pull it off, will there be any loot to split up?"

"They expect it to be."

"What do you think the chances are of my getting in on the action?"

"I don't know, mate. But I suppose it's possible."

"Could you put in a good word with Alf, for me."

"I'll get Alfie's ear and he's sure to carry it up."

"Carry it up?" Tungee asked, "I thought Talbot was the big fish."

"No. But he's big enough."

— NINE —

Fritz Cheny's call to reef was the beginning of a long night. The deep and heavy swells were a harbinger of that night's foul weather. They had just started the reefing process when orders came to furl all canvas fore, main and mizzenmasts. They rode out the next eight-hour storm carrying only the jibs, stays and the spanker.

Tungee's first impression about the ship was born out, she was solid and handled rough seas with the grace of a ballet dancer. Watch sections, to the man, got little sleep for the next twenty-four hours. And several crew members learned more than they ever wanted to know about seasickness. Heave to the lee, not into the wind.

Dobbs joined the men that took to their bunks. Tungee approached him and could immediately see the pea green complexion accompanied by cold sweat. The invalid waved a limp arm and signaled Tungee to come closer. Then he said something between a whisper and a croak. "Forget that talk we had. The one about my speaking to Alf about you."

"Why, did you change your mind?"

"I did nothing of the sort. I done talked to him and he told me straight that there was nothin' in the deal for you."

"Doesn't want me in, huh."

"No, thank you very much."

"It's Ok, Dobbs. Don't give it another thought, you just relax and try to get your sea legs back under you."

Tungee walked back to his hammock and worried about the turn of events. Alf and his gang must figure since I've sailed with Foster before, I'm in his camp.

Tungee came out of the forecastle and spotted Foster near the helm. The captain turned and went into the chart house. Tungee took a quick look around and when he didn't see anyone looking, slipped into the chart house just behind the captain.

"What are you doing here, Tungee?" Asked a startled Gideon Foster.

"We've got to talk."

You in trouble up there?"

"You might say that. Someone in the thick of things has apparently figured out where I stand."

"How do you know that?"

"Don't know for a fact. But it sure looks that way."

There was a rap on the door and Captain Foster ordered, "Come on in."

"Fritz Cheny rushed through the door with excitement written all over his face. "Talbot's used the knife again.

"Who was it this time?" Foster demanded.

"One of the Aussie's Dobbs is his name. It was just a scrape and from what I can tell it was done to intimidate."

Tungee said, "In a round about way, this Dobbs knifing may have been caused by me."

"How so, Tungee?" the captain asked.

"Well, Dobbs seemed to be pretty cozy with Talbot and I asked him, Dobbs, to pass the word that I was interested in joining Talbot's group. The answer came back that Alf wanted no part of me. Dobbs may have pushed a bit too hard on my behalf and set Talbot off."

"Put him in irons," Gideon Foster ordered.

"Hold on, skipper!" Tungee exclaimed. "I have it on pretty good authority that Alf Talbot is not the top man. I figure we may be better off by giving them a little more rope."

Foster puffed on his cigar and said anxiously, "All right, Tungee, but not much. If we give that gang too much rope, we might wind up on the wrong end of it."

Tungee left that meeting and immediately collared Gene Blakely. "Follow me up the mast, we've got to talk."

The youngster followed Tungee and they climbed to the starboard side of the fore upper topsail yard and found themselves comfortable positions.

Tungee got Blakely's attention and said grimly, "Kid, I'm not sure you understand the danger we're in. Something bad is going on and if it turns out to be a mutiny, there'll be some killing. Now, I have a feeling that you know a lot more about what's going on than you've told me so far. I haven't pressed you before, but I'm going to now."

Gene Blakely swallowed hard. Then said innocently, "I guess I should have told you earlier. But I was afraid to. I'm scared to death of Alf Talbot."

"What do you know?"

"Well, it's a lot of bits and pieces and I don't know if it amounts to much." The kid looked pleased to be getting it off his chest. "A day or two after we put out of San Francisco, I heard Talbot jawing to a small group in the forecastle. He mentioned a half-breed and his gold. He said that would be a sizeable bonus that they could figure to add on to their original cuts."

Tungee's face flushed. "Did he mention a name?"

"No, but he said the old man would put the whole thing together in a day or two. Alf Talbot was excited. He said the gold is just pouring out of California."

"Anything more about the half-breed?"

"No. Not then," Blakely said earnestly, "and of course I had no idea about who the half-breed or the old man was at the time."

"Now you do."

"Yeah. I guess you're the half-breed and the old man is Thunder Parker."

"I expect you're right about me, but how does Thunder figure into it?"

"Because the Aussie's call him the old man and he's as cozy as he can be with Alf Talbot."

"Well, I'll be damned." Tungee muttered.

Fritz Cheny yelled up the rigging. "We'll shorten sail. You top men loafing around the deck. Shake a leg and get to your masts. You'll take in the skysails and the royals, and then stand by for a tack change. Helmsman, port your bow by ten degrees."

*　　*　　*

Tungee's hammock mocked the gentle roll of the ship as he relaxed under soft lantern light. He read his notes in his attempt to sort out the players. The ship's bow was cutting through a medium chop and mixing its low-level noise with the singing of the wind as it passed through the rigging. A distant din of voices from the card players got Tungee's attention. He slipped out of the hammock and casually walked back to the card game, leaned against a supporting post and watched the play.

Simms said, "You want in, mate?"

"What's the game?"

"Dealer's choice."

"What are the stakes?" Tungee asked.

"Big game, penny and raise to a nickel," Simms declared.

"Take a seat, mate. Fresh meat is always welcome."

Tungee recognized everyone at the table, but as he was sitting down the affable Simms said, "This here is Alf Talbot, Matt Benton, Leon Stark and me, I'm Oliver Simms."

Tungee threw in his ante and Matt Benton dealt out a hand of five-card draw. Tungee lucked out with the first hand; drawing to three deuces a king and a queen and took the first small pot.

The engaging Simms said, "This here ain't your first trip to sea is it, mate?"

"No. But it's the first time I was ever signed on with a club."

"Very exclusive, mate, our club. Very exclusive."

"Exclusive, my arse," Leon Stark grumbled. "Where did you come up with that seven dollar word, exclusive, Oliver Simms?"

"Never you mind, mate. Learnt is learnt."

Tungee said, "Listen fellows, I've spent a lot of time locked up in Cabin C, maybe you can answer a question for me. I hear we left San Francisco as the Orient Leaf. Now we're called the Marcus F. Childs. How come?"

The question was met with silence. The players looked toward Alf Talbot, but the big Aussie clammed up.

Tungee said, "Maybe I got the wrong information. There was no name change."

"There's been a change," Alf said quietly.

"Why? What was the reason?"

Simms grinned. "Fact is, mate, we ain't privy to that there information."

"Not even a guess, huh."

"There's plenty of guessin'," Talbot said, "but we don't know and further more we don't much give a damn. One name's as good as another as far as I'm concerned."

A voice called from the forecastle door, "Is Tungee Cahill down there,"

Before Tungee could answer, Jeff Randolph shinnied down the ladder and crossed the room to a position just behind his friend. Jeff, in an effort not to disturb the game, put his hand on Tungee's shoulder.

Tungee turned and said, "Randolph, what brings you down here?"

"Nothing, just came down to say hello."

Talbot snarled. "Well, you've said it."

Jeff recoiled. "How's that, mister?"

Tungee sat quietly, realizing Jeff had made an error by coming into the forecastle.

"Funny thing, mates, I don't see a damn thing," Simms said cynically.

"You're wrong, Mr. Simms. Why, I can plainly see a dark shadow ... Or is it just a darkie?"

Without a word, Jeff turned and made his exit.

Alf Talbot glared at Tungee. "Are you a Nigger lover?"

"I never gave it much thought, Alf," Tungee said casually, attempting to brush off the slur.

"Well, you best think about it, mate," Talbot declared, "You bein' Injun and all -- you ain't but a cut or two above the black, you know."

Tungee knew he was looking into the eyes of an evil man, but he kept a calm face and shuffled the cards.

Jeff signaled Tungee across the chow hall and silently mouthed, "Meet me in Cabin C."

They arrived moments apart. Jeff locked the door, paced the room and shook with nervous energy.

"I'd like to apologize for those low--"

"Thanks for the thought," Jeff held up his hand, "but that's not important, this is. Less than an hour ago Thunder Parker and Alf Talbot were in this room and spelled out their plan."

"What?" said an unbelieving Tungee?

Jeff shook his head. "I was about to open the door and heard Thunder's voice. "He said, 'That be a dumb trick, Alf.' Alf said, "'It warn't near so dumb as lettin' that Injun know what we're about.' Then Thunder said, 'If you be using that knife too freely on our own men, we ain't gonna have enough hands to pull this thing off. Just be mindful of what I tell you, Alf. Are all the guns in place?' 'You bet, Thunder.'"

"Is that it, Jeff?" Tungee asked.

"Not by a long shot. Thunder said, 'This'll be the night, Alf. You make shore that Foster, Cheny and the cook all go over the side. And when that's done, the rest will be a piece of cake.'"

"You're sure it was Thunder and Alf."

"As sure as I'm standing here."

"Why, that old fox," Tungee shook his head, "what a performance."

"What now, Tungee?" Jeff asked.

"You wait here, I've got to talk to Foster and Cheny."

Jeff quietly unlocked the door and Tungee slipped out of the cabin and jogged toward the captain's quarters. He gave a light tap on the door and walked right in.

Gideon Foster looked up from his map. "What's the bad news, Tungee?"

Thunder Parker is heading up this whole thing. It seems that Parker and Talbot were in on the plot before we left San Francisco."

Fritz Cheny shook his head. "We paid for both of them as part of the shanghaied group."

"That's just it, gentlemen," Tungee shook his head. "The way it figures now, there were only a few of us actually shanghaied. The rest are all members of the conspiracy."

"Damn their hides," Foster groaned.

"That's the reason we couldn't hear anything. They didn't need to talk about a plan that had already been worked out."

"Did you hear any details?" Fritz Cheny asked.

"Yeah," Tungee said and you won't like them much. They plan to kill you two along with Brett Herman."

"Can't get much worse than that," Foster muttered.

Fritz Cheny said evenly, "When does the killing start?"

"Late today or tonight," Tungee told him.

Cheny snapped, "Then we'd best grab Parker and Talbot right now."

"No. It's too far along for that," Foster said. "We've got to keep them thinking we're still in the dark. Tungee, you get back to the forecastle and quietly alert the people you can trust. Fritz, you do the same thing on deck. And be careful. Now, I want every trusted man to take his time and work his way aft to the quarterdeck." Then the skipper began to pace. "Further instructions and authority on board this ship will stay in my hands with you two as my lieutenants." Then he went to his desk, picked up a full crew list and ticked off the name of every man he thought was a good bet to be loyal.

Tungee found Jeff in Cabin C. "Give me the gun, I've got to go back to the forecastle and I may need it."

Jeff handed him the small weapon. "What do I do?"

"Go aft and find Captain Foster or Fritz Cheny, tell them I sent you. They'll tell you what to do."

Tungee gritted his teeth, put the gun in his boot and headed back to the forecastle.

— TEN —

As Tungee walked forward from the quarterdeck, he saw Thunder and Alf huddled near the bow. Unseen by them, he slipped into the forecastle and shinnied down the ladder.

There were more than a dozen men milling about the crew quarters and the regular card game was in progress. He gave a quick nod as he passed the card players and walked directly to his hammock.

Dobbs and Blakely were in their bunks and he had to figure a way to send them aft without drawing attention to what he was up to. He went to his hammock and picked up the jar of salve he had used on his belly burn. Then he went directly to Dobbs' bunk and asked in a voice loud enough for anyone to hear. "How's your cut?"

"It'll heal I suppose."

Blakely leaned over the side of his bunk to listen.

Tungee held up the jar, winked toward the kid and said to Dobbs. "Think this stuff might help?"

"If it's what the saw-bones put out, I got my doubts."

Tungee leaned in and spoke in a low tone. "Do you want to throw in with me and Captain Foster?"

"What are you talkin' about, mate?"

"You know damned well what I'm talking about," Tungee insisted. "I want to know where you stand?"

Dobbs paled. "I ain't sure, I ain't sure of nothin' right now."

"You don't want to be a party to murder, do you," Tungee said stoutly.

Dobbs took a short breath. "Not really, but I---"

"We're on to their scheme."

Dobbs hesitated. "May be, mate, but I think they're on to you as well."

"You could be right, but I need to know where you stand?"

Dobbs opened his mouth and nothing came out. Then he took in a long breath and stammered, "I'll throw in with you and Captain Foster."

"Ease out of your bunk," Then he tapped Blakely on the shoulder, "now the two of you need to work your way aft. Find Foster or Cheny and tell them I sent you."

"Tungee slipped back to his hammock and dug out his crew list. Two men the captain was counting on were presently in the forecastle. Will Farmer and Dan Thurston and they were both within the sound of his voice, but what could he say to them that wouldn't tip his hand?

There was a loud noise at the other end of the forecastle he heard shouts and swearing. It was a scuffle, maybe a fight. He heard shuffling feet and lots of commotion. He moved in the direction of the disturbance and saw two men being herded from the shadows toward the center of the room. The card game broke up and the players scattered.

"Dammit. Dobbs and Blakely didn't make it," Tungee said softly. He watched as Alf Talbot and Thunder shoved them toward the middle of the room. His heart was pounding like a drum inside his rib cage. Calm down now and stay in control. Play their game. He took a deep breath and moved toward the action.

"Thunder Parker, what are you doing down here with this riff raff?"

"You'll be fer knowin' soon enough, Injun," Thunder Parker growled.

Alf Talbot snapped. "I think we best put the knife to all of them we ain't sure of."

"That be your way of handlin' everything," Thunder bellowed, "But it ain't mine." Then the old man pulled a long pistol from his belt, waved it and motioned everyone forward. "Now, do like I told you, Alf."

Then he gestured toward Dobbs and Blakely," tie 'em up. Stark you and Benton, go up the ladder and guard the door." Then Thunder waved his gun and said, "Get over there, Tungee. I got somethin' to say to you."

"What's going on, Thunder?"

"Well, it be this way, Tungee. This here ship is gonna take on a new skipper and she's gonna sail a new course."

"What does that mean?"

"You'll know soon enough, if you join up and if you don't -- it won't make no never mind."

"Does that mean you're taking command?"

"That's the way she squares."

"Why didn't you let me know what was going on. At least I would have had a chance to think about it"

"That there is just what I didn't want, Tungee,"

"Then you mean I don't have a choice in the matter."

"Not much ... It's that time, Tungee. You be with me or agin me. You call it."

Tungee knew what he had to say, but he was concerned about how Dobbs, Blakely and the Foster people would take it. I'd better say what I've got to say now and explain later, he thought. "I stand with you, Skipper."

Thunder then turned To Alf. "Tie this one up with the others."

"What would you have done if I'd said no," Tungee said easily.

A grin cracked Thunder's hardened face. "Well, that there don't make no never mind now."

Tungee cringed at what he figured to be the true answer.

"Belay what I said about tying up the Injun. But do what you see fit with them other two, Alf," Thunder Parker said as he gestured toward Farmer and Thurston.

Tungee looked toward the tough Foster men and admired their character. They apparently couldn't be bought with gold or intimidation. However, in the present circumstances, he had to question how wise it was to stand that firm on principle.

Thunder waved Tungee down an isle, pointed to a bunk and said, "Sit ye down." Then he took a seat on a bunk near by.

Parker's face was flushed, but Tungee realized he was not looking into hostile eyes.

Thunder said, "I reckon you've noticed that things ain't always what they seem. All them lies I made up back there in Cabin C. Well, they had a reason."

Tungee just shook his head and listened.

"When I got into this thing, it was for one reason and that was for the gold. We all stand a chance to be rich. Now that brings it around to you. By all rights, you're a dead man, Tungee Cahill. You was to be dumped into the Pacific a day or two out of port. It was planned that way back in San Francisco. And it were me that put a stop to it. Now you may not believe that, but it's the God's honest truth."

Tungee was stunned, but mumbled. "I have no reason to doubt you Thunder. But what do we do now?"

"We go for the big score. Take this ship and set ourselves off of Panama and wait."

"For gold shipments headed for the states?"

"That's it, son...The gold." Then Thunder's eyes danced as he said, "There's tons of it, and just waitin' to be took."

"What about the Navy, won't they be escorting the shipments?"

"Too much ocean to cover. The Navy ain't got near enough ships to escort the gold that's comin' out of California."

"That may be true, but you can't expect to dodge all the escorts. Is it wise to tangle with their big guns."

"I don't plan to stand up and fight no naval battle." Then Thunder grinned, "If push comes to shove, we could stand and fight, cause we got some heavy artillery of our own. But I don't plan on that. Hell, we can out run anything they got and I'll stake my life on that."

"Who put this thing together?"

Thunder hesitated and rubbed his face. "Now I like you well enough not to kill you, Tungee, but not enough to put myself in that same fix."

Tungee gave a long reflective look and Thunder broke the silence. "I hope I can depend on you, my friend. But I'll tell you straight out, iffen you cause me grief, I'll just do what I was told to do back in San Francisco."

"You can count on me," Tungee declared.

Thunder stood and gestured that they should join the others. Tungee followed the old man and knew he was walking a very thin tightrope.

Dobbs and the kid were tied up in sitting positions and their backs to a large support post. The three Foster men were still standing.

Thunder asked, "What are you gonna do with these three?"

Alf said, "Give 'em the same as we gonna give Foster and Cheny I suppose."

Thunder Parker looked directly at the men and said, "So you ain't got no taste for the gold."

Tungee weighed in. "Thunder, these fellows may change their minds when you take full control. And something else, you've got to keep enough men for a crew."

Thunder looked at the men and said, "You got a choice, you can be rich or you can be dead, it's up to you."

Farmer and Thurston stood like mutes and then all of a sudden Alf suggested, "Maybe we best tie 'em up along with the others and decide later."

"I think that's best," Thunder said, then he signaled two of his men to come forward and give Alf a hand.

Tungee looked at all the men in the room and he finally spotted two of Foster's old timers who had crossed over, second boatswain, Dave Johnson and one of the stewards, Lowell Riker. Foster had counted both of them as solid crew members, but the gold was apparently worth more than their loyalty. How and when did they become a part of the plot?

The puzzle was beginning to fall into place, but he still couldn't tell which side had the upper hand.

Thunder Parker pointed toward one of the guards and ordered, "Break out the guns, Matt."

Matthew Benton walked to the aft bulkhead of the crew quarters, opened a hatch and crawled inside.

Tungee knew he had only minutes before their arsenal would be out of the hold. *Maybe I could knock off the two leaders. But one misfire and I'd be dead. Another thing to consider, a firefight in the crew quarters would put the tied up men right smack in the middle. No, that small handgun was not a big enough bargaining chip. Better* to do nothing for now than make the wrong move. Without realizing it, he started to pace back and forth.

Alf Talbot barked, "Hey, Injun. Cain't you settle down."

Tungee turned and raised his palms and gave the big Aussie a wide sheepish grin.

Matt Benton saved the moment when he poked his head out of the hold and called, "Hey, lend me a hand with these guns."

Half dozen men rushed over, took the weapons and laid them neatly on the nearby bunks along with ammunition.

Thunder said, "Pass them guns out and get 'em loaded."

Alf looked toward Tungee and said, "Thunder, I'd feel a whole lot better if we didn't give the Injun no gun. In fact I think we ought to tie him up with the others."

Thunder didn't hesitate. "Go ahead and do what you think best."

Alf was an expert at his task and in minutes had Tungee neatly tied up and sitting on the floor with the others.

Thunder walked over and knelt down beside Tungee and said, "If I was a odds maker I'd put some pretty low numbers on a certain proposition I got in mind." He smiled. "I'm bettin' there's a little old pistol tucked inside that right boot."

Tungee chuckled and in less time than it would take a pick pocket to steal your wallet Thunder was holding that little palm gun with two fingers. But despite it all, Tungee had a good feeling about that old pirate. Thunder put the tiny gun into his pocket and in the same move drew out a gold watch. He flipped open the face and it read nine o'clock. Parker closed the watch cover, returned it to his pocket, took a brief look around the room and announced, "Well, men, it's time to go."

Tungee was already making what seemed to be a futile effort to free himself.

Thunder pointed toward the hatch and said, "Give me ten minutes after we all clear into the hold before you start your action."

He squeezed his portly frame through the hatch and into the cargo hold followed by six of his men, two carrying lanterns.

Tungee figured they would exit somewhere near the stern. If this is a correct assessment, Thunder plans to strike from Foster's rear while Alf attacks over the main deck. He ruled out the mid deck's companionway as Thunder's exit. That wouldn't be smart at all and would provide nothing more than a shooting gallery for each side. But he was concerned about Foster, had he considered an attack from his rear.

Alf Talbot closed the hatch as the last of Thunder Parker's men disappeared into the hold.

A clock went off in Tungee's head and he knew they had less than ten minutes to work a miracle.

The big Aussie took a cursory look at the men tied up by the post and then joined the mutineers that had gathered beside the ladder. The door at the head of the ladder was swinging free, allowing outside sounds to enter. The ship was still under way, but probably making no more than three or four knots.

Tungee spoke quietly, "Anybody got a loose rope?"

The only response came from Dobbs and that was negative. Tungee was not tied to the post and he worked himself around near Farmer. And in a short time, he had Farmer's hands untied. Soon Tungee's hands were free but the clock in his head was racing, not ticking.

Alf Talbot and his men paid no attention to their prisoners, which allowed Tungee and Farmer to work around and untie the other men.

A good portion of the mutineer's arsenal remained on the bunks nearby. Thunder and his men had taken two lanterns and the dancing shadows caused by the one that remained gave Tungee an idea. He whispered, "Have you got your ropes off, Dobbs?"

"Almost."

"Can you see the rifles and ammunition on that near bunk?"

"I can."

"Get to them and load a rifle?"

"Gotcha, mate. I'm on my way."

Dobbs moved like a cat, slithering into the shadows near the bulkhead and in no time at all he slipped behind the bunk and began loading a weapon. "Now you just tell me what to aim at."

"The sea lamp," Tungee said in a hoarse whisper. "When the place goes dark, you other men figure a way to get to one of those rifles and load it. When you get that done, just stay in place and cover the forecastle door. Dobbs and I will follow Thunder and his men through the hold."

"I'm all set, mates," Dobbs said deliberately.

Talbot and his men had all gone through the door, with the exception of one man left to guard the prisoners.

"Go ahead, Dobbs, do it."

The muzzle flashed, the rifle cracked and the forecastle quarters was thrown into total darkness. Then as one, the men moved to the guns and as they picked up their rifles and began the process of loading, the noise level rose.

"Keep it down," Tungee ordered. "They can't see us, but they're not deaf."

═ ELEVEN ═

Tungee crawled through the hatch and Dobbs immediately shoved two rifles in and followed. They had expected a light source from the other men's lanterns, but instead they were met with an overwhelming darkness. Once their eyes began to adjust they could make out a feint glow at the aft end of the ship.

Will Farmer stuck his head through the hatch and asked, "Should we follow you?"

Tungee said, "No. You guys stay put and use your rifles to keep Talbot's men out of the forecastle."

"All right," Farmer whispered, "but holler if you need help."

"Never you mind about that, mate. If we need you, we'll scream our bloody heads off," Dobbs told him.

It was hot and stuffy inside the cargo hold. They inched their way across the grain sacks on hands and knees and felt their way over and around cargo. The heat was stifling and it was difficult to breathe. Sweat beads popped out on their foreheads and perspiration dripped into their eyes and ears.

Dobbs grumbled, "Gawd it's hotter than all billy hell in here, mate."

"Yeah, yeah, Dobbs, but keep it down."

They crawled along at a slow and deliberate pace toward the yellowish glow at the other end of the hold.

"What do you say, we take a few shots in the area of them lights," Dobbs suggested, "stir things up a bit."

"No, let's not tip our hand yet."

As they made headway, the glow at the end of the hold got brighter and made it easier to maneuver around the cargo.

"When we get near enough," Dobbs asked, "do we take out the lights or the men?"

"Go for the lights first, and after that just return their fire."

When they got closer to the light, they could hear a din of voices, but couldn't tell what they were saying.

Tungee and Dobbs had both dropped to their bellies and did a kind of serpentine slither, using their elbows to propel themselves forward. That ten minute clock was still ticking in Tungee's mind and he figured there couldn't be more than a minute or two remaining before the overall attack began.

They breathed heavily as they clawed their way over a large mound of grain sacks. Their effort paid off, when they got to the top they could see two distinct lights.

"Hold it right here," Tungee whispered. "Check your rifle and get into a firing position. You take the port lantern, Dobbs, I'll take the starboard."

"Please, mate. Give it to me in right and left, I'm still confused about this here shipboard lingo."

"Ok. You take the one on the right, I'll take the left."

"Now that makes more sense, mate."

"Now, get set and cock your piece. We'll go on three."

Tungee said in a hoarse whisper ... "One. Two. Three."

The rifles flashed and cracked out an ear splitting blast that reverberated around the hold. There was a momentary black out, but just as their eyes were adjusting to the total darkness, a strange kind of light flickered into life.

That new light quickly got brighter. Then someone shouted, "Fire!" And feet could be heard stomping the floor.

"Damn, that's a problem we could do without," Tungee blurted.

"I hate to say this, mate, but we might have just cooked our own bloomin' goose." Dobbs sat up on his haunches. "And I do believe a hasty exit might be in order."

"Point well taken, Mr. Dobbs," Tungee said gravely.

The firelight gave Tungee an exact location. "Follow me, Dobbs. There's a hatch just forward of our position. "Now, stay close and let's get going."

"Close you say, mate. Close I'll be. You'll be wearin' me like a bloomin' glove."

Tungee located the hatch at about the same time a thick acrid smoke moved like a giant cloud out of the fire area and began to obscure the light advantage the fire had provided. Tungee crawled up on a box, jumped to the ladder and climbed to the top and pushed on the hatch, but it didn't move. Then he climbed another rung, trying to get some leverage and forced it with his head and shoulders, but it wouldn't budge.

Dobbs climbed up beside him. "Let me have a go at it, mate," but he had no better luck. Then he slammed the butt of his rifle into the stubborn hatch. That didn't work either. Tungee climbed back into position and ran his fingers around the edge of the hatch and found the inside lock. "Stand back, Dobbs." Tungee coughed. "I'll shoot the lock off."

"Hurry up, Mate. I can't breathe."

The shot blasted the lock off and with one swift move Tungee forced the hatch open and back on its hinges. Then the outside sounds became clear and they were greeted by sporadic gunfire. Bullets could be heard singing across the deck in both directions.

"Gawd, Mate. I just had a thought."

"What's that, Dobbs?"

"Now I don't want to sound pessimistic, but I just had this thought. Both sides up there are gonna be takin' pot shots at me, don't you think."

Tungee swallowed smoke as he laughed, but it was no laughing matter. We have to make some kind of a move and chances be damned, Tungee thought. Better to take a bullet than stay in the hold and suffocate. Smoke billowed past the two men as they moved close to the opening. But they couldn't see or breathe without sticking their heads out and into the line of fire. A rock and a hard place came to Tungee's mind.

They could probably count on a few seconds of indecision. Both sides would likely figure the men coming out of the hold were allies. The deck location of the hatch was four feet aft of the mainmast base that was stepped down and raked toward the stern. They were lucky, because that construction gave them some protection from Alf's men. The black smoke pouring out of the hatch was bending toward the stern, obscuring Foster and his people from view.

"Are you ready to make a run for the quarterdeck, Dobbs?"

"Ready as I'll ever be I suppose. But you go first."

Tungee chuckled. "All right, keep your head down and follow me. Let's go ... Now!"

They exploded out of the hold and sprinted across a part of the deck that could only be called no-man's-land. Tungee yelled, as they approached Foster's makeshift breastworks, "Cahill and Dobbs coming in, Captain." And moments later, they scrambled over the grain sacks that made up most of the skipper's defenses.

"Where's the fire located?" Captain Foster demanded. Tungee pointed down. "Two decks below. And something else, Captain, Thunder Parker and six of his men are in the same general area of the fire."

"We heard the gunshots down below and I sent Fritz Cheny with a detail to look into it." Foster told him.

"They had planned to attack you from the rear, Skipper."

Tungee grinned. "I guess luck was on our side, they got delayed by the fire."

Fritz Cheny sent word back to the bridge that they had secured their position below and they had killed or captured all of Thunder Parker's men. But they had a problem; the fire was getting out of hand. They couldn't get to the bilge pump so Foster gave orders and Hank Jensen immediately set up a bucket brigade to fight the fire. They used every kind of container imaginable to scoop up seawater and pass it along to douse the blaze. Some of Thunder's men who had just surrendered to Fritz Cheny had a quick conversion and immediately picked up water buckets and joined the regular crew.

Following a coughing spasm to clear the smoke from his lungs Tungee looked around and was pleased by what he saw. The three-inch deck guns discovered by Foster had been brought topside and aimed out of the breastworks toward the mutineers. Gabe Toombs was in charge of the three-inch guns. But even with all that firepower, men on the quarterdeck were at a disadvantage. Sniper fire was coming in from the foremast and kept them hunkered down below the grain sacks.

The captain cupped his hands and called around the corner of the chart house, "Ahoy, you men at the forecastle. Stop your firing."

Alf Talbot responded with a cynical sneer. "We're takin' your ship, Gideon Foster."

"You've got your facts wrong, Mr. Talbot." the skipper said bluntly.

"You may as well give it up, Foster."

"Wake up, Mr. Talbot. We already have seven of your men, captured, wounded or dead. Thunder Parker is among the wounded." The captain hesitated and then shouted, "Just in case the smoke blinded you, Mr. Talbot, take a close look, we found the deck guns you'd planned to use after your takeover and they are presently aimed at you and your men."

"You're a foul mouthed liar, Gideon Foster. We'll take your ship and drive you to hell in the bargain."

"You'll do nothing of the kind, Mr. Talbot. You and your men have just two minutes to put your hands in the air and gather at the mainmast. If you don't accept that offer, I'll blow you off the forecastle."

"Save your talk, Foster," Alf Talbot snarled.

Foster yelled, "You men there in the rigging, give it up. I don't want your blood on my hands, but damn you all, we'll blow you to kingdom come if you don't give up this plan of mutiny and piracy."

"We'll see who has the bloody hands," Alf Talbot shouted.

Then he turned to his men and ordered, "Load your weapons and fire."

The men on the quarterdeck crouched low behind their breastworks. And in the next few minutes the rebels laid down a withering hail of gunfire.

When the guns fell silent, Alf Talbot's voice rang out, "Draw your saber's and charge the quarterdeck."

Alf Talbot led his men across the deck with a saber in his right hand and a pistol in his left.

Gideon Foster ordered, "Mr. Toombs give them a whiff of the grape."

"Aye, Captain," the gunner, said as he touched a hot ember to the short fuse.

The port side cannon immediately belched out a tight load of grape that hit Alf Talbot in full stride. He was cut in half and the concussion of the shot catapulted his body over the side.

When the mutineers saw Talbot go into the water, they stopped dead in their tracks and threw their weapons to the deck.

Tungee took a deep breath and turned his attention toward the stern and saw a worried look on Doc Dawson's face as he kneeled beside Thunder Parker. The old man was laying near the stern and seemed to be struggling for air. The doctor looked undecided for a moment as Tungee walked over and made eye contact with him. But after a brief pause the doctor just shook his head picked up his bag and moved on to his next patient.

Tungee knelt beside the dying man and thought about the many faces of Thunder Parker. One of the best skippers he'd ever known. The man was a scoundrel and yet Tungee considered him a friend. "How are you, Thunder?"

"I ain't no good, Tungee."

"Anything I can do for you?"

The old man held up a cup. "You might find me a little mite of rum."

Tungee picked up the bottle left behind by Doc Dawson and filled the cup.

Thunder's hands shook as he pressed the cup to his lips and took a swallow. "You be a wonderin' why, don't you, Tungee?"

"How in hell did you get mixed up with the likes of Alf Talbot."

"He were a hired hand, same as me."

"Who did the hiring?" Tungee asked urgently.

"The one that brung me in was a banker named Albreght."

"Mason Albreght?"

"One and the same."

"Was this plan put together the day before the ship sailed?"

Thunder shook his head. "No, Tungee. It were a long time before when they hatched the scheme to pirate for gold."

"They? Who do you mean, they?"

"Some pretty big folks back in San Francisco."

"How did you get mixed up in it?" Tungee asked.

"They needed a skipper for the gold operation and they bought me, Tungee. They was gonna make me rich." Then the old man coughed and chuckled. "There was to be a big bonus from a special bank account. I didn't know who owned the account till we got out of Cabin C and Alf told me."

"Why did they bother to shanghai me? Seems like it would have been simple enough to dispose of me back there."

"Bodies turn up too easy to suit them. Leastwise that's what I was told."

"I was supposed to just disappear?"

"That's the way they planned it. They said to kill you and dump you over the side."

"Why didn't you?"

A warm gentle look came over Thunder's face and he said. "I ain't never had, no stomach for killin'," then he looked directly into Tungee's eyes and grinned, "and ain't no way I'd go a killin' my friends."

"What about the ship, Thunder? With all the ships tied up in the bay, looks to me like they could have bought one rather than hijacked."

"They didn't want no ownership papers comin' back to haunt 'em."

"They thought of everything, didn't they?"

Thunder took another swill of rum and gave a deep rumbling cough. Then he closed his eyes and began to mumble, "Be the wind a holdin'?"

"Holding steady, Captain."

"We gonna make Liverpool in record time."

"Looks that way, Skipper."

"There ain't no need to be a puttin' into Madeira."

"The men have all backed off, Captain."

"I told 'em it ain't no need to go a changin' course."

Thunder sucked in all the air he could. Then he shivered.

"Thar be a squall workin' up out there."

"No signs of one, Thunder."

"Maybe you cain't see it yet, but it's there." The old man pointed toward the western horizon and held his arm steady for a long moment before letting it fall limp to the deck. Then he looked toward the sky and fought hard for his last breath. "God forgive me."

Then the light faded from Thunder Parker's tired old eyes and Tungee reached over and closed his eyelids.

— TWELVE —

The mutiny was over and the fire was out. Half burned grain sacks were tossed over the side and dead bodies were assembled amidships.

"Get me a head count of the dead and wounded, Fritz," Captain Foster ordered as he paced the quarterdeck.

"And what do we do with the mutineers, Captain?"

"For the time being, keep them on deck."

"Aye, Skipper."

"Keep them near the bodies."

"How's that, sir?" The first mate questioned.

"I want them to see what they've done. Maybe if they stay close to it long enough, Fritz, it'll sink in."

Two decks below, Doc Dawson moved rapidly from bunk to bunk and ward to ward, digging out bullets, setting and splitting broken limbs. The doctor had enlisted Jeff Randolph as a temporary assistant. And they worked tirelessly in their efforts to save lives and provide some comfort to the injured men.

The last patient on Doc's emergency list was on the operating table suffering from a mangled left arm. Jeff Randolph recognized the patient. It was Oliver Simms one of Alf Talbot's associates. Jeff remembered him as a big-mouthed bigot who had thrown slurs at him from time to time. But that was no matter now; he would do his best to concentrate on the man's wounded arm, not his bigotry.

The patient's elbow was shattered and one inch above that wound a bullet had gone through flesh and bone, leaving a jagged hole. Doc Dawson had made the decision to amputate the arm just above the bullet hole. The belt they had used for a tourniquet had stopped the bleeding, but the patient was in great pain.

Walter Greenleaf moved about the room and it was apparent that he had assisted the doctor before.

Doc Dawson gestured. "Get me a bottle of rum, Walter."

The rum was no substitute for laudanum or morphine, but under present circumstances it had to do. Walter poured several ounces of rum into a tin cup and placed it in Oliver Simms' good hand. The patient knew what he was in for, but couldn't bring himself to admit it.

"You ain't takin' my arm off, are you, Doc?"

"I don't see any other choice," Doc Dawson said earnestly.

"But you ain't really sure, are you?"

"I'm only sure of one thing, Mr. Simms, if we don't take it off, gangrene will set in and you'll die a slow death."

Oliver Simms writhed with pain, but grabbed onto the rum cup, pulled it to his lips and downed it in one big swallow. "You don't give much latitude, do you, Doc?"

Dawson shook his head sympathetically. "There's not much to give."

Simms managed a half smile. "Do what you gotta do," and shoved the cup back to Walter Greenleaf for a refill.

The doctor looked toward Jeff. "We need another man or two for this operation. See if you can round up a couple."

Jeff Randolph hurried out of the room and soon returned with two unlikely volunteers, Everett Dobbs and Gene Blakely. They both paled when they saw the bloody mess inside the sickbay.

The rum was beginning to take effect and Oliver Simms rose to a half sitting position and slurred, "Come on in, mates and join the party."

Dobbs attempted a smile and winked at his friend as he reluctantly entered the room.

Doc Dawson nodded and greeted his new help, "Gentlemen."

"What do you need us for?" Blakely asked timidly.

Walter Greenleaf put his finger to his lips and quietly said, "We're here to assist. Just do what the doctor tells you."

The surgeon told Blakely to hold down the left leg and motioned for Dobbs to take the right.

Jeff had been instructed earlier to hold down the left upper torso and arm.

Walter Greenleaf took a full bottle of rum, held it in the air as a kind of salute, took a healthy swig and passed it along to Dobbs who took a solid drink and handed it to the kid. Blakely pushed it away, but Doc Dawson urged, "Go ahead and take a hefty swill. You'll be thankful you did later on."

The young man did as he was told grimaced and handed the bottle off to Jeff.

Oliver Simms grinned and spoke with all the humor he could muster. "Gents, as long as we're havin' this here shindig at my expense may I have another sniff or two of the grog?"

Doc Dawson filled the order by holding his patient's head up and putting the cup to his lips. Oliver Simms took the last dregs of the cup and with a fixed smile on his face as he began to grind his teeth.

The new men paled at the sight of the instruments the surgeon would use in the operation. The tools could just as easily have come from a carpenter's toolbox. There were knives with razor sharp edges and an assortment of handsaws and drills.

Jeff noticed Blakely's ashen face and pushed the rum bottle back into the kid's hands urging him to have another shot of courage.

Doc Dawson picked up a small wooden block from the tray and held it to Simms' lips. "Put this between your teeth and bite down on it, hard. Now, I want you to either close your eyes or look straight up at the overhead and don't let go the block until I tell you."

"How much time does this here surgery take?"

"Less than a minute, I expect."

"I can manage that, Doc."

"Of course you can." Then Doc Dawson looked around the table and ordered, "Take a good hold, gentlemen."

The surgeon's years of practice showed from the outset of the operation. He took a single scalpel and carved a full circle to the bone, put the knife back on the tray and picked up a small saw to cut through the bone. Simms held up well until he heard those tiny saw teeth digging into the bone. That shattered his brave front and as his grit and determination deserted him, he spit out the wooden block and screamed as his body writhed, kicked and jerked. The assistants held him down and in less than a dozen strokes of the saw the bone was cut clean through.

Doc Dawson put the saw away, took a handkerchief, mopped his brow and examined the results of his surgery. Walter Greenleaf nonchalantly picked up the lower end of Simms' arm and tossed it into a corner waste barrel. Gene Blakely paled and gagged at what he had just seen, lost consciousness and slipped silently to the floor.

Captain Foster gave the men no time to sit and brood over the tragedy. He used basic psychology and put the crew on double time clean up details. The hired mutineers were given the task of cutting and sewing old sailcloth into a coffin like shroud for each dead crew member. Then following the completion of their work, they were forced to sit upright in a semi circle facing those shrouds to finish out their penitence.

The MFC crew was a buzz with activity. Cheny and Jensen called out a string of orders to remove the half burned cargo from the hold and throw it over the side, dismantle the cannon and breastworks, then rearrange the cargo for ballast and weight distribution. That work continued at a breakneck pace up to and including the 0400 watch. At that time Cheny told everyone, with the exception of a small skeleton crew, to hit the sack and get some sleep.

Tungee stayed on as part of that small crew and once the men had gone below, he had a wide expanse of deck to pace and await the dawn. He listened to the sound of the sea with its light chop and was reminded of the night he and Charlie Boone buried Davy.

The sun rays finally peeped over the horizon and lit the shrouds and warmed the day. Those living mutineers fulfilled the captain's orders, sitting with the dead in a kind of forced atonement.

Fritz Cheny cupped his hands to his mouth and made the pedantic ritual call. "All hands -- bury the dead." Then he followed up with orders the seated mutineers had long awaited. "Gentlemen, you may now stand."

In less than five minutes from the time Cheny's haunting burial call went out, the whole ship's company had assembled amidships, with all faces turned toward the quarterdeck. In a strict sense, there were only two men attending duties relating to the operation of the ship. Tuck Rogers standing at the helm and a lookout perched high above in the crow's nest.

Captain Foster walked onto the quarterdeck and looked around at the men. He took his time and finally spoke in the gentle tones of a country preacher. "I would like to call the names of your dead mates as they were entered into the ship's log."

The captain took a slip of paper from his pocket and read:

"William "Willy" Baxter

Matthew "Matt" Benton

Dave Johnson

Jack "Thunder" Parker

Leon Stark

Alf Talbot." The captain looked up and had to suppress a grin. "As most of you know, Alf is not among these shrouds."

Every man aboard the MFC got the meaning of the captain's remark about Alf. And while decorum remained in tact, there was a slight easing of tensions along with a snicker or two.

Gideon Foster opened the Bible and read in a thoughtful monotone. "Unto Almighty God we commend the souls of our brothers departed, and we commit their bodies to the deep, in sure and certain hope of the resurrection unto eternal life through our Lord, Jesus Christ...Amen."

Fritz Cheny gave a hand signal and each of the boards containing the dead were lifted and the shrouded bodies, as one, slipped feet first into the sea.

Tungee stood and watched the captain as he went through the ceremony and figured that Gideon Foster wore a placid facade, not so much to deceive, but to hide his own emotions from the outside world. For as those shrouds plunged into the sea, there were tears in the captain's eyes.

Captain Foster then drew a deep breath and stood erect. "I have an announcement to make and I advise you all to listen well. Gentlemen, I have no desire to cause any further grief among this crew. You men involved in the conspiracy have done quite enough on that score.

This ship needs a full compliment of men and to get those numbers, you who caused this tragedy will pull extra duty beginning today and extending to Cape Horn. That extra duty work will concentrate on making repairs to damage done to the ship and in some small way compensate for harm and hurt you have brought on yourselves and others in this ship's company.

After your work has been completed, I'll take a report from the mates and add my own observations. If the reports are good, for my part, the mutiny will be behind us.

Then following a brief pause the captain looked up into the rigging at the small pennant flying high above the sails for a reading of present wind direction and then a glance at the waters around and he called, "Mr. Rogers, port your helm by five degrees. Mr. Cheny, prepare to make all sail. We shall sail close haul on the port tack."

Every sailor heard the order, but held his place for the first mate's announcement. "All hands prepare to make sail. Top men, both port and starboard watch go to the rigging, unfurl and make all sail, and set your braces for a close haul on the port tack. Now get about your business and shake a leg, gentlemen."

The MFC had been carrying just enough cloth for proper steerage. The men from both watches climbed into the rigging and just minutes later the braces were set, clew lines untied and let the sheets fall into place. Then as the sails caught the wind, the MFC shook off her lethargy and began to glide smartly through the low chop.

Warm winds blew out of the north and sweat poured off the sailors, accenting their tans. A crew of happy faces grinned out a newfound life. The night before they had flirted with death, but today these same men climbed to the rigging and felt alive doing the things a sailor lives for, working a tall ship and sailing on a gentle breeze.

*   *   *

Gideon Foster assembled the war party for a victory celebration. And by the time Tungee arrived at the captain's quarters everyone had a drink in his hand, Foster, Cheny, Herman and Greenleaf. Tungee looked around the room and at that moment he began to appreciate how lucky they were. All the men marked for assassination had survived.

Was it fate? Perhaps, but the fact is every man killed in the mutiny had been a part of the original conspiracy.

There was a party atmosphere in the room and someone pushed a mug into Tungee's hands. They all raised their cups in a salute to Gideon Foster and he immediately returned the favor with a toast. "To the winners. Thank you, gentlemen, for your hard work and your loyalty."

Glad hands were extended, slaps on the back, more drinks poured and tossed down. Good-hearted banter consumed the next half hour before the skipper waved his hand for attention. "Scuttlebutt circulating throughout the ship says the MFC is putting into Valparaiso. It has no basis in fact. Our next port of call is St. Katharine Island. That's what it was when we sailed out of San Francisco and that's what it is today."

"What follows St. Kat, Captain?" Tungee asked firmly. "Where do we drop the cargo?"

The captain pursed his lips and said tartly, "Liverpool."

Tungee didn't believe that and furthermore he didn't think the captain believed it either.

Fritz Cheny passed out new watch lists that reflected the current makeup of the crew and Tungee chose that time to make a request. "Captain Foster, I have a request," The chatter stopped and he asked, "Would you consider giving Jeff Randolph top side duty, Sir?"

The response was immediate, a pained expression from Fritz Cheny and a dirty look from Brett Herman.

"Now why do you want to go making waves, Tungee?" The first mate asked.

"Well, Jeff has requested the change. He proved himself during the mutiny and I personally believe he'd make a damn good top man."

Brett Herman growled, "I want him right where he is. He's a good hand in the galley."

Captain Foster gave a slightly twisted grin. "Mr. Herman, I believe you just answered the question. Randolph is a good man and like Mr. Cahill just said, he showed it during the riot and black or not, give him a chance up top, if that's what he wants."

"Thanks, Skipper," Tungee said as he held up his drink in a salute to the captain's confidence.

— THIRTEEN —

Tungee walked back to cabin C and as he reached for the door handle, a force reeled him backwards and slammed his body against the bulkhead. He braced himself upright and with a strong effort lunged for the door. He grabbed the handle and turned it only to find himself being hurled across the cabin. He grabbed the edge of the porthole and looked outside. The sea was running through mounting swells and the ship dove and rolled in her attempt to stay upright.

Jeff hung onto his bunk for dear life. "What in hell is going on, Tungee?"

"Thunder Parker said a squall was working up just before he died." Then Tungee grinned, "Looks like it's here. You just hang on, Jeff, I have to go topside."

He pulled himself through the cabin and scrambled up the ladder and onto the deck. Thank God, he thought, the sea is giving us a warning. The winds had yet to hit the ship with gale force. He moved along the deck holding onto the side rails and finally saw Foster and Cheny standing beside the binnacle.

Fritz Cheny called out above the noise of the sea. "The barometer's moving up and. down like a sea saw."

The captain remarked. "The squall may have missed us, but let's play it safe and pull the canvas."

Cheny gave the order. "Ahoy, you men in the mizzen, get all the sail in save the jibs, stays and spanker. Pass the word."

The MFC was off her tack and she was bobbing and weaving like a punch-drunk fighter. The good part was that her sticks were still pointing toward the sky.

Tungee moved along the deck, holding onto anything he could get his hands on. He finally worked his way to the base of the foremast and laughed at what he saw. While the crew hurried onto the deck and began to climb into the rigging the capricious winds quit. And within a couple of minutes the waters flattened out to a gentle rise and fall.

The squall had reached out and grabbed and shook the MFC for a moment, then drifted off to the northeast.

Tungee stood near the foremast for a while and thought about that sharp encounter. Nature could be giving us an idea of what to expect from the waters around Cape Horn.

The captain threw up his hands and said, "Belay that last order" tie the sails back to the yards and, helmsman get ready to ware ship to starboard."

Tungee grinned as he entered Cabin C. "Congratulations, Jeff."

"For what?"

"You're out of the galley, that is if you still want to work up top."

Jeff hesitated. "What did Herman think about it?"

"Hated the idea and Cheny wasn't too thrilled either."

"Then what makes you think they'll let me out of the galley?"

"Overruled by Captain Foster."

"Cheny could make it tough on me."

"Hell that'll add character, Jeff," Tungee declared. "And besides, Cheny will come around."

Jeff took a long moment and said guardedly, "When do I make the change?"

"Next watch, so I suggest you gets some sleep. You've got work ahead of you, Mr. Randolph."

Then Tungee rolled into his own bunk and closed his eyes. But as he tried to go to sleep, he kept hearing the captain's voice repeating the word Liverpool.

Captain Foster figured the squall that had just missed them was a warning and he began preparing for the Cape. All hands were ordered to turn to and work and make the ship watertight. They would add extra tar, caulk every crack and put on a fresh coat of paint. The young sailors who had never had to weather Cape Horn found it hard to understand and grumbled about the extra duty. By the time they strung up lifelines around the deck and Walter Greenleaf issued foul weather gear, sou'westers, oilskins and boots they began to get the idea.

A sea gull perched on top of the mizzen royal yard a half dozen mews were flying a hundred feet above the ship and almost stood still as they labored against a steady breeze.

Tungee stood back from the foremast and looked up as Jeff, Dobbs and Blakely worked hard to repair a frayed halyard and a slipped brace on the fore upper topsail yard. The talkative Dobbs yelled down. "Just look at that bunch of birds, mates. Makes a pretty picture, don't you think."

Tungee called up, "Do you know what they are?"

"Not a clue."

"They're mews and some folks call them bad weather birds."

"Does that bad weather bird mean what it sounds like?"

Tungee smiled. "I'm afraid it does." Then he pointed to the gull back on the mizzen. "There's another part of the bad weather group."

Dobbs chuckled. "Many more of them birds in the rigging and we'll take on the look of Noah's Ark."

"It's just a rest stop," Tungee said. "Their natural instinct tells them to move away from the storm."

"Smart little buggers, ain't they."

In final preparation for weather ahead, Captain Foster gave the order to remove all light sailcloth and replace it with heavy canvas. The crew turned to and by mid afternoon of the following day the changes had been made. The ship plowed through a medium swell at more than ten knots on a close haule starboard tack. Valparaiso was far astern on the port quarter.

A school of dolphin showed up off the port beam and put on an exhibition doing jumps and spins to the delight of the crew. The playful dolphin stayed with the MFC for two full days before making a final circle around the ship and heading into the sunset.

By the numbers the migration of bad weather birds had increased and you could see a buildup of clouds to the southwest, darkening and boiling down to a running sea.

Captain Foster called, "Mr. Cheny, let's begin to take off some canvas. We'll reef sail on fore, main and mizzen masts from t'gallant's down."

"Aye, skipper." Then Fritz Cheny cupped his hands round his mouth and blasted Foster's order verbatim.

The mizzen royal yard had become a resting-place for gulls on their way out of the area. Mews and terns had flopped down in the water for food and rest some one hundred yards aft. And the weather was changing; there was a definite chill in the air.

Gideon Foster had already decided to take the longer route known as Drake's Passage round the Horn, not chancing the sometimes treacherous, if shorter, Strait of Magellan. Keeping to the open sea had its merits, but it did put you nearer Antarctica and those frigid ice flows. The past two days had seen the midday temperature drop from a balmy seventy-five degrees to two points below freezing.

Almost to the man, the crew was wearing their oilskins. Hank Jensen had apparently found a supply of rum and was using it to help ward off the chill. For the past three days he had staggered from mast to lifeline, fallen into and then dragged out of the scuppers, soaking wet and quoting everything from the Bible to Shakespeare.

The crew had just shortened sail and most of the port watch top men had dropped down to the main deck. Jensen had gathered quite a congregation at the foot of the mainmast. The gathering storm in the path of the MFC and a heavy blanket of darkness seemed to encourage the tale telling second mate. The performer took a swig from his bottle, steadied himself against the mast, wiped his mouth on his sleeve and croaked out his version of an old seafaring tale.

"Twas on a dark and cheerless night to the southward of the Cape." He quoted every verse and added a few of his own. Then he wound up with, "The Sea all round was clad in foam and just up on our lee, we saw the Flying Dutchman come a bounding o'er the sea."

There were mixed emotions among the crew regarding that old canard. Some believed the thing was true while others called it nonsense.

But whether they believed it or not, every man in the audience gave Hank Jensen a good round of applause for his efforts.

Gene Blakely looked across the waters as if he expected to see the Dutchman come bounding over the horizon.

Dobbs added a cryptic note. "It's been seen you know, that bloody old Flying Dutchman."

The barometer had been steadily dropping along with the temperature. And not to be caught with his sails billowing out full when the gale struck, Foster had done the prudent thing by taking off large sections of canvas. All the sailors in the rigging were holding on a bit tighter as the running sea preceding the high wind caused the masts to sway like some giant pendulum swinging it's circle and exerting enormous centrifugal force.

Tungee was on the port side of the fore royal yard and saw the sky light up with a flash followed by the rolling crack-bang thunder bouncing off the building waves. Jeff was on his right Dobbs and the kid were below on the fore upper topsail completing their furl.

"Hang onto to what you've got now, men. The wind from the squall line is going to hit any minute," Tungee yelled.

Dobbs declared, "I've got me a grip on this here foremast that lovers just dream about, mate."

Cheny raced from the quarterdeck and took a position halfway between the main and foremast, leaned back and yelled new orders. "Yo, fore and main top men spill and secure your outer and inner jibs and all stays.

The men in the rigging had just gone to work on Cheny's order when the man in the crow's nest bellowed, "Land ho."

"Give me a point and what you see," Captain Foster ordered.

"Broad on the port bow, sir. They are distant, sir, but they are hills, make no mistake about that, sir."

The skipper knew that Wellington was behind them, present position had to put them off the Strait of Magellan. The crow's nest must be reporting the hills of Punta Arenas.

"Give me a distance," Foster demanded.

"I'd reckon a score of miles, sir."

"Helmsman, we'll wear ship to a starboard heading of one hundred ninety five degrees."

The MFC was nearer land than the skipper had intended and with that starboard maneuver the ship would likely be on a collision course with the storm. But Captain Foster figured it was better to stick his bow into the turbulent waters rather than drift toward the shoals and in the end be broadsided and slammed onto the rocks by the storm's fury.

All top men had returned to the deck and ducked inside the forecastle by the time white pebbles began to bounce off the mast and decking.

Tungee held onto a lifeline and made his way back to the quarterdeck where Foster and Cheny stood just outside the chart room observing the helmsman. They would soon find out how the ship handled in a real storm. She had weathered some rain and gale force winds, but nothing like old Cape Stiff could dish out.

Tuck Rogers was at the wheel and was as good a helmsman as you'd ever want to see, especially on tack and close haul sailing. By the time hailstones began to collect in the scuppers, intermittent sprinkles of freezing rain started to fall. The sea was running wild and a monstrous roller built up and moved ominously toward the starboard bow. The big one missed, but all of a sudden the men on deck were looking down at a trough below.

Captain Foster yelled, "We can tie the wheel down, if you'd like, Mr. Rogers."

"If you don't mind, I'll stick with her for now, sir."

"You feel you have some steerage then."

"Aye, she's a bit cranky, but that's to be expected in these crazy cross seas."

The ship rode the top of that giant wave for a few brief moments and then she plunged and dove down into a canyon. Dirty gray walls of water churned up on either side of the ship and they still hadn't hit bottom. When those huge walls collapse we'll be overwhelmed, Tungee thought. They bottomed out and he was forced to his knees. He knew the sides would come crashing in, but they didn't. Those gray walls held. The ship was in the pit of the trough and just as fast as they had fallen to the bottom they were spat up and out again.

The wind was not much more than gale force and it was somewhat dryer than they had expected, so the skipper ordered a modest sail change. "Call out the watch, Mr. Cheny. "I'd like to set the stays and jibs."

Tungee peered into the black night and worried about the overcast and how the captain planned to navigate when there was no chance to shoot the stars.

And before the night was done, the MFC had collected a veneer of ice that covered both deck and rigging. The storm raged and screamed as it blew in off the South Pole and sent the thermometer's mercury retreating far below zero.

— FOURTEEN —

Sleet was changing to a freezing mist as a dreary dawn struggled to break through the heavy overcast. Ragged underbellies of the clouds were so low at times they touched the waters. Waters cluttered with brash ice ranging in size from a bobbing apple to that of a full grown pumpkin. Ominous thumping noises caused by frozen chunks hitting the sides of the hull were underscored by the steady beat of a crew working the bilge pump. Those were the sounds they heard above an almost still ship that lay as near to dead in the water without being so as you would ever see. Ocean currents gave more movement to the ship than did the jibs and spanker, the only sails that were set.

Captain Foster, Fritz Cheny, Hank Jensen, Gabe Toombs and Tungee all stood on the quarterdeck in the teeth chattering cold, their hands stuffed deep into their pockets. No one said anything. They waited, watched and listened. But for what, none of them was quite sure. Two nights had passed since they'd had a clear shot at the stars with their sextant. Navigation anywhere near the South Pole was a tricky business at best. And considering the wild compass swings down in that region along with merging currents of the Pacific and Atlantic Oceans pushing and pulling in contrary directions you were left with only one formula for navigation, dead reckoning. And under their present circumstances that was almost worthless.

Foster and Cheny were both schooled in navigation, but neither of them had a real fix on their present location and they were worried.

Gabe Toombs asked, "What do you make of the ice, Captain?"

Foster thought for a moment. "We may be too far south, Gabe."

"What does that mean?"

"We get too deep into these freezing waters we could get hung up."

"You mean ice bound."

"That's what I'm saying."

Gabe Toombs rubbed his hands together, spat a mouthful of tobacco juice over the side and drawled, "Gawd."

Fritz Cheny was less pessimistic. "We're not in trouble yet and if we get a break in this overcast we won't be."

"Do you think we're south of the Drake Passage?" Tungee asked.

"To be honest, I'm not sure. I doubt that we're that far south, but all this ice makes me wonder," The captain said bleakly.

"Then you think the ice may have drifted farther north than is normal," Tungee commented.

"I think that is just the case," Fritz Cheny said. "The way I see it, the wind hasn't been strong enough to carry us to longitude sixty. But the currents, on the other hand, are something else."

"Then we could have drifted faster and farther than we've sailed."

"That's the rub, Mr. Cahill," Foster cautioned. "With the running seas we've experienced for the last two days and nights along with no chance to shoot the stars, we're guessing. Damn I hate to admit that, men. But we're reduced to calculations based solely on an educated guess."

"Better In nothin' I suppose," Gabe Toombs said dryly.

The youthful voice of Gene Blakely called out from the bow. "Yo, there on the quarterdeck, listen up."

Captain Foster moved toward the kid and the others followed. As they walked forward the captain demanded, "Avast, you men on the bilge pump."

After the noise of the pump ceased and the captain's group arrived at the bow, they all stood looking at Blakely.

He had just crawled back from the bowsprit and stood stark still with his hands cupped behind his ears. He was looking and apparently listening in a direction off the port bow. He finally took his hands down and while he cleaned his glasses with a handkerchief he almost whispered, "Breakers, Captain. Way off in the distance."

The earlier conversation came to Tungee's mind and he wondered if they were south of longitude sixty and hearing waves pounding the shores of some small Antarctic island. Could that be the real reason for all the brash ice? There was an eerie stillness in the air and the kid may have heard breakers, but no one else did.

"Mr. Jensen," Captain Foster said quietly, "go and get my long glass from the chart room. Mr. Cahill, you and Mr. Toombs get the chains and find what kind of depth we've got."

Jensen scooted for the captain's long glass while Gabe and Tungee removed the lash from the measuring chain and began to play the lead out over the side.

Jensen returned quickly and handed the long glass to the captain. Foster put his hand on Blakely's shoulder and said, "Now point to where you think the sounds are coming from."

The young man pointed in a direction that would be off the port beam. "That's where I hear it, sir."

Tungee reported, "The regular chain is all paid out, Captain and we find no bottom to report."

Foster and Blakely continued to look and listen, but after several minutes the captain lowered his glass and shook his head, indicating he hadn't seen a thing.

The calm and quiet was broken by the noise of a sea gull. The crew watched as the bird skittered through the low hanging clouds, made an approach and gently settled onto the mizzen royal yard. The gull looked to be at home. There was a smile on every face, as that bird seemed to bring the crew some measure of hope.

Captain Foster asked thoughtfully, "Mr. Cheny, what was our last barometer reading?"

"It was 29.01 and dropping."

"Go back and take a look and I'll predict she'll be on the rise."

Fritz Cheny almost ran toward the quarterdeck and moments later he called out, 29.19."

The captain gave thumbs up to Cheny. Then he put his finger to his mouth and a hush fell over the deck.

Tungee mused the kid had a great set of ears. There were breakers out there pounding onto something all right. But what? Then something else positive happened, a stream of sunlight found it's way through the cloud cover. That old sea gull must have known a thing or two and every man on deck smiled as they looked up at blue spots of sky replacing the dark ragged clouds present only moments before. There didn't seem to be any wind direction, but there was a hint of a breeze. The jibs and spanker began to move slightly. True they were only small signs of improvement, but Captain Foster said, "Mr. Cheny, call all able bodied seamen to stand by. Mr. Cahill and Mr. Toombs, keep those chains busy."

"Aye, Skipper," Gabe Toombs, replied. Then he turned and said, "I wager he's on to somethin', Tungee."

"Like an old coon dog that's just picked up a sent," Tungee declared.

Cheny called the order down to the men in the forecastle and Foster took a slow walk around the deck looking down at the water for signs of any movement. Then suddenly he began to bark out orders. "You men on the bilge pump, get back to your tasks. Mr. Jensen, go and find Walter Greenleaf and you two fetch me that canvas sea anchor."

"Aye, Sir."

Fritz Cheny's wake up call had done the trick. Men poured onto the deck, some still sleepy eyed. Doc Dawson came up along with his last and most injured patient, the one armed Oliver Simms.

Jensen and Greenleaf had the sea anchor ready to deploy as soon as the skipper made up his mind where he wanted it placed.

Tungee and Gabe Toombs continued to pay out the chain and call out marks, but had yet to find any ground beneath the MFC.

The sound of those waves crashing onto some shore was now clear enough to where anyone on the deck could hear. But what were they crashing on to, an iceberg or a small frozen island?

Captain Foster pointed to a spot and Jensen took that gawky piece of canvas and sailed it a dozen yards off the stern to starboard. It landed flat and didn't sink much until he yanked on the rope a time or two. Then it dropped like a stone until he gently tugged at the guide lines and finessed the sea anchor into position.

Gabe Tombs observed the same things and commented, "Don't seem to be much flow one way or another."

Tungee nodded in agreement and kept calling out his marks.

A small breeze came from somewhere flooding the jibs and a few seconds later the sea anchor took hold and the stern of the ship was yanked to starboard.

Gabe Toombs looked aft. "Sea anchor took hold, Tungee."

Their drift toward the shore was halted just as larger patches of blue sky began to show through the dark ragged clouds.

The captain looked to the top of the main mast and the small directional pennant as it began to flutter in the light breeze coming in from the west-southwest.

While the crew turned to their various tasks, Gene Blakely remained vigilant, listening for the sound of the breakers. He finally saw it and shouted. "Land ho, Captain, land ho."

All eyes turned toward that phantom beach. Tungee nudged Gabe Toombs and chortled, "Rock ho might be more like it."

"Ain't that a bitch," Gabe Toombs drawled.

There it stood Cape Horn. The Horn itself, jutting out from Tierra del Fuego. The place that's thought of as lands end South America is that solid piece of rock that towers some six hundred feet up from the water's edge. Cape Horn seemed less intimidating that day and Tungee figured that rock was a welcomed sight compared to the cold alternative they had all speculated about earlier in the day.

Gideon Foster reached back to his boatswain's days and bellowed orders directly to the crew. "You men on the chains, stay at your task and the rest of you loafing about the deck, prepare to set all sail to the royals. Now get the lead out of your britches and shake a leg. Mr. Rogers, stay alert, we'll wear ship to starboard. Mr. Jensen and Mr. Greenleaf, get that sea anchor out of the water, please."

Earlier in the day, Gideon Foster had doubted his own abilities as a competent skipper. That morning he had about reconciled to a huge navigational error that could have easily ended with the MFC foundering and freezing among the ice flows of Antarctica. But that was earlier, now his self-confidence had returned along with a full measure of enthusiasm. "Mr. Rogers, give me two more points to starboard, please and you top men brace up for a close haul starboard tack."

Then Captain Foster strode forward, inspecting every sail for angle and capacity and when he finished his inspection he called out, "That's it, Mr. Rogers, keep her as close as she'll lie." And cupping his hands, he leaned back and admonished, "You, in the crow's nest, keep to your business. Mr. Cahill, you and Mr. Toombs, don't let those chains get dry. Search men, search. If there's any bottom, I want to know about it."

Without a word, Cheny and Jensen had taken over Tungee's and Gabe's positions on the fore and main mast, shouting orders and working the men as if they did it every day.

While continuing to call out marks, Tungee looked over his shoulder and took a measure of pride as he watched his raw recruits performing their duties like veterans.

The MFC and her crew took advantage of the day's good weather and fair winds that were coming in cold from the southwest. The weather conditions were perfect for the ship to show off her overall speed. After leaving the tall rock faced Horn, she posted an average speed of fourteen knots. With only three long shallow tacks and helped by a low choppy sea and a good quartering wind the ship left that mariner's nightmare, that dreaded Tierra Del Fuego and the Horn area. They passed close on to the southeastern tip of Staten Island.

Tungee and Gabe received their only report of ground with the deep-sea chains, which produced a reading of close to one hundred fathoms. The ship's company fell back into a regular routine with port and starboard watches alternating and every man on the ship getting his chance at some well-deserved sleep.

By sunset on the day following their experience around the Horn, the MFC had a trailing wind and the skipper took dead aim at a point just east of the Falkland Islands. From there they would intersect latitude forty and bend to a northerly heading for a direct shot at the Rio De Janeiro area and to be more specific -- St. Katharine Island.

Buenos Aires and Montevideo were far off the port beam when Gideon Foster kept his promise to the ex mutineers and canceled their extra duty. The captain had inspected and declared repairs complete to the riot damage and as far as he was concerned, the matter was over and done with.

The Atlantic Ocean, which can throw a tantrum now and then, seemed more hospitable than the Pacific had been the week before.

The Clipper was presently plowing through the Atlantic's blue waters and the men stood on deck and watched flying fish explode out of the water and fly across the ship like darting missiles.

All hands had assembled and Captain Foster paced the quarterdeck. Then he smiled and faced the crew. "You men will be at liberty to go ashore at St. Katharine, one watch section at a time."

The men broke out into yells; whistles and some danced a jig. And from the look on Foster's face, he had seen too much enthusiasm. He stood for a moment and glared before he said accusingly, "Gentlemen, if that outburst was an indication that you'll be looking for better arrangements on the island, think again." He took a long moment and chewed on the end of his cigar. Then he took the stogie out of his mouth, spat a slug of juice over the rail and in a threatening tone, laid it out. "St. Kat is a company port. There are plenty of island police and guards to control the situation. So if any of you are thinking about jumping ship, you best think again. I plan to use every resource at my disposal to carry out my orders. I have a ship to command and a cargo to deliver, a'hem, to Liverpool."

Tungee smiled as he watched the captain's performance and thought, now some people just can't bring off a lie. Then he shook his head. I swear I believe Gideon Foster is one of the worst liars I've ever run across.

Dobbs elbowed Tungee. "What do you make of that bilge, mate?" Guards and island police."

"Hadn't thought much about it."

"Now, mate, you best get up to speed. They been jawin', about that up in the forecastle since Cape Horn."

"Is that the same bunch that took part in the mutiny?"

"Some I suppose, but there are others too."

"You heard what the skipper said."

"You mean about the guards and that."

"If you plan to get off at St. Kat, you better give it some more thought."

"From what I've heard, there are plenty of hiding places on that island."

"What good does that do you, Dobbs?"

"Gives you time to think things over and then hitch a ride on another ship."

"You didn't listen, Dobbs. It's a company port, most all the ships belong to the same people."

"Hadn't thought about that."

"Another thing, Gideon Foster is not a half bad skipper compared to some I've seen."

"It ain't right though, mate the way I was signed on. And the same goes for you too, it just ain't right."

"I know, Dobbs, but making things worse for yourself isn't any kind of an answer, is it?"

"Then you think I'd be steppin' on me dick if I joined in."

Tungee hooted. "Where did that saying come from?"

"I'm not sure, but it may have originated in Sydney. I think it was back home where I first heard it, but the Ducks use it quite a lot in San Francisco." Then he gave one of his funny laughs. "Now this is going to sound outrageous. But when Alf got his and was blown over the side. Well, that was my exact thought at the time, Alfie sure has stepped on his this time."

A wry grin broke over Tungee's face. "Well, you just try and jump ship at St. Kat and you could very well use the phrase on yourself, Mr. Dobbs."

"Oh, mate. What a terrible thought."

"Land ho, showing two points off the starboard bow."

Tungee had just come on deck to prepare for the dogwatch when a call came down from a lookout. He ran toward the bow scanning the horizon, waiting to confirm what he already knew. St. Katharine Island with its low sandy hills carpeted with green vegetation.

Crewmen who were usually last to answer watch call crowded the forward area of the ship trying to get a look at land they could expect to stand on soon. For the old hands two and a half months was nothing, but for the new it probably seemed like a lifetime.

Nightfall came quickly and the sky blossomed with stars. A three-quarter-moon rose over St. Kat as the MFC nudged into the lee side cove of the island. They were the second vessel to enter the small harbor in the past hour. The one just ahead of the MFC had sailed in from the north and a third that was already resting at anchor.

"Cut her loose men," was the only command Captain Foster gave to drop anchor. And almost at that same moment men from the starboard watch scrambled to get on board the liberty launches with port side crew members left to grumble about having to wait until tomorrow.

A soft northeast breeze drifted out from the island bringing sounds of life on St. Katharine. Tungee and Jeff were in Cabin C preparing to turn in when Jeff said, "I like the sounds coming from the island, Tungee. How's the nightlife?"

Tungee looked up with a sly grin. "You'll like it."

— FIFTEEN —

The MFC was anchored in St. Katharine Bay and most of the starboard watch crew had returned from their first night's liberty. Some of the brawlers nursed cuts and bruises some were still a bit tipsy and a small minority came back wearing the wide smile of satisfaction.

The longboat ferrying port watch sailors was half way to the dock when Dobbs said, "You ought to be ashamed of yourself, Oliver."

"Well, facts is facts," the one armed Simms declared.

"You may be right, Mr. Simms," Tungee remarked, "but I think you scared the wits out of the kid."

"It was you, Oliver, me mate," Dobbs said with relish, "who furnished the straw what broke the camel's back."

"Now just how do you figure that, Mr. Dobbs?"

"Why it was when you lumped fresh meat, virgins and whores into one of your little outbursts, that's what done the trick. Why he almost flew out of our boat and into the launch."

Oliver Simms chuckled, knowing full well what he'd done to the kid. It was one big joke to him but not, to the not quite dry behind the ears, Gene Blakely. The kid may well have had his first drink in sickbay the day Oliver Simms arm was amputated. However following that time Captain Foster had been fairly liberal with the rum, especially in those dark days just before the Horn. Blakely had taken on enough once to get sick and heave his insides out. Then tie that happening to the recent razing and you wind up with a very frightened young man.

Oliver Simms grinned. "He's a virgin you know. He ain't never been laid."

"Now how would you know that, Oliver?" Dobbs asked, "He ain't told you has he?"

"Of course not. You don't go around announcing the fact that you're a bloomin' virgin. Smarten up, Dobbsy, my mate."

Tungee and the others stepped off the longboat onto the dock and stood for a moment feeling good to be on dry land. They faced an open market that occupied both sides of the street near the quay. The street was crowded with horses, wagons, carts and people in bare feet. skin colors and clothing varied. Women wore long skirts, brilliant colored blouses and most of them wore a wide brimmed straw hat. The men were more scantily clad and generally wore only a pair of pants and no shoes.

There were still a few slaves on the island, although most had been freed, at least they had been given papers, as Jeff Randolph had, that gave them a release from bondage. However, most would never live long enough to pay off their debts to the company store and very few had any hope of eventual freedom.

Most of the sailors only hesitated briefly on the dock before hustling up the street in the direction of Papa Joe's Bar or the One Eyed Bull Saloon located farther on up Main Street just below the red light district.

Tungee hung back and walked into an open-air coffee shop located at the north end of the market. He observed Foster and Cheny come ashore followed by Gene Blakely. The three of them stood on the dock for a while and talked. The kid was the first to leave and as he passed by the coffee shop Tungee called to him. "Where you going?"

Gene Blakely joined Tungee. "I just asked the captain about the best place to eat and he said the restaurant in the Main Street Hotel."

"Is that where he's going?" Tungee asked.

"No, he's got to check in at the company office first. Said he might see me in the restaurant later. Are you going for supper?"

"Maybe later."

Gene Blakely gave a salute and walked up the street. Tungee then turned his attention toward the captain and his first mate. Fritz Cheny purchased a couple of mangos on their way through the market. The captain and first mate took their own good time as they meandered up the sandy street. They eventually arrived at the corner of Main and Spice Street, finished their mangos and dropped the pits into the waste barrel. They stood and looked toward the Company office, which was located in the Main Street Hotel. The hotel's large veranda ran along the Main Street side and curved around and down to the end of the building on Spice Street. Foster finally shook his head and took the two steps onto the veranda. Cheny followed close behind as they moved past white wicker tables and chairs that outlined their path.

As Tungee sat and sipped his coffee he had a sense that Captain Foster had the same kind of reluctance about entering the company office as he'd had during their first meeting in his cabin on the MFC. There was no doubt in Tungee's mind that Foster was troubled about something. Something he hadn't been able to bring himself to talk about.

Gideon Foster stood for a moment looking up at a one by four, hand tooled, mahogany board sign reading "The L.A.G. Spice and Tea Company" that hung above double French doors. He finally reached for the shiny brass knob, turned it and opened the door. The large office was functional and well appointed. Three good sized working desks and chairs, the walls were decorated with pictures and maps. A large oil painting of Lindsay Arthur Griffin, the company owner hung alongside a print of the old Marcus F. Childs.

Oscar L. Hooper stood up behind the middle desk and extended his hand. "Morning, Gideon, Fritz."

The two returned halfhearted greetings to Hooper and Findley Smith, the local company manager. Smith seemed ill at ease and simply nodded before he turned away from the others and concentrated on his paper work.

"What do you think of the ship, Gideon?" Hooper asked.

"She's a good sailer, but we took a few battle scars off the coast of Panama."

"What do you mean by that?" Hooper asked.

Foster told the bare bone facts about the mutiny and ended his short report by saying, "You'll get the rest when you go over the log."

Hooper asked a dozen pointed questions about the mutiny and

other trivial matters. Both Foster and Cheny grinned at his ploy. They knew he was offering small talk to avoid the subject they had come to discuss, namely facts and figures regarding their cargo that was destined for Liverpool.

The skipper made a point of striking a match on the sole of his boot and lit his small cigar. Then he inhaled and blew the smoke out. "Cut the crap, Oscar. You never were any good at small talk."

The squint eyed Hooper peered over his gold rimmed glasses and coughed. "How many men do you need?"

"We can make out with what we've got," Foster turned his head, "don't you think so, Fritz."

"Sure Skipper, assuming we've got stevedores at Liverpool."

Foster stared down Hooper. Then taking his time he blew a half dozen of his famous smoke rings.

Every man in the room had been down that road before, including the innocuous Smith who stayed out of the conversation and shuffled his papers. The office was silent for almost a full minute. Hooper finally broke the quiet by saying, "Liverpool. A' hem. Yes we would need stevedores at Liverpool, if that was your destination."

"All right, Mr. Hooper, then why don't you just tell me what our destination is?" Foster exploded as he slammed his fist onto the desk. "The orders read Liverpool."

"Those are the papers you were given in San Francisco, Gideon. But, you see, all that's changed."

"Who says so?"

Hooper gestured over his shoulder toward Griffin's portrait.

"I knew something was rotten when I saw those sham orders." Gideon Foster blurted. "In the first place there was no consignee for the cargo and second, with the name change of the ship, it appeared to me it would involve insurance."

"You're right on the money, Gideon."

"Then I suggest you spell out the new orders."

"Mr. Griffin didn't really want to put you into this situation, knowing how you feel about the trade."

"Lindsay Arthur Griffin never gave a damn about putting anyone into any situation that would turn a buck for him. Now damn it, Oscar let's get down to cases."

"The fact is we need, a' hem, the company needs you to make another run to Africa."

Tungee frowned as he looked toward the company office picturing in his own mind Gideon Foster as he reluctantly opened the door and wondered what was on the skipper's mind. As he sat drinking his coffee he had seen Hank Jensen, Dan Thurston, Will Farmer and several others hot footing it up Main Street. He had no doubt as to what they were looking for.

The long lanky Gabe Toombs was all smiles as he shuffled into the coffee shop. "Did you hear what I heard, Tungee."

"What's that, Gabe?"

"Captain Jubal Mosby of the Morning Glory made a bet with Captain Foster."

"What kind of a bet?"

Gabe Toombs grabbed Tungee's arm and walked him to the street. "Hundred dollar gold piece says the Glory's crew can best the MFC bunch in a bawdy house challenge."

Tungee laughed and scratched his head. "Now, I can see old Jube Mosby making the bet, but I can't believe Foster went for it."

"Must have," Gabe Toombs said brightly.

"Where do they plan have the contest?" Tungee asked.

"Madam Picard's place."

"You mean the whorehouse just above the One Eyed Bull?"

"Yeah," Gabe strung out the word. "What do you say we go on up to the Bull and see if we can't get in on the action."

"Okay," Tungee said as they sauntered up Main Street. Not that he was much interested in that kind of game. He'd been with whores before, but he wasn't at all comfortable with the idea of participating in some kind of arena seduction.

They arrived at the entrance of the saloon, stepped inside and stood for a bit looking into the dark place. It was a dingy dimly lit room with a long wooden bar occupying the north wall with tables and chairs scattered around in front of the bar. There was a gambling area in the rear set off by a low rail. The saloon was decorated with smoke covered palm fronds, fishnets and cork floats. A wide backdoor opened onto a path that meandered past the outhouse and up the hill.

*　　*　　*

Gideon Foster paced between Hooper's desk and the front door, chewed on his cigar, then he relit it, puffed and fumed before settling back into his chair. He eyed Hooper and said, "I'm not sure I'm gonna go along this time."

"We need an answer, Gideon. And one more thing, you have another year left on your contract obligation to us. And you know as well as I do what a stickler Griffin is when it comes to honoring your personal contracts."

Cheny said, "Skipper, why don't we just do it and get the damned thing over and done with."

Foster agreed with Cheny, but shook his fist in Hooper's face and blustered. "Damn your hide, Oscar, you sat in that same chair two years ago and handed me the same bull." He leered at Hooper. "It never changes, does it? Those blood-sucking vultures up in Boston could care less about morality. For God's sake, Oscar, how long are they going to keep up this kind of business? They're not just slave traders, they are cheating insurance companies, playing games with manifests and registrations."

"No, it's not all on the up and up, but as long as we and I do emphasize we are still in the trade, we must do it in the most profitable way we can. And we don't really involve the insurance companies. After all, Gideon, in the event you are caught with a load of blacks aboard the non registered MFC, we simply pay your fine and the insurance company is none the wiser. As you know, they don't insure that kind of cargo, do they?"

"Scum of the earth." Foster grumbled and shook his head.

"The whole damned lot of us."

"Gideon, why don't you just settle down and let's go over the plan."

Fritz Cheny enjoyed the moment. He nodded and smiled in agreement with Oscar.

"All right, let's have a look at the new orders."

Hooper gave a sigh of relief as he took the papers out of his desk drawer and handed them to Foster. He had won the argument, but in truth, it wasn't Hooper who had won, it was that imposing figure hanging on the wall behind him, Lindsay Arthur Griffin, that had gotten his way again.

Foster pulled on his cigar as he thumbed through the paper work. "New wrinkle, Fritz. Not Senegal this time."

"Where is it?" Cheny asked.

"North shore of the Gulf of Guinea," Hooper explained.

Cheny said, "Don't remember being there before."

"Nope, brand new to me too," Foster said thoughtfully.

Hooper got out of his chair and walked to a wall map, picked up a stick and followed along a line he had previously drawn indicating their proposed route. "Had to make some changes, Gideon. The old route got too risky. Now, you will be dealing with the same people."

Captain Foster asked, "Where do we off load?"

Hooper pointed and said, "It's a little island off the Georgia Coast called Saint Simons."

"How many passengers?" Fritz Cheny asked.

"Three hundred and fifty," Foster said as he rifled through the pages. "What tribes, Oscar?"

"We don't know that. It's up to Becker and what's available, I suppose."

Gideon Foster said irately, "No tribes spelled out."

The three men just looked at each other and collectively shook their heads. Knowing well that some tribes were easy to get along with and some could give you nightmares.

"Is this the first run over the new setup?" Foster asked.

"No. Bonner just finished one, not out of St. Katharine, his originated in Boston, West Africa, Saint Simons and back to Boston."

"So, he's back in the old man's good graces. Last I heard, Al Bonner had been kicked down to first mate."

Hooper grinned. "It was easy for Griffin to reinstate him. Bonner's not a bad skipper and the old man needed a favor." He looked up and said, "Same as he's asking of you, Gideon."

Foster chuckled. "Fritz, would you mind breaking out the hip boots, it's getting pretty deep in here." Then he looked toward Hooper, "Is it ballast to Boston?"

"No, you take on a load of cypress, change the name back to the

Orient Leaf and ship to Boston. Turner will give you new papers at Saint Simons Island."

"Well, that's good news, Fritz," Foster said jovially. "Damn nice of Mr. Griffin to make honest merchants out of us for at least one leg of our voyage."

Tungee and Gabe Toombs stood at the bar nursing their watered whiskeys when a disturbance in the far corner of the room rose above the din of the crowd. An excited quarrel erupted at a poker table. "This is a crooked game," one player shouted as one of the other players pummeled the small man making the disturbance.

"Hank Jensen's in the middle of that," Tungee declared as he hurried toward the action.

The dealer sat calmly, tilted his shade up and snarled. "You're just a bad poker player and a sore loser."

Jensen dove across the table, grabbed the dealer and pulled up his right shirtsleeve revealing several hidden cards and a mechanical card dispenser. Jensen held up the man's arm and yelled, "I knew it was a crooked game, you're nothing but a bunch of thieves."

Two other players friendly to the dealer pulled Jensen away. Tungee followed the action and when he arrived at the table he grabbed the hustling dealer by the collar, yanked him to his feet and delivered a vicious right cross to his jaw. Then in a split second Tungee grabbed a wad of cash from the dealer's pot and stuffed it into Jensen's shirt pocket.

Gabe Toombs had followed along and took on the man that was roughing up Jensen. Dan Thurston and Will Farmer arrived from their table across the room and joined the fray. A roar came from the crowd and blood oozed from the puffy lips of the dealer as he reached into his pocket and pulled out a revolver. Tungee grabbed the gun hand and forced it down just as it exploded harmlessly into the floor. He wrenched the weapon from the dealer's hand and kicked it across the room.

The MFC crowd quickly pulled Jensen away from his attackers and dragged him toward the front door as he shouted his defiance. "You blood suckers will all roast in Hell."

Tungee and the others elbowed their way through the hostile saloon regulars until they cleared the entrance and moved into the street.

Once they got the second mate settled down Tungee declared, "Let's go down the street and find you a pot of coffee."

"I don't want to go that way. I already paid my money. I gotta go up to the Madame's," Hank Jensen complained.

"It's all right, Tungee I'll take care of him," Gabe Toombs said as he flashed a wide grin.

Tungee figured it was an impossible situation and turned to walk down the street when Will Farmer called excitedly, "Tungee, ain't you going up to the contest?"

Tungee nodded and gave a wry grin. "I think I'll pass. But if you fellows don't mind, let me know who wins the hundred dollar gold piece."

— SIXTEEN —

Papa Joe's Bar was owned by the company, like most everything else on the island. The bar was decorated in a traditional way, a long L shaped bar with a grand mirror back of it. But it probably had more than its share of paintings on the walls. There were several excellent paintings along with some bad. There was an oversized portrait of a beautiful brown skinned girl wearing a flower in her hair and that was all she wore, well almost all, she was smiling.

Papa Joe was a large man with a paunch; he had a full shock of gray hair and a trimmed beard. There were only two rules in the place wear a shirt and don't get out of line. And Papa Joe was the sole arbiter of those rules.

The big man was toweling down the bar when he turned and answered a routine sailor's question. "There are plenty of places to hide, but no place to go."

Jeff pressed his point. "How far is it to the mainland?"

"Too far for a small open boat," Papa Joe said as he turned to serve another customer.

Jeff turned to Tungee. "What do you think?"

"About jumping ship?"

"Yeah."

"Well, Jeff. I'll tell you what I told Dobbs, not that I'm in love with the idea, but put your money on Foster and the MFC. We'll eventually get to Boston and be paid off."

"Then what?"

"What ever you like."

Jeff frowned. "That's my big problem, Tungee. I don't know what to do when I get there." Then he arched his brow and looked up. "Keep running--"

"And never look back?" Tungee said, using Jeff's own words.

Tungee and Jeff stayed at Papa Joe's Bar and during the course of the evening they had talked to most of the men on the port watch. Early on, several seemed in the mood to jump ship, but by the end of the talk they decided to go along with Captain Foster and the MFC.

Jeff pointed to a tall colorful drink Papa Joe had just mixed for a customer. "What do you call that?"

"Papa Joe special."

"What's in it?"

"Four different rums, two jiggers of gin and some fruit."

Tungee said, "Sounds like a good start for tomorrow morning's hangover."

Jeff looked at the painting of the girl and the flower. "Wonder who painted that."

Tungee said, "I believe Papa Joe did a number of them."

Then he called out, "Hey, Papa Joe, did you do the girl?"

"I'm afraid I have to plead guilty."

"Who's the model?"

"Oh, she's a local whore."

"Hum. You wouldn't guess it," Tungee said, "she's quite attractive and she has a real look of innocence about her."

"I guess you're right about that, but she's still a whore." The bar owner hesitated a moment and said, "I suppose she's like everything else on this God forsaken island, even the fruit spoils the day it falls off the tree."

"You don't like St. Kat, do you, Papa Joe?"

"Nobody does."

"You mean you're locked in here too?"

The man behind the bar seemed to peer into the distance before he shook his head. "No, not by the company, I've done it to myself. I guess I'm like the locals, when it comes to leaving the place it's always manana." Then he squinted and pointed to one of the tables. "There's the girl in the picture."

Jeff and Tungee turned and saw her sitting with another girl at the table with Dobbs and Simms.

"I would have guessed Maria, or perhaps Juanita," Dobbs said easily.

Oliver smiled, "Rose is a flower too, so I'm going to call you Rosie."

"But my name is Flora."

"Don't you pay Oliver no mind, my dear, you can be any flower you choose." Dobbs pointed down the bar and slurred, "You see that young fellow with the specks on?"

Flora cooed. "Oh, he is young. And he looks so sweet."

"Well, I can't speak to that," Dobbs said, "but I'll tell you a little secret -- he's a virgin."

"You don't mean it." Flora giggled.

"He's a virgin all right," Simms announced.

Dobbs drew the girl close and whispered, "I have an idea that might be fun for you two girls. Go and talk to him, Flora. Then you and Anna take him into your place and seduce him."

Flora needed no further prompting; she got up and walked directly to Gene Blakely. The kid's head was swimming from drinking Papa Joe's specials. He turned and looked at the beautiful Flora. "I must be dreaming. I could swear I just saw you behind the bar -- right there in the picture."

The girl put her arm around the kid. "Do you like what you see in the picture?"

"Oooh, yeah. My goodness. Yes, I'd have to say yes I do."

Flora draped his arm around her waist, nudged him forward and they moved unsteadily across the room to a hallway opposite the bar. Anna, with a slight prompt from Dobbs and Simms, followed Flora and Blakely.

Dobbs and Sims rubbed their hands together and laughed heartily at their success in setting up the kid as they got up and stumbled toward the bar.

"I'm taking all bets, gents," Dobbs said laughingly.

"What's the proposition?" Tungee asked.

"Well now, you've turned a pretty good phrase there, mate. Proposition is what it's all about ... Flora just gave the kid as nice a proposition as you would ever dream of. You see, in my way of thinking, the kid needs to be saddle broke and that's what I suggested to the girls, didn't I, Oliver?"

"We did it, Dobbs, the two of us. But that is essentially correct, mates. The girls are going to seduce that kid into manhood."

"How are you setting the bets?" Jeff asked. "That the girls can or that they can't?"

"I'm saying the girls can make it happen, mates." Dobbs said through a slightly inebriated grin. "After all, I just happen to know their work first hand."

The room was sparsely furnished, one large double bed, two chairs, dresser, washstand with mirror and a number of Papa Joe's paintings on the walls. The girl's were well schooled in their profession and the fact that the kid was a virgin added a touch of excitement to their normal routine.

Gene Blakely had had just enough booze to be relaxed as those two maids of the night began their task. Flora was kissing Gene and at the same time removing his blouse. Anna took off her own scanty sarong. The boy smiled at the two on one situation and protested. "Hey, just a darn minute."

Flora planted another kiss on his mouth and quelled his protest with her tongue. Gene's manhood grew in proportion to his desires, but like a young bull, he didn't quite know how to go about satisfying them. However, as he observed Anna disrobing and the feel of Flora's hot moist tongue glide past his lips, the kid's sexual senses were set aflame.

Flora and Anna were well aware of the kid's lack of experience, but the two professionals began to work their magic and in a few brief moments Gene Blakely's lust was fired and the games began.

* * *

Tungee and the others sat around Papa Joe's Bar and speculated on the kid's possible performance. More than an hour had past and Dobbs and Simms were becoming concerned about the folly of their wagers.

"Do you know something, mates," Dobbs lamented, "my gut tells me that there little four eyed character is making monkeys out of us."

Loud laughter coming from the street got everyone's attention and just moments later Will Farmer and Dan Thurston entered the front door and crossed the room to join their mates. Dan Thurston licked his lips and announced, "It's all over."

"Did they get a winner?" Jeff questioned.

Dan Thurston urged on by Will Farmer proceeded. "You guys gotta hear this. Let me give you the setup. You see this here ain't no rip roaring orgy, you know what I mean, with ladies and gents all drunk and running around bare ass." Then he staggered and belched. "You gotta remember, Madam Picard's place is fixed up like a palace. And in the middle of all these fancy furnishings is a naked lady spread out on a tiger skin rug. And she ain't no plug neither; she's a looker, maybe like one of them Italian paintings. Well there she is relaxing on silk cushions while we're all standing around with our hands in our pockets holding it down. Then the one who's turn it is drops his pants to half-mast, the Madam moves in for a close inspection and when she's satisfied he ain't drippin' she backs off, folds her arms and glares at the bloke."

"Dripping? What do you mean by dripping?" Jeff asked innocently.

Danny gave Jeff a, what a dumb question look.

"If it's dripping," Tungee suggested, "he's likely got a dose of the clap."

Jeff gave an understanding nod.

Then the storyteller grinned and looked at the others for approval before he continued. "Now I know what you're thinkin', piece of cake. But it ain't. Fact is with everyone standing around lookin' and sneerin' and makin' catcalls it ain't that easy. And none of us in line, waitin' our turn, are wishin' him well," Danny chuckled, "cause we'd all like a shot at that beauty on the rug, not to mention the hundred dollar gold piece."

"Well, for God's sake, man what happened?" Dobbs shouted.

"Time after time they'd get into position, drop their pants and he'd be all firm and at attention. But then us bystanders would begin laughin' and makin' a ruckus and the Madam glarin'. Well just about the time he's ready to plug it in his cock goes as limp as a jib in a calm."

"Are you telling us they had no winner," Tungee said with some sense of disappointment in his voice.

"Oh, they got a winner right enough, but they went through a dozen men alternating between MFC and Glory crews before it happened."

"Who won, mate?" Simms asked impatiently.

Dan Thurston, thirsty for another drink, chewed on the question for a long moment before a slightly drunken smile played over his face. He held the audience as long as he dared. "One of our own."

"Who, for God's sake, Danny? Spit it out," Dobbs said with total frustration.

Will Farmer punched Danny with his elbow and took his cue. Then he leaned forward favoring a slight port list and announced, "Old Gabe Toombs did us proud, mates. I'm bound to tell you, he popped it to her good and proper. And before he was half done the gal on the tiger skin rug groaned and kissed old Gabe like there wasn't another soul in the room."

Keeping a tight secret on St. Katharine Island is like trying to call a halt to the Sunset. Just what Foster didn't need was a wholesale defection of his present crew. The rumor mill was churning out stories and scuttlebutt had it that the MFC was about to set sail for West Africa. So far the skipper had deflected any direct questions about Africa as a typical island rumor. He told them there was no more truth to that than the one about Valparaiso that surfaced before the Horn. It worried Foster though and the rumor was damned persistent.

Gideon Foster, Oscar L Hooper and Findley Smith were all gathered in the company office along with a carpenter by the name of Gordon Hayes.

Hayes was a large beefy man with an intelligent look and he was not happy about the delay in his work. Most of his task had to be completed before they dock in Africa. Refitting the MFC from a regular cargo vessel to a slave ship and it would require many hard hours. The carpenter was making his case for going ahead with the work before putting to sea. "We have two other ships in port right now and I know three good carpenters that could lend me a hand if you'd let me start now."

Foster frowned and shook his head. "My crew's as jumpy as a cat with a scorched tail just from this slave scuttlebutt floating around. I don't like the idea of the rumor becoming a fact while we're still in port."

Oscar said, "If you need extra help I suppose we could scavenge from the other two ships."

"I won't buy that," Gideon Foster said, "we might be trading trouble for trouble. But all things considered we could be a mite short handed," then he pursed his lips, "I wonder if we could scrounge a half-dozen able bodies seamen from your locals."

The taciturn Findley Smith looked up with a half grin. "I can manage that, Captain Foster."

"We sail on tomorrow's outgoing tide."

"You'll have your extra men," Findley Smith said with authority.

Tungee, Dobbs, and Simms were in a longboat twenty yards ahead of the captain's launch. A call from shore got everyone's attention. They looked back and recognized Gene Blakely racing down Main Street with his shirttail flying. He ran past the hotel, through the market and over the dock where he dove into the water and swam toward the launch.

The swimmer called out, "Hey, wait up."

"What kept you, kid?" Cheny yelled.

Dobbs cupped his hands to his mouth and shouted. "You shit."

"Pace yourself, Gene," Tungee warned.

Jeff yelled, "Come on, champ."

"You little creep," Dobbs cried.

"Careful of the sharks, lad," Simms called out with his perverse sense of humor.

"You young fart," Dobbs yelled, "I'll fix your wagon."

The youngster, huffing and puffing reached the captain's launch and Foster, with an assist from his first mate, hauled in the exhausted sailor.

In the longboat Tungee asked, "What set you off, Dobbs?" Then he recalled the prank in the bar. "I don't know what you're crabbing about, you won all the bets."

"She was my girl," Dobbs whined.

Tungee arched his brow. "Your girl?"

"Well, she didn't exactly belong to me, but I saw her first and I had her first."

"You set the whole thing up, Dobbs," Tungee said disarmingly. "You sicked the girls onto him, you know."

"Think about it, Dobbs," said Jeff, "You fixed the bets."

"I suppose you gents are right, but who'd have thought the kid would turn out to be a champion stud. It's disgusting to think that little four eyed character was able to keep both the girls occupied and happy every bloomin' minute he was on the island."

Fritz Cheny called out, "Mr. Cahill, keep your port watch men on deck and prepare for a general muster."

"Aye, Mr. Cheny."

"Who's done it this time, who's screwed up the works for the rest of us," Dobbs protested not aware they were about to haul anchor and get under way.

Fritz Cheny yelled, "Oarsmen, get to your boats, capstan crew, standby to haul in the anchor. And the rest of you men get to your regular duties, stow the gear and prepare to get under way."

Hank Jensen assumed the master coxswains duties on the longboats. He tied a twenty five-yard stern line to each boat and made the other end fast to the bow stem of the MFC.

A quick signal from Captain Foster put the capstan crew in motion turning round the hub in circles drawing the anchor chain taunt. In just two more turns the anchor broke loose from the bottom and the ship gave a sharp lurch to port.

There was no visible shadow cast by the rigging, with the exception of the yards, as the sun stood square on top of the MFC and burned straight down to generate a hundred and fifteen-degree temperature. The ocean was stirred ever so slightly by a feeble swell that barely broke on the sandy beach. The present breeze was listless, stifling still and broken only by a vision of heat waves rippling just above the waters.

Captain Foster shaded his eyes and called to Hank Jensen and his men, "Put your back's into your work men and pull."

Foster repeated the word pull once, twice and the men at the oars as well as those on deck picked up the cadence and all with one voice began to chant, "Pull, pull, pull."

The captain timed his move right down to the minute and in less than a quarter of an hour after the pull chant had begun the tide shifted and you could feel the tug of the ropes and then see movement as the MFC began to slide past North Point, a small sliver of land that lends protection to St. Katharine harbor. The MFC had cleared Lands End by no more than a hundred yards when they began to get the push of the outgoing tide as well as the pull of the oarsmen. Top men in the rigging were letting go the clew lines, preparing to unfurl sail.

The sometime afternoon breeze, not nearly so predictable as the tide, was making a subtle appearance out of the east-southeast. When the ship was fully clear of North Point, Captain Foster called for a direction change. "Mr. Jensen keep your lines taunt and move your bows to starboard. Helmsman, cheat your wheel just a little in that same direction. Mr. Cheny, prepare to make sail."

Fritz Cheny called out the routine orders and the men who were already in the rigging scrambled to set the jibs, stays and spanker.

The timing was almost perfect. No sooner were the fore and aft sails out when they began to flutter gently in the light breeze.

"Mr. Jensen," Foster called, "secure your oars and prepare to come aboard." Gideon Foster had given that last order none too soon as the ship began to make her way through the shallow waves as Jensen and his longboat crews were hard pressed not to be run down as they hustled into position for recovery.

— SEVENTEEN —

One day out of St. Katharine Foster and Cheny were in the captain's quarters doing a quick calculation on time and distance of the voyage to West Africa. They knew there was only so much work the carpenters could do in the shop before they had to begin installing the new lattice hatch covers that would provide circulation to the hold. As soon as the first open cover was installed the old timers would be aware of what their actual mission was about.

Fritz Cheny saw anxiety on the captain's face and he finally said, "It's gotta be done, Skipper and to my way of thinking, the sooner the better."

The captain paced the cabin, searching his mind for ideas and ways to sugarcoat the slave business. He finally sighed. "I'll stress the extra bonus and hope it'll be enough to keep most of them in line."

Carrying more than half the ship's canvas on a close hauled port tack and traveling at about a dozen knots, the spray off the bows gave cooling relief to the shirtless MFC crew that lined up to face the captain.

Gideon Foster looked down from the quarterdeck and with a twisted grin said, "Gentlemen, it looks like these meetings are getting to be a habit." He scanned the faces of his men and coughed.

Tungee stood with the others considering the captain's words. Maybe it was a look in Foster's eyes or perhaps it was his attempt at levity. The fact was his last statement didn't register with the crew and only garnered a halfhearted response.

Gideon Foster grinned. "To those few men who, back in St. Katharine, asked me point blank about the African scuttlebutt I owe you an apology -- I flat out lied to you."

Oliver Simms pushed his good arm into the air and threw caution to the wind. "Ask me no questions, I'll tell you no lies, is that it, Captain, sir? Which side of Africa and just how long does this here bloody voyage last, sir? And what is our final destination?"

"We terminate the voyage in Boston." Then Foster pursed his lips. "And if all goes well we should complete the trip this side of ninety days."

"Now, that's gettin' down to cases," Simms said, "Thank you Captain, sir."

"I can do without the commentary, gentlemen."

Dobbs pulled Simms good arm out of the air and said, "Leave off, you bloody fool."

"Men, keep this in mind. There will be a damn good payday when we get to Boston." The captain said with authority, "The company has assured me that this whole crew will receive a generous bonus, and that's in addition to your regular pay." The captain's statement received light applause in some quarters. Captain Foster almost smiled as his audience began to turn in his favor. "We drop this load of grain in West Africa and take on three hundred and fifty black Africans."

"Oh, Captain, sir," Simms said with a bitter tone, "You mean we're becoming a bloomin' slaver and you say we take on three hundred and fifty of them monkeys."

Jeff collared the one armed man. "One more crack like that, Simms and one arm or no, I'm going to punch your face in."

"Piss off, Nigger," Simms said defiantly.

Jeff pushed the bigot away, wound up and delivered a hay maker that Tungee slapped down as he quickly stepped between the two.

"Knock it off, Simms," Tungee spat, "or I'll personally finish the job Randolph started."

Captain Foster pulled a pistol from his belt and fired it into the air just as Dobbs called out, "It's all right, sir. We've got things under control."

Gideon Foster fumed, but put his gun away. "I've just heard some remarks that don't accord with my thinking. Some of you apparently think the black man is less than human."

A voice in the crowd said, "They ain't human."

And a mixed chorus called out, "Animals."

"Jungle bunnies."

"Niggers."

The captain raised his voice. "Settle down. I'll not try and convert you to my way of thinking. But this is an order! You will keep your personal opinions, about those people, to yourself. I expect some of you will find that difficult. Now if it becomes too much of a burden for you to keep your mouth shut, I'll begin issuing extra duty assignments." Then he pursed his lips and began to speak in a quiet voice, "Now I have just given you men a generous offer and a chance for all of you to earn some serious money."

"What if we don't want your serious money, Captain," Jeff said irately.

The captain frowned. "If any of you would like, you may report to me and we'll talk man to man. And I'll consider putting you off in West Africa, if that's what you want. In the meantime we are in route to our pickup point. There's work to be done refitting and preparing for the new cargo. Any of you who want to talk to me, see Fritz Cheny or Hank Jensen and they'll arrange a meeting."

Then Captain Foster turned on his heels and disappeared below, leaving some grumbling and the rest trying to get a handle on exactly what to do. There was talk of a rebellion, take over the ship and sail it to the states. Tungee scratched his head as he listened to the prattle and figured that for the most part it was just men letting off steam.

Tungee was alone in Cabin C, relaxing on his upper bunk thinking about San Francisco, how to play the game and get back there alive. He mused at his present situation, the MFC was moving away from California at about twelve knots per hour. An attempted takeover was sure to cause more killing. And making a slave run made him sick to his stomach. There was a light tap on the door. "Come on in."

Dobbs and Jeff entered the cabin, both shirtless due to the oppressive heat.

"I'll not do it," Dobbs said sullenly, "I'll not be a party to the trade."

Jeff paced like a cat and Tungee followed him with his eyes. "What about you, Jeff?"

"I feel the same as Dobbs," he said as he continued to pace.

Tungee slid to the floor and stood beside his bunk. "I hear some of the men plan to leave the ship in West Africa, you fellows plan to join them?"

Dobbs grumbled. "I ain't decided yet. First I'd like to know where in West Africa?"

"If we keep to our present heading it will likely be around the Gulf of Guinea," Tungee said evenly. "And if that is the case we'll be square on the Equator. It'll be damned hot there."

"Hot or no, mates. I, for one, don't see how that could make a whole heap of difference about gettin' off a bloomin' slave ship."

Tungee shot back, "What if it's the only game in town?"

"What do you mean by that, mate?"

"I mean, what if all the shipping in the area is part of the trade. Think you might get a better deal with someone else?"

"I see what you're gettin' at," Dobbs muttered. "Could be stuck in that hot spot."

Tungee took a deep breath and said, "I've just about made up my mind to go along with Foster."

"What the hell are you sayin', mate?" Dobbs said accusingly. "We was supposed to talk about it first. Shit, we just got here and now you say you've already made up your bloomin' mind."

Tungee held up his hands in surrender. "Now, now, Dobbs, just listen. I'm not telling either of you what to do, but listen to my reasoning before you get you nose out of joint."

"All right, have your say," Dobbs sputtered.

"The way I see it is, trust the devil you know rather than the one you don't." He looked at Jeff, "I don't discount your feelings about the whole mess, but you're a fool to think of anyone but yourself when it comes to survival."

Dobbs' sharp mind immediately picked up Tungee's meaning. "Hadn't thought about it that way." Then he rubbed his hands together and turned his position one hundred and eighty degrees. "Look at it this way, Jeff, my mate. What'll you be doin' in a slave tradin' port? Why the chances are pretty good that you'll be picked up and thrown in with the other Africans. Now you may hold free status back in the states. But I doubt if it would count for much with them traders."

Tungee looked out the porthole and chuckled at Dobbs' practical assessment of the situation.

Dobbs walked to the door. "I've had about all of this slave talk I can handle for one day. Think I'll go play some poker."

Jeff and Tungee gave the departing Dobbs a high sign. They were both silent for a long moment before Jeff sighed. "I suppose you and Dobbs are right, but it kind of leaves me between a rock and a hard place."

A wry grin came over Tungee's face. "Why, that should make you feel right at home, Jeff. Seems to me we've been in that fix since we first woke up in this very cabin."

Tungee gave a light tap on the captain's door and a voice inside said, "Come on in, Cahill."

He chuckled at the captain's awareness as he opened the door. Foster walked in a wide circle around the cabin and puffed on his cigar. "Sit down if you want to, Tungee."

"Thanks, Captain Foster," sounding rather formal, "but I'd sooner stand."

Tungee stood near the chart table and watched the captain make three complete turns around the room.

"I guess you think I lied to you and Thunder and the black -- "

"Randolph," Tungee interjected.

"Yeah," Foster nodded, "right here in this cabin during our first meeting, if I recall correctly." Foster continued to pace and puff on his cigar. "I had a lot on my mind at the time, some of it having to do with you and Thunder being on board. Another thing was that I had just opened my sealed orders telling me to change the name of the ship."

"Did those orders mention Africa?"

"No, Tungee, but I suspected as much."

"Dammit, Captain Foster! If I had known that I might have joined Thunder Parker and the others." Then he glared at the skipper, "If you ask me, there's more honor in consorting with pirates than associating with the trade."

"Tungee, the orders didn't mention the trade. That was just an educated guess. I wasn't told until we got to St. Katharine Island. I swear, all I had earlier was a hunch."

"It showed on your face, Skipper," Then Tungee laughed, "you aren't very good at hiding a lie."

"I'll take that as a compliment, Tungee."

Gideon Foster finally went to his desk and sat on the front of it, put his cigar in the ashtray and interlaced his fingers like a cathedral and moaned. "It's a damned dirty business."

"Well, if you're looking to me for sympathy, Captain, you'll not get any." Tungee glared at the skipper. "Why in hell didn't you tell them to shove the whole proposition up their ass?"

Gideon Foster took a long moment and then said sadly, "No guts, I guess."

"Guts has nothing to do with it. It's character, Captain Foster, character and integrity. And the way I see you and your whole crummy company is that you're are all a bunch of greedy bastards." He glared at the captain and saw Gideon Foster wilt.

"If I was smart, Mr. Cahill, I'd have you drawn and quartered for those remarks." Then the skipper grinned. "But the fact is, you're right. Oh, hell, I've threatened not to go along, but in the end it always comes down one thing. If I want to keep my master's license I've got to follow orders. It's as simple as that."

"Company orders."

"You could say it's the company, but it really comes down to one man, Lindsay Arthur Griffin."

"Couldn't you fight him in court?"

Foster shook his head and there was fear in his eyes. "I'd rather go to court and face the charge of slave trading than stand up to that son-of-a-bitch."

Dammit, Tungee began to consider his own position. Shit, if I had any guts, I'd be up in the forecastle talking rebellion, not compromise.

Foster picked up his cigar and began to pace. "I'm just trying to figure a way to come out of this thing alive and I'm asking for your help."

Tungee walked to the porthole near the chart table and looked out for a long moment before he turned back to Foster. "I guess what I just said to some of the men stands." Then he fixed the skipper with a hard look and said without humor, "Trust the devil you know."

Gideon Foster grinned, took a deep breath and gave an agreeable nod. "Then let's get this trade business out of the way and head on up to Boston."

Tungee, Dobbs and Blakely stood on deck watching the carpenter, Gordon Hayes work on the amidships hatch covers.

Hayes looked up from his work and grinned at Dobbs. "You're the one that was giving the youngster such a hard time, weren't you? Something about a gal back in St. Kat?"

"You got that right, mate. At least you got it half right. Actually there were two ladies in the bargain."

"Don't leave out the part you played in the whole setup, Mr. Dobbs," Tungee chided.

"The greatest tragedy of my life, that there is what it was. And it was my own doin'. The two most beautiful ... er ladies of the night, Flora and Anna. I handed them to this one time virgin, handed them to him on a silver platter, expecting him to whet their appetites and return the ladies in short order as frisky as a couple of little kittens. But no, mates. What happened was this young virgin turned into a ragin' bull. And he kept Flora and Anna occupied and happy the better part of our stay in St. Kat. Oh, mates, it still pains me to no end."

The kid blushed, Gordon Hayes smiled and said, "That's a couple of Papa Joe's girls, sounds to me like you've got pretty good taste, son."

Somewhere south of Lagos in the Gulf of Guinea, the MFC was on a port tack and a northeast heading. They were just one day out of a three day calm and nerves were settling a little as every man on the ship had decided for his own reason to tag along with Captain Foster, man the slave ship and take the money at Boston. Less than a dozen men had gone in to see the captain and talk about the issue. Some had their own grievance regarding the slave issue, but for the most part they wanted to know the bonus figures. The captain gave them no satisfactory answers; the probable reason was that he didn't know the figures himself.

Tungee, Foster and Cheny stood on the quarterdeck near the chart house. "What kind of port facilities can we expect at our pickup point?" Tungee asked.

Gideon Foster pursed his lips and said, "It's not a port, not in the true sense of the word. From what I've been told, it's a floating dock." He gestured, "Come on inside the chart room and I'll show you."

Tungee and Cheny followed the captain inside. A large map of South America, the South Atlantic and about half of the African continent was spread out on the table.

Captain Foster pointed to a location on the map. "Here we are right now," then he moved his finger over the map to a place called Lagos. "Look right here on the coast just past the Niger River outlets, you see the Bonny River. Now follow on to the east, there's Opobo. Right here, we'll be aiming for a spot half way between the two places."

On the evening of the sixteenth day out of St. Katharine Island, the MFC arrived at her designated point off the African Coast. About an hour after making visual contact with their people, a near full moon made an appearance. And soon after the moon came out, three long dugout type canoes were spotted slicing through the nearly still waters and heading directly toward the ship.

A very tall African man wearing an English business suit stood in the bow of the lead boat and when they came near to the MFC that man called out, "Oh, Captain, sir. I bring you greetings from Bonny."

Captain Foster acknowledged the signal and allowed the man in the suit to come aboard. As the African scrambled on to the deck, he began to parrot a phrase, "I you pilot, I you pilot." It soon became apparent that he was short on an English vocabulary, but that didn't seem to bother him. He handed the captain a piece of paper signed by one H. Becker, the L.A.G. Spice and Tea man on the West African Coast.

The new pilot immediately went to work, picked up a coil of rope and pointed out over the bowsprit toward the dugouts. They were already positioning themselves ahead of the ship. Cheny and Jensen complied with his broken English and hand signals and fixed three ropes to the stem of the ship. The African then tossed the loose ends to his men in the dugouts. It only took a few minutes for the men watching from the deck of the MFC to realize that those natives handling the paddles were experts at their tasks.

Those three small boats working in unison took less than three hours to haul the ship across more than a mile of open sea, maneuver her into position and tie up alongside the floating dock at the place called Bonny.

— EIGHTEEN —

Tropical heat and humidity made crew life aboard the MFC miserable during their stay at Bonny Dock. The midday sun was almost unbearable, but most afternoons they got a break from the heat just before sundown when a light breeze would drift in from the Atlantic. However it didn't last long and when it got dark and the breeze quit the sultry heat would return. Most crewmembers spent their nights on deck and only distant drums and the sounds of animal life in the nearby jungle broke the suffocating stillness of the night.

Black Africans were hired to do the heavy stevedore work, removing cargo from the ship's hold. And once the grain was unloaded the crew was put to work cleaning and painting the ship while Gordon Hayes ripped out the cargo cleats in an attempt to make the hold more habitable for the passengers who would soon be using that area as living quarters.

Prompted by the sounds of life in the jungle Tungee borrowed Captain Foster's long glass and invited Jeff to come along and they climbed to the crow's nest for an extended look at the countryside. The green jungle spread out from a level coast and gradually rose to an undulating plateau. It was a beautiful landscape and with the naked eye they could see a rugged hill country on the distant horizon. Between the jungle and those hills there was a huge plain dotted with patches of short grass, scattered shrubs and trees. And it was on that great savanna where they spotted some of West Africa's animal life lions, leopards, giraffes and elephants.

Tungee saw it first when he lowered the glass and scanned the near jungle. He spotted a village on the east bank of the Bonny River, apparently the hub of the local slave trade. And just south of the village he saw great holding pens filled with captured natives. He drew a deep breath and after a few moments of hesitation, he handed the glass to Jeff and pointed.

An immediate frown came over Jeff's face as he got his first close look at the ugly and sinister heart of the slave operation. Moments later he began to shake with indignation. "I don't know if I can go through with this, Tungee."

"You've got to, Jeff. I've said this before and I'll say it again, our best chance of survival is with Foster and the MFC." Then he took the glass from Jeff and squinted at the village. "It's disgusting and I know what we're about to do won't square with any decent standard of morality, but jumping ship is not an option -- that would be just plain suicide."

The loading process would begin at sunrise and Captain Foster gave orders to the crew, to prepare to make sail on the afternoon tide.

Streaks of red in the east foretold the dawn as Tungee paced the quarterdeck. Gordon Hayes climbed out of the cabin area a duffel bag in one hand and his carpenter's toolbox in the other. Tungee called out, "You're leaving us, Mr. Hayes."

"And not a moment too soon I should think."

Tungee got the gist of the comment, but didn't add to it. He just hesitated and said, "You going back to St. Kat?"

"Yes I'm on my way to Port Harcourt. I'll hitch a ride to Rio and someone from the company will pick me up there."

Tungee laughed. "Might be fun in Rio."

Gordon Hayes looked over his shoulder and said, "It better be."

Tungee smiled and waved as he watched the carpenter descend the aft ladder and walk jauntily toward the African village.

It was at that early hour when the crew first saw the company man at Bonny Dock. Henry Becker wore round gold-rimmed spectacles, a dandy's mustache, a shock of gray hair hung neatly across his brow.

He wore a suntan colored military jacket with matching trousers and a wide brimmed straw hat. His chubby boyish face made him look more like a Sunday school teacher than a slave trader.

Standing on the quarterdeck Foster, Becker and Cheny were all busy making their own separate count as the Africans boarded. Those people came in a long single file and were hustled onto the dock and then forced to climb one of three boarding ladders. They all wore some clothing, men generally wore a loin cloth draped over one shoulder covering their bodies to mid calf. Women wore long one-piece dresses of bright cotton calico. And the children usually emulated their elders.

The guards were black Africans, their uniform was short sleeved khaki shirts and cut off trousers. And every guard carried a cat-of-nine-tails style whip to back up his commands.

Henry Becker turned to Foster and said, "I see a number of new babies in the group and since they're not in the tally, you ought to come out all right, Captain."

"I'd figure you to put the best light you could on it." Foster chuckled. "Hell, I'd do the same if the shoe was on the other foot." Then he frowned. "Some of these folks can be difficult."

"You won't have any trouble with these Ebo's, Captain Foster."

"It's really not them or even the trip that bothers me, Henry, it's Turner's bellyaching on the other end," Gideon Foster said tartly.

"Most will be sold into plantation labor, won't they."

"Maybe all and I know what you're about to say. Yes, many already have some farming skills, but you know just as well I do that some of the Ebo tribe are about as stubborn as a mule. For blacks, they probably think too much."

"Captain, you just tell Turner that Henry Becker said that Ebo was what was available and Ebo is what he gets. And one more thing, tell him this too, these people are quite intelligent and that a kind word will get a whole lot more than a switch of the cat."

Tungee, Jeff and Dobbs stood near the starboard bow watching the boarding process, all still wrestling with and trying to rationalize their own actions as they were unwillingly drawn into the trade.

The long black line was getting shorter, most of the men disappeared into the hold while many women and children milled about the amidships deck. The boarding process was almost complete.

One of the last to walk across the dock and climb the aft most ladder was a tall majestic man with sad, but determined brown eyes. Instinct told Tungee that he had just seen an important man, possibly the king of some region. The man was dressed about the same as other African men, but there was something different about the way he carried himself.

On the far side of the dock a white man who appeared to be the ramrod looked over the shoulder of a counting clerk sitting at a small desk, turned and called out to his boss, "Mr. Becker, that's it."

"What's the final tally?" Becker demanded.

"It's right on the money, three hundred and fifty, not counting the new babies."

Foster, Cheny and Becker conferred and agreed with the ramrod's tally. Fritz Cheny handed some papers, on a board, for signature and in the end keeping some and handing Becker a sheaf. The slave trader put the papers into his pocket and descended the aft ladder to the dock.

Tungee and Jeff had been asked to share Cabin C with Hank Jensen and Gabe Toombs due to the packing into every available space, the people they had just taken aboard. The general order was for women and children to be kept on deck, also some of the below decks cabins would be given over to the new mothers. However, in emergency situations the people living on deck would be crowded into any available space below.

Twenty-four hours after departing Bonny Dock, Tungee, Jeff, Dobbs and Blakely were at the chow table having their noon meal. Jeff had made it a point to talk to some of the guards that boarded at Bonny. He quickly found out the reason for blacks selling other blacks. And it was very simple, greed, in the name of cold hard cash.

Jeff looked up from his food and grinned. "There's a king onboard, you know."

"A king, did you say?" Dobbs asked.

"That's what I said, a king."

"Well, he must be a king without a crown, or maybe he was not wearin' it when he came onboard, leastwise I didn't see it." Dobbs turned to Tungee, "Did you see any of them folks wearin' a bloomin' crown, mate?"

"No," said Tungee.

Jeff smiled at Dobbs humor. "They may not know about crowns, but they do know about leaders and from what I hear they call them kings. Anyhow, it seems we have one among the prisoners."

Hank Jensen rushed into the chow hall and ordered, "Port watch, get to you're work stations and make it snappy."

"What's it's all about?" Tungee asked.

"You'll be told when you get on deck."

"Every man in the room made a dash to the ladder and hauled themselves up to the main deck. Tungee arrived just in time to hear a report from the crow's nest. "One's flying the British Union Jack and I can't make the second, but it could be the Stars and Stripes."

Foster called, "Are they both man-of-war."

"Aye, man-of-war, they are. You bet, sir. The nearest is a British sloop, the one farther back I make out to be a frigate and they've got guns all right, sir."

"Keep a sharp eye and call down any course change."

"Aye, Captain."

Captain Foster called, "Jensen. Have some of the guards round up these people on deck and take them below."

Jensen and the guards immediately herded the on deck people down the ladders. The numbers overwhelmed the limited space as those people squeezed into the already crowded cabins while others huddled in the narrow companionway. Tungee and Jeff had already given up their bunks in Cabin C and moved into the forecastle, but that did little to eliminate those awful conditions below.

"Make all sail," Foster bellowed, "I want every inch of canvas put to work. Get your men aloft, Mr. Cahill. You too, Mr. Toombs."

The crow's nest reported, "They've fired a shot from the sloop, Captain."

"Are you sure about that?"

"Aye, aye, sir. I just saw it hit the water, short, sir. Way off the mark and a mile short, sir."

As they climbed the rigging, Jeff called to Tungee and asked, "What if they catch us?"

"I've never been on a slaver before. All I know is what I've heard."

"What about the slaves? Think they'd be better off."

"Not if the guards have orders not to get caught with cargo."

"What do you mean by that?" Jeff asked guardedly. "They may have been told to throw them overboard."

"Oh, mate." Dobbs said disbelieving, "You've got to be wrong. They wouldn't do that, would they?"

"I don't think Foster would order it, but I have no idea about the guards. It wouldn't be the first time though."

"Well, they'll bloody well have to toss me with 'em gents. Cause I for one ain't gonna stand by and watch no wholesale murder."

"That makes two of us, Dobbs," Jeff said defiantly.

Fritz Cheny ran forward from the quarterdeck to take a look at the progress in the rigging. The MFC was on a close haul starboard tack with the sheets trimmed flat and every thing from the fore, main and cro'jic to the royals full.

Cheny leaned back and cupped his hands around his mouth and was apparently about to give some kind of reprimand when he looked up and didn't utter a word. The fore and main were already flying full, all the sail she could carry.

Tungee noticed Fritz Cheny's action and called down, "What was that you're were about to say, Mr. Cheny?"

Fritz Cheny said laughingly, "Don't be a smart ass, Mr. Cahill. And furthermore get into position to brace the yards to begin a port tack as soon as I get the word."

"Then the skipper thinks we can outrun them to the southwest."

"He doesn't just think, Mr. Cahill. He knows damn well we can."

Fritz Cheny was correct and on the heels of that short conversation, the captain's orders came to brace for a close reach on a port tack.

The men in the rigging came alive and seemed to enjoy the challenge. This change was a model of efficiency and with both watch sections in action it took them less than five minutes to brace and lock the yards into position.

"The frigate is definitely flying the American flag," the man in the crow's nest yelled, "and she's changing course, hard to port, sir."

"You're saying the lag ship is turning hard to port," Foster called back.

"Aye, sir. She's on a hard port tack, sir."

When his work in the rigging was finished, Tungee shinnied down the pole and jogged back to the quarterdeck. "Captain, I'd like a word with you, if you don't mind, sir."

"Go on in, I'll be along in a minute."

Tungee walked into the chart house and crossed to the map table. Fortunately the same map they'd looked at before was spread out on the table. He knew he had to be careful in what he was about to say to the skipper, but he had to say something. And as Gideon Foster came into the room, Tungee looked up from the map and said, "Captain, this is just between you and me -- man to man."

The captain gave a respectful, if guarded, "What is it, Tungee?"

"Well, um ... I want you to tell me something."

Captain Foster cocked his head.

"If we are overtaken by those warships, what happens to the Africans?"

Foster gave an embarrassed chuckled. "Let's cross that bridge when we get to it."

"No, Skipper, I want an answer."

"Nothing's going to happen to those people, because we'll not be caught."

"What if, Captain?"

"What if is not a damned question? I just told you they'll not catch us." Then he chewed on his cigar. "And one more thing, the mercury's dropping."

"Are we heading into a storm?"

"Maybe. But this is my thinking, if we can open a little distance between us and then hit the leading edge of the front, it's just possible we could skirt the heavy weather and leave that for those fellows to wrestle with."

Tungee looked square into Foster's eyes and saw a gambler full of confidence. He figured old Thunder Parker might have played it the same way. "It's a crap shoot, Skipper, but it wouldn't be the first gamble that ever paid off."

Captain Foster's tack changes and added canvas finally gave the MFC an advantage. The British sloop and American frigate had steadily dropped back and eventually the crows' nest reported he had lost sight of the warships.

During the last eight hours the barometer had a slight rise and then a sudden drop. Cumulonimbus clouds were building up to the southwest and they rose thousands of feet into the sky. Nearing sunset the tall clouds took on an ominous hue as their color changed from white to dark gray.

Captain Foster summed up the condition and passed the word along to all hands to prepare for imminent gale force winds and rain. A large part of the captain's concern was for the women and children whose regular living quarters was on the open deck. He called on Walter Greenleaf and the carpenter to rig several low canvas tents that would provide some shelter from the rain.

The wind picked up as it made a ninety 'degree shift from southeast to the southwest. And just as the sea began to reflect the storm and the rollers grew in height Foster gave orders to bend to a starboard tack that would give them a northwest heading and begin to pull away from the Equator.

They were braced for close haul sailing and even with heavy seas, the MFC was making a good ten knots. They had just secured the braces when a warm rain began to pelt down and the wind swirled just enough to bathe the bodies of crewmen on deck and in the rigging.

"Yo, there on deck. Sail ho!" The lookout called down, "Starboard, abaft the beam."

Fritz Cheny yelled. "Can you recognize her?"

"There are two of them, Mr. Cheny. Same ones as before, the Britt and the American."

Tungee, Captain Foster and Fritz all raced for the aft starboard rail. But none of them could make the sighting from the deck.

The captain called to the lookout. "Ahoy, crow's nest. Can you still make out their masts?"

"Aye, Captain Foster. But only with the glass, they are quite distant, sir."

"Those tenacious bastards ... Mr. Rogers, port your helm by twenty degrees ... Mr. Cheny please call to the rigging and begin to brace for a close haul on the port tack."

Fritz Cheny gestured to Tungee to get back to the rigging and then he belted out the skipper's orders. Cheny then turned to Foster and said, "I hope you know what you're doing, Gideon."

"We're going into the eye of that monster," Foster said wryly, "let's just see if those bastards have the guts to follow."

Then the captain paced the deck between the quarterdeck and the forecastle and demanded. "You men on deck see to it that all blacks are taken below."

Gideon Foster continued to pace until he determined the time was right, then he reared back and bellowed a new set of orders. "Top men reef every square sail on all masts from fore upper topsail down in preparation for heavy gale force winds and rain. Now get about your business, gentlemen."

Then he climbed up and planted his feet squarely on the quarterdeck and watched until all changes were made and the ship's bow was pointing directly into the storm.

— NINETEEN —

Tungee finished his work, dropped down from the rigging and was on his way to the forecastle when he noticed a half dozen children huddled beneath the canvas. They should have already gone below, and when he motioned them to follow him they didn't budge. When he called to them and they crawled toward the back of the tent. He spotted Jeff and hailed, "Jeff, give me a hand. We've got to get these children out of the weather."

Jeff ran over and kneeled down. "Come on, you've got to go inside."

Then a youthful voice said in English. "No. Too many people packed in. No room. No, sir we stay here. No breathe down below."

"You can't stay here," Tungee said.

They understood, but pushed their little bodies farther back into the tent.

Then Tungee said, "Come on, Jeff, "we'll take them to the forecastle, carry them if necessary."

Jeff reached in and took one quivering hand. "Come with us, we'll find room for you."

It didn't work out exactly like the Pied Piper, but all of them eventually followed Jeff's lead and Tungee herded from the rear.

Simms was the first to spot the children. "Hello. What do we have here?"

Tungee declared, "Guests, Mr. Simms."

The jovial Dobbs added, "Watch your language, gents."

Simms furrowed his brow and grumbled, "I'm not sure we need any blackbirds in the forecastle."

"Oliver Simms, why don't you take your mean spirit and go heave it over the side," Dobbs said accusingly.

"Cut the crap, Mr. Simms," Tungee demanded.

These children had apparently been separated from their parents and they were frightened and in tears.

Tungee spoke to the children in gentle tones, "Which one of you speaks English?"

A young boy stepped forward and raised his hand. "I speak some little English, sirs."

"What's your name?" Tungee asked.

"Kulando, sirs."

"You're very polite, Kulando," Jeff said.

"I respect my elders, sirs."

"How did you learn English?" Tungee asked.

"From my mother and father, they learned from the missionaries and the Great Book."

"Bright little bugger, ain't he," Dobbs enthused.

"Kulando, tell your friends what we've been saying and that we won't harm them," Tungee advised.

The youngster did as he was instructed and the other children smiled and seemed to relax just as the ship lurched and yawed. The timbers stretched and groaned as the sea began to run and swell, twisting the hull. And the winds whined through the rigging.

Fritz Cheny cracked the forecastle door and called down. "Port watch, lend a hand. We've got some furling to do."

"Aye, Fritz," Tungee replied as he turned to the men and called, "Port watch needed topside. Let's turn to." Then he had second thoughts about Blakely's spectacles. "And you, Mr. Blakely, I don't want you in the rigging tonight. Stay on deck and man the halyards."

As the men climbed the ladder and forced their way through the door, they were hit with a drenching and blinding rain. The sea lanterns attached to each mast and the one over the binnacle were barely visible. Every man going into the rigging that night knew they would have to climb by feel and instinct more than sight.

Captain Foster stood between the helm and mizzenmast shouting orders to Cheny who was standing between the mizzen and main. Jensen standing between the main and foremast relayed the word from that position. The noise made by wind, rain and the roaring sea made it impossible to hear orders in the top rigging when called directly from the bridge.

Tungee and Jeff hit the foremast first and since the orders were to furl all the rectangle sails, Tungee headed straight to the top to lend a hand with the sky sail and royal. He directed Jeff to help with the fore royal.

Gabe Toombs bellowed from the main. "Mr. Cahill, get back to the deck and grab Jensen. The spanker just blew out and Captain Foster wants you fellows to jury-rig something. We can't do without a spanker."

"I'm on my way, Mr. Toombs." Then he yelled to his crew, "This is a rough one, gentlemen. Hang on and I'll see you later."

Dobbs was half way up the forecastle ladder when he turned and realized Simms was in foul weather gear and following him to the deck. "You don't need to go on deck in this kind of weather, Oliver."

"What do you mean I don't need to be on deck?"

"You don't need to act like a hero."

"Hero, my arse. Its just part of me bloody job and I can damn well handle it."

"Ask Tungee or Cheny, they'll tell you that you ought not to be out there tonight."

Dobbs knew Simms was out to prove he could hold his own with the rest of the crew, handicap bedamned. Their friendship went back to Sydney, Australia and Dobbs knew Simms was a hard case. He could do crime of any sort and he was a bigot, but in those areas Dobbs tried to look the other way and they remained friends.

High winds beat the rain into the MFC's deck leaving it awash and slippery. Recognizing it was impossible to maintain one's footing, Dobbs called back down the ladder, "Hang on and be careful of your footing, Oliver."

"I can get along without a nanny, if you don't mind."

"All right you horse's arse. I've said me last on the subject." Dobbs then moved straight up the foremast and climbed quickly to the top.

Perhaps if he moved fast enough he would discourage Simms and he wouldn't follow. But the one armed man paid no attention to his friend and simply began his methodical and tenacious climb into the rigging.

Barely able to hang on, he muscled his way up the foremast past the foresail, then the fore lower topsail.

Dobbs joined Farmer, McCoy and Thurston and the four of them spread across the yard of the upper topgallant.

Jeff finished his work up top and began to ease his way down the pole. It was impossible to see more than a dozen feet as the wind whipped sheets of rain through the rigging. Jeff squinted to focus on the object. He was sure it was a man in foul weather gear struggling to hang onto a yardarm.

The wind and rain slashed at the bodies of the topmen and the old salts as well as novice crew members tenaciously fought to hang on.

Jeff yelled over the din. "Yo there. What's your problem?"

The man in the foul weather gear asked, "Are you calling me?"

"Yeah," Jeff said, recognizing the accent. "Is that you, Simms?"

"One and the same."

"What the hell are you doing up here?"

"I'm working the port side of this here fore upper topsail and what's it to you."

"Get back to the deck, Simms."

"What for, Nigger. You think a one armed white man might show you up."

"Cut the crap, Simms. You could be hurt up here. Get your ass back to the deck."

"Don't you worry, I can handle myself."

Jeff called out, "Mr. Cheny!"

"What's your problem, Randolph?"

"Simms is in the rigging. Do you think he should be up here in this gale?"

"Hell no. Oliver Simms!" Cheny shouted.

"Aye, Mr. Cheny."

"Get back to the deck, Simms."

"Never you mind about me, I can handle myself up here."

Simms had worked himself out the fore upper topsail yardarm. He stretched and leaned over the yard, grabbed hold of the short clew line and feverishly tugged at the sail. Then he lost his balance as the foot rope he was standing on swayed back and forth.

Cheny saw the man's problem from below. "Just hold what you've got, Simms."

Jeff Randolph worked himself down the fore upper topsail yard. He ran into the same problem Simms had and that was simply locating the elusive footrope. "Hang on, sailor, I'll be there in a minute."

The one armed man had been able to secure just one foot on the foot rope, the other was irrationally kicking out at the darkness in search of the rope.

The MFC bucked like a wild bull and the masts circled with a centrifugal force that made it nearly impossible for healthy seamen to hold their own, let alone an impaired one armed man.

Jeff Randolph inched his way out the yard and strained to move into a position near the stricken Aussie.

"Don't move, Simms. I'm almost there."

"I can't hold on much longer -- help me, Randolph. I can't find the bloomin' foot rope."

"Never mind that, just hug your chest close to the yard."

"Please, for God's sake, Randolph."

The wind swirled a solid sheet of water into the reefed sail causing the canvas to puff out. And with that jolt the clew line, held by Simms, ripped out of it's mooring and tore along the sail.

Jeff saw what was happening and made a desperate lunge for his mate.

The wind held Oliver Simms motionless for a long moment before he let go. Then he fell backwards, grimly holding onto the short clew line. Then a violent gust of wind picked him up and tossed him, screaming, into the darkness, where it dropped him in amongst the foamy waves.

"Mr. Cheny! Simms has gone over the side," Jeff wailed. "I'm sorry, I couldn't get to him."

"You did all you could. Now stop the self-pity or there will be two of you out there. Do you hear that, Randolph?"

"Aye, I'm all right, Mr. Cheny."

"You other men, up there, shape up. You know your jobs, now

get on with them or you'll answer to me later," Cheny said brusquely. "Secure those sails and get you butt's back to the deck."

Captain Foster observed from the quarterdeck what had happened and hurried to Cheny's side. He said, "We could send out a long boat, I suppose, but we'd probably never get it back."

"The odds are no good, Skipper," Cheny yelled. "Risking a dozen to get one back makes no sense."

"That's my thinking, Fritz."

The usually talkative Dobbs hadn't said a word as he watched the scene unfold. And he didn't wait to complete the furling. He quickly dropped down from the mast and ran to the stern, looking over the vast ocean, hoping to spot his friend. Dobbs thought back to his mild admonishment aimed at keeping Simms below. I should have made a stronger case, he moaned.

Everyone in the rigging knew what had happened and a group gathered at the stern rail. They all strained their eyes as they looked out at the churning waters, desperately searching for something that might lend hope for Simms' survival.

Gene Blakely stepped up beside Tungee and asked, "What about a longboat. Couldn't we at least take a look?"

"It's awfully rough out there," Tungee told him, "but I suppose anything is possible."

Foster and Cheny walked up and heard the exchange. Fritz Cheny answered, "I think not, Mr. Cahill."

"There must be something we can do," Young Blakely said plaintively.

"We might launch a boat, but we'd never get it back."

Gideon Foster looked around at the men and said, "Maybe my not launching a boat seems too final and perhaps even cruel, but I don't want to lose any more of you out there."

Dobbs looked over the stern rail and scanned the waters. He was in a world by himself and called out in a last hopeless effort to will his friend back..."Oliver. Oliver."

Captain Foster's gamble had paid off the ship weathered the storm and sustained only slight, repairable, damage to the rigging. In the following twenty-four hours the MFC maintained a northwest heading with an average speed of twelve knots. And there had been no sightings of the sloop or frigate during that period.

The usually talkative Dobbs had been in a depressed silence, lamenting the loss of his friend. Even Jeff, who by all accounts could have really hated Simms, had his quiet moments of reflection about the man who had slipped out of his grasp and plunged into the sea.

Captain Foster kept the crew busy making those few repairs as well as constant tack changes. About once an hour they would change from a close haul to a close reach, alternating port and starboard tacks, and all the while moving toward the U.S. mainland.

The guards and cooks whose primary duty it was to keep order and feed the Africans had a continuing routine during the daylight hours. Beginning at first light, food would be served in groups of two dozen per sitting and continue until they had all been fed. The morning meal was seldom finished before eleven o'clock. The evening meal started serving around four thirty and had to be completed before nightfall. The diet fed to the Africans was a corn meal mush, which they alternated with rice and beans. Yams were served once in a while as a treat.

Tungee's observation back at Bonny Dock had been correct. The distinguished man he had noticed toward the end of the long black line was in fact a king and his name was Kumi. The king sat on the deck in leg irons and chains that connected him to his friend and confidant, Ekoi. Ekoi had a medium, but muscular build, a kind face and a mild manner.

They sat beside three ladies who all wore calico. Siepe was trim; dark eyed and had an innocent charm. Isbele was outgoing, if sometimes abrupt and prone to grumble. She was slightly overweight, but had a disarming smile. Sasika was the youngest of the three, a slim beauty, bright, and her warm brown eyes sparkled. She wore her plain green calico dress with the style and grace of a model. Those four were King Kumi's inner circle and at the present time they were making the best of a bad situation and quietly enjoying the late afternoon sun. Speaking in their own tongue, they continued a conversation that had been ongoing since their departure from Bonny Dock.

Kumi rocked back and forth. "The only doubt I have is the uncertainty of our never knowing the final results."

Siepe frowned. "King Kumi, you of all people must show no sign of weakness."

The king gave a benevolent smile. "Please, everyone listen to my words. I am very confident about our plan of action. My only concern is for our future generations. You see if our actions are not passed on to our descendents then our purpose is lost."

"Not in the eyes of God," Ekoi said with conviction.

"The actions we are taking are not for God," King Kumi told him, "they are to open the eyes of man."

Siepe said, "Aren't we talking about the same thing."

The king smiled. "Perhaps my desire to know the results are selfish. We believe this is the only way to remain free. But what will be the thoughts of others in the future? Will what we do make any difference to them?"

Siepe nodded. "They will, Kumi, they will."

"Not if word of our convictions and our action is not passed on to others."

"Why should we worry about what they think?" Isbele snapped.

Kumi looked at the lady and gave a benevolent smile. "We are all brothers and sisters and one generation must pass the things we know along to those not yet born."

"Please," Sasika sighed, "Isn't that why we are here, the business of choosing our messenger."

"It would be simple if I only had a son," Kumi said in thoughtful contemplation. "But you are correct Sasika, we must get on with that important work. Will all of you please give this matter some thoughtful prayer."

— TWENTY —

Tungee and Jeff came on deck just in time for the early half of the dog watch only to be greeted by shouts coming from the hold. They quickly ran to and dropped down through the amidships hatch. Once they got use to the dull darkness, they saw a small group of guards encircling two young African men who were fighting. They were exchanging body blows until one fighter backed off and swung a wicked punch that connected with the other fighter's jaw. Blood spattered, but the guards seemed content to look on and cheer, as if they were watching a cockfight.

"Don't just stand there, separate them," Tungee yelled.

One of the guards said cynically. "Leave 'em alone.

Those two are going to fight. Let 'em finish it now?"

Jeff stepped between the fighters and forcefully threw them apart. They ignored Jeff and stood glaring at one another.

"Is king Kumi your Moses, Butawa?" the tall one taunted sarcastically. "Can he part the waters and make you free?"

"King Kumi is no Moses, but he does not practice your skull and bones magic nonsense either," Mark fired back.

Jeff held them apart and barked, "Knock it off."

Neither of the young men understood Jeff's words, but they didn't mistake the tone. Both glared at the referee and Butawa shouted, "You are not of us."

156

"Get these two on opposite ends of this ship, now!" Tungee demanded.

Fritz Cheny followed Tungee and Jeff back up the ladder and onto the deck. "Tungee, you and Jeff best back off next time and don't get involved with these people."

"Did you see what happened, Fritz?" Tungee asked.

"I caught most of it, but I don't want you fellows weighing in like you did. It could stir up trouble for us," Cheny admonished as he walked away.

"You know something, Tungee," Jeff said, "I'm beginning to see bits and pieces of myself mixed in with these folks and it bothers me."

"Well, you could look at it this way," Tungee said easily, "until we get to Boston and get paid off, we're in the same fix as they are. If I recall correctly, we're not exactly here by choice."

Jeff grinned. "You're got that straight, Tungee."

"Why don't we just try and put blinders on, at least until St. Simons Island."

The fight below decks had drawn Kulando's attention and he ran to report the incident to the king. "They are fighting again, sirs."

"Mark and Butawa." Kumi said.

"Yes. They were fighting again."

"They love one another and yet they fight." Siepe sounded addled about the matter.

"If they truly loved, the way of our people, they would not fight," said Sasika accusingly.

Kumi held up his hand. "They are brothers and both fighting for what they think is right. That is good. One should stand up for what he believes. They are discovering life and each wants the other to accept his ways and his beliefs."

Siepe was distraught. "Is resorting to force the only way man can resolve any kind of problem?"

Kumi, with a look of despair, slowly shook his head. He knew it was not the only way, but it was still the chosen way of the young warrior.

Jeff saw Kulando walking aimlessly around the deck, and in a friendly tone said, "You look sad, Kulando."

The young man looked up. "No. Not sad, but I am worried."

"You were taken from your parents and your homeland. You have every right to be worried."

"That worry is long time. That began when I was captured. This is another worry," the boy hesitated and then added, "this one is short time worry."

"What do you mean?"

"Some talk about action."

"Action, what kind of action, Kulando?"

"Something or someone-will make action." The boy frowned, "But I do not know what kind or when."

"Why does that worry you?"

"I worry because I feel something bad about this action."

"Who spoke of it?"

"Please, sirs. I would rather not say."

"Kulando, if it's as bad as you think, I'd like to know what it is."

"Mr. Jeff, I must like to listen more. Maybe then I can tell you better."

"Tell me as soon as you can," Jeff said with concern, "we wouldn't want it to be too late."

King Kumi requested and Captain Foster allowed him to stay on deck overnight. Six bells sounded as Jeff Randolph came topside to watch the dawn. The king sat cross-legged near the forecastle and appeared to be in deep thought.

Sensing Jeff's presence he looked up and spoke in quite good English. "I didn't expect your captain to honor my request to stay the night up here."

"Captain Foster is not your typical slaver," Jeff said.

"Since I was a boy, I've been told there are many white devils." Then the king paused and smiled. "I personally know some black ones. My people on this ship and I are here as a result of some of our own devils that captured and sold us."

Jeff nodded. "I've noticed that a number of your people speak English. The boy, Kulando speaks very well. He said he learned from his parents and the Great Book."

"In the gone by days, missionaries crossed our lands and as they taught lessons from the Great Book, our people learned to read the English." He looked up and said with a great deal of pride, "And I might add, talk some too."

"Did you sleep well out here on deck?"

"I had no wish to sleep," Kumi said evenly. "I asked to stay on deck so that I might examine some of my thoughts."

"The night does have a way of clearing the mind."

"That is so. The night is very important to my people and our association with the spirit world. Sometimes my ancestors come to me by night."

"Did you speak with your ancestors last night?"

"I had no wish to speak to them last night. I was here to listen. I listened for another voice."

"A voice from the Great Book?"

"Perhaps, but I was truly listening for the voice of freedom." After several moments, Kumi leaned back and with a wry grin, said, "It was only a whisper, but it was as clear as the waters of a rambling brook."

"You heard something that means freedom?"

"For me, I have long time known the way." Then he looked straight at Jeff and asked, "Do you consider yourself free?"

"Not just now. You see I was shanghaied onboard this ship in San Francisco."

"What is shanghai?"

"Same way you and your people were taken. I was made a prisoner. Taken along to work against my will."

"How long must you work this shanghai."

"Until we get to Boston."

Kumi snorted dejectedly. "This thing they do. They make us slaves, it is not right. My people have always been free to move about the land as they pleased. Look at the birds," Kumi said openly, "they are free to fly in any direction. Now that is what I consider freedom."

"Somewhere in the future, your people will find a way out of slavery," Jeff said.

"How do you know this? I know that when one is made a slave one does as one is told, lives where one is told, go here or there. Do this or that as you are told, lest you be tied up and beaten."

"All masters are not cruel or even free with the cat."

"What do you know of slavery?"

"I was born into slavery. My mother and father were slaves."

"How did you escape?"

"I did not escape, I was given my freedom by my master."

"Were all given their freedom?'

"No and that is the problem. They were not all freed."

"I shall not become a slave!" Kumi said adamantly. "I am a prisoner now, but I will never become a slave."

"I wish there was some way I could help."

"Your thoughts are kind," Kumi grinned, "but we are quite prepared to take matters into our own hands."

"Then you must have a plan to escape."

Kumi pondered the word for a moment. "I wouldn't call it escape -- deliverance may be a better word."

"You and your people will find deliverance?"

"Not all. Some will follow, but not all."

"Then you do have a plan."

Kumi looked up with a broad smile, but he did not give an answer to Jeff's question.

Tungee came out of the forecastle and saw Jeff walking toward him with concern written all over his face. "What's on your mind?"

"Come with me," Jeff said quietly, "I don't want anyone to hear."

They stepped down the short ladder from the quarterdeck and walked to the base of the mainmast. Jeff took a deep breath. "I feel like a Judas for saying anything, but I think you ought to hear this."

"What's it about?"

"I'm not quite sure, but I believe these people are planning some kind of escape."

"How do you figure that?"

"Kumi, the king, just said something kinda strange. In some ways it sounded like an escape plan. But not in a conventional way."

"What other kind is there?" Then Tungee stopped short. "Of course some of those people practice Voodoo and Black Magic."

"Yeah, some do. But that's not what it sounded like to me, Tungee." Jeff took his time and spoke deliberately, "During our talk,

I used the word escape and he said no, not escape -- it would be more like deliverance."

"Did he say what he meant by deliverance?"

"No, he didn't. But he said this, 'I am a prisoner now, but I will never become a slave."

Tungee rubbed his day old whiskers and frowned. "Now if we add that to what Kulando said about a plan of action we might just have a problem. Did the king say when they would carry it out?"

"No."

"In a way, I'd like to help them," Tungee said softly, but not while they're still onboard. Too dangerous. That kind of thing could turn into a slaughter. We've already seen enough killing on this ship. And I'll tell you straight, Jeff, I've got one thought on my mind and that is to finish this voyage alive."

Jeff nodded a silent agreement.

It was late in the day when Kumi gathered the council for a meeting. Ekoi, Seipe, Isbele and Sasika sat along with their leader in a circle, meditating, holding hands, each trying to relax and clear their minds for the important work they had ahead of them.

For the most part, the Ebo tribe had denounced witchcraft although most tribal ceremonies still held some of the old ways and in certain respects included behavior associated with witchcraft and ways of the cult. Kumi had never demanded that his followers give up all of their individual beliefs. However, he did not allow them to practice their skull and bones magic in-group meetings. Kumi and all the members of his own inner circle had grown up with the missionary's teachings and the Bible and they were all strong in their belief in God. But none of them could dismiss the fact that some parts of their old spirit world remained with them. And all of them had some self-doubt as to their own knowledge and spiritual reservoir for guidance. But they felt that collectively the right answer would eventually come to them.

Kumi opened his eyes. "Was I dreaming?" There was no answer. He shook his head. "I heard the drums of night and a thousand voices gently humming in my ears. Sarai clutched my hand, kissed my lips and disappeared. I ran after her. For days I ran, finally I was totally exhausted and my legs grew weary. Then darkness came. There was not a single star and no moon to light my way."

"Kumi, please!" Isbele exclaimed, "You are torturing yourself. All of our tears and prayers cannot bring queen Sarai back. She is gone."

Kumi rocked on his haunches. "God's will be done." Then he took a long breath. "These are the times I long for the simple answers that our forefathers would have given," he laughed, "they had an answer for everything. Their skull and bones magic and witchcraft."

"Do you think it good to mock our ancestor's belief's?" Siepe asked anxiously.

"God knows, I'm not making light of their ways, I am stating a fact. The power and beliefs they grew up with. Their gods and goddesses were all knowing, they had all the answers to life's needs. I am only saying I sometimes wish my God made it that easy for me."

Sasika said, "Perhaps you ask too much from one God."

If those missionaries and the Great Book had not caught you early in life, Sasika," Kumi chuckled, "there is no doubt in my mind that you would have become a charming witch."

As Sasika blushed and looked down at the deck Kumi thought that had polygamy been practiced among his people, there was no doubt in his mind that Sasika would have certainly been one of his wives.

Ekoi called for attention. "My friends, the hour draws near. So, could we please get to the subject."

Kumi nodded. "Give us your thoughts, Ekoi."

"Mark and Butawa were always high on my list as candidates for our chosen messenger." He stopped and then said deliberately, "Not anymore."

"Why?" Isbele snapped.

Ekoi took a moment and then said with candor, "They are no longer innocent."

Siepe said, "They may have grown past the age of innocence, but I believe Mark has the honor of his ancestors and could be an honest messenger."

Kumi leaned forward. "Perhaps a younger person would carry the word with some less bias."

"I believe Butawa to be honest and could tell with complete truth," Isbele reminded the others.

"Ah," Kumi said, "Then we have a difference of opinion."

He looked into the eyes of each person in the circle and said judiciously. "You see, what I just said about the old ways. In those days there was a definite age when a man lost his innocence, and both Mark and Butawa, by those old standards, no longer qualify."

"Well, who do you propose?" Isbele said with a tone of irate frustration.

"Calm down, please," Kumi said. "I have called this meeting to listen and I plan to do just that."

Ekoi gazed at the ladies for some time before he spoke..."I propose that we name Kulando."

There was no immediate consensus on the matter. The debate went on for an hour and at times there was irritation bordering on hostility. Kumi had not made a nomination and the ladies had stayed with their original selections, but were eventually worn down by Ekoi's calm and rational arguments.

Kumi listened and meditated at some length before announcing Kulando as his choice. Then after the final vote was taken, the selection was judged fair and was unanimous in numbers if not spirit.

Kumi was determined to impart all the knowledge he could to the young man designated as the official teller to the next generation. The Ebo tribe had no written language and as their ancestors had done before, they in turn must pass along the stories and tales relating their heritage. Some fables and legends passed down through the years were somewhat larger than life. Warriors and hunters sometimes grew in huge proportions to the ways of their real life.

Following his selection, Kulando was asked to join the circle and was quite honored by his appointment to the position of official tribal messenger. The boy, up to that point had assumed the tribal storyteller was old. Actually in the past, more women held the position than men. Kulando had always been a good listener. He was bright and possessed a good memory.

The ritualistic and symbolic objects from the past, which included talisman, charms and masks, could not be excluded from Kulando's hurry up introduction. The boy's first thoughts as he was thrust into his position were that he was being groomed to become their next witch doctor, not at all what he wanted to be. Speaking before the group, he said, "I believe the teachings of my father and my mother and I also believe what I know of the Great Book. How can you expect me to become a witch doctor?"

"No, no, no, Kulando. You misunderstand, witchcraft is not a part of our doctrine," Kumi explained. "You will be our tribal messenger. You will tell the heritage of our past. The stories our ancestors passed to us and the history of our generation."

"Am I the only messenger?"

"No, but you will be the official messenger and any dispute about our past heritage, you will have the final word. For all the days you remain on this earth, Kulando, you will have the respect of our people and you must always remember that honor and truth must be guarded and handled with care."

The boy was wide-eyed and pleased as well as a little frightened concerning his future responsibilities. "Must I just tell of the past, from this day back to all our yesterdays?"

"No, my son. You will be the teller not only of our yesterdays, but of today as well as tomorrow."

"This is a great honor," Kulando sat for several moments as tears came down his cheeks. "I wish my father and mother could know of this day."

No one spoke, but there was approval in the eyes of everyone present.

Kumi nodded and smiled at the young man. He was more assured every minute that the right choice had been made.

"Why do you give me this honor now?"

"We did not choose the time, my son, the time comes when it comes."

"You must listen, Kulando," Ekoi said, "and many of your questions will be answered. But first, take in what we say as we have taken from our gone befores."

The boy said nothing, but gave a serious affirmative nod. He was prepared to hear the folklore of his ancestors, the gone befores. Kulando had had little experience with the old ways. His mother and father told him very little of the spirit world that he was now going to hear about. He had seen a witch doctor belonging to another tribe and had heard whispers of spirits, towns of the dead, skull and bones magic that meant nothing more to him than tall tales made up by the conjure man or woman.

Kulando remembered talk among his own family. One uncle especially use to tell tales of their ancestors, mighty hunters and warriors who had been saved from certain death by spirits of their gone befores. As he grew and heard stories told and read from the Great Book, there began to merge in his mind, the tales and people who were his direct ancestors with characters from the Bible. It seemed to Kulando that these people were one and the same. Then a word began to spin round in his head, begat was that word and Jesse begat David the king, and David the king begat Solomon. And the boy looked up and smiled.

He was now prepared to listen. But there was something inside that told him he already knew the words he was about to hear.

— TWENTY ONE —

Captain Foster sent word for Tungee and Jeff to join him in his cabin. Fritz Cheny and Walter Greenleaf were already with the captain when the other two arrived. Foster prowled the room like a cat, puffing on his cigar. Cheny and Greenleaf sat in two of the canvas chairs, which were now turned with their backs to the desk. The captain turned to the new arrivals. "Cahill, you and Randolph tell me what you know about this scuttlebutt that's floating around, the thing about the blacks."

Tungee glanced at Jeff and then back to the captain. "We probably heard the same things as you did, Skipper."

"You must know something, Randolph, I've seen you talking to that fellow they call the king."

"Yes, sir, I've talked to him," Jeff acknowledged. "But all he's said to me is how him an his people hate what's happened to them."

Captain Foster took a long drag on his cigar as he looked into Jeff's eyes. "I want to know what he actually said."

Jeff was frustrated and nervous. He stood on one foot, then the other and finally turned to Tungee for help.

Tungee took his time. "This is what Jeff and I know. "The boy, Kulando came to us and said he was worried about something he had heard. Action was the word that disturbed him. He thought some kind of action was going to take place. That's part of it. Then Jeff followed up on the boy's story and asked the king if action meant escape. The king said no, it would be more like deliverance. He didn't want to say

166

anything more about it, but in my way of thinking, the term might mean escape."

Jeff broke in by clearing his throat. "Something else the king told me. He said, 'I am a prisoner now, but I will never become a slave.'"

Captain Foster stroked his mustache. "Now, how do you figure that?" Then he turned to the chart table and pounded it with his fist. "Damn nation." Then he began to walk, circling the room and chewing on the end of his cigar. "By God, back at Bonny Dock, I was told about these people. They are Ebo, gentlefolk, I was told. But I'm thinking that when you put 'em in shackles and chains, they might get desperate enough to do something stupid. What do you men think?"

"There is no doubt in my mind that those people are frightened," Tungee declared. "Slave tales have a way of getting around and you can bet they've heard horror stories about the trade. How their people have been tossed overboard by some captains to avoid being captured with contraband."

"How much time to anchor, Gideon?" Walter Greenleaf asked.

"Not more than a dozen days, I should think. And if the wind kicked up a little, it could be less than ten."

"Seems to me we ought to talk to that fellow, Kumi," Walter Greenleaf suggested.

Foster took a deep breath. "Randolph, go find him and bring him here."

"Right away, Captain."

Jeff returned with two men. He stuck his head in the door and called. "Captain, the king asked if he might bring his friend along."

Captain Foster simply gave an affirmative nod and motioned for Jeff to find seats for them. The two men settled that question by sitting on the floor next to the chart table and crossing their legs.

The room was quiet for some time before Foster began the questioning. "Are you the leader of these people?"

"My name is Kumi I am known as King Kumi."

Gideon Foster chewed on his cigar. "Scuttlebutt has it, you're some kind of a Moses."

Kumi sat back and smiled. "No, I'm hardly a Moses, Captain, but I am their leader."

Tungee watched the expression on Ekoi's face and from what he could tell, the man was showing something between a good poker face and passive indifference. The friend was probably there as a lightening rod. Maybe just to listen to the tone of the conversation, he had never let on that he spoke English.

Captain Foster said abruptly, "I've heard that you and your people are planning some kind of action. Do you plan to use some kind of skull and bones magic to make an escape?"

"Captain, I do not practice any kind of magic. And as for planning an escape in the middle of the ocean?" Kumi laughed and said, "I don't think so."

"Maybe you plan to wait until we get to port?"

"Captain Foster, if all you have to worry about is the possible escape of my people from your ship then please calm your fears."

Gideon Foster stood for a moment and then walked over and kneeled down on one knee. He got close to Kumi's face and looked him in the eye. "Would you make a promise and shake on it that you and your people have no plans to escape from this ship."

"I can only answer in this way, I know of no plan and I am not ordering any such escape." Then a wry grin crossed his face. "Now I can't tell you that some person or persons in our ranks will not try such a thing. I am not a witch doctor and I do not read minds."

Foster grimaced and stood up. Then he struck a match and relit his cigar.

Tungee stood back and watched. He couldn't tell if the captain believed the king or not. He believed him, but that was only to a point. In his way of thinking, there was something going on, a lot more than had surfaced so far.

The captain continued to pace. "I've seen you talking to women from time to time, are they your wives?"

Kumi spoke softly. "No, but they are all long time friends."

The captain asked, "Is your wife aboard?"

"Queen Sarai has passed on to another world. She was tortured and killed by the same people who captured us and sold us into the trade."

"I wasn't aware of that," Foster said, "I'm sorry."

Kumi looked at the captain showing more than a little contempt. "No, Captain. If you were truly sorry we would not be on this ship."

"My comment had only to do with your wife." Then the captain changed his tone. "There's a rumor that you've said this, 'I'm a prisoner now, but I will never become a slave. Did you say that?"

"Yes, I probably did," Kumi said openly.

"Well, that leads me to believe that you have some kind of plan to escape and if you don't, how do you expect to pull it off -- not becoming a slave, that is?"

"Perhaps I would not perform the duties of a slave."

"Then the chances are pretty good that your master would use the cat on you."

"You mean they would beat me if I did not do as they ordered."

"There is that possibility, yes." Foster then shook his head and looked around at the other men in the room and asked, "Any of you fellows have anything to add. Is there any ground I haven't covered?"

No one said anything. Foster rubbed his hands together. "Randolph, take these two back to the deck."

Kumi and Ekoi got off the floor and walked toward the door. Foster moved to Kumi and looked him in the eye. "I expect you to keep your word about the escape proposition."

The king froze in place, glared at Foster and spoke sharply. "I am a man of honor, Captain."

After the door closed the cabin became unusually quiet. The men had all heard the same words and maybe they were all thinking the same thoughts, but Tungee's gut feeling was very near to what he felt after that first meeting with Foster -- it wasn't what had been said so much as what was left unsaid. In the meeting just concluded it was probably things the king hadn't said.

Captain Foster turned to Fritz Cheny. "Pass the word along to the crew that following the evening meal, all adult African males, with the exception of the king and his friend will be locked down in the hold. None of the men will be allowed topside before the morning breakfast call. If the king and his friend elect to stay the night on deck, so be it, they will remain there all night. There will be no going back and forth. One more thing, Fritz, all of our men on an active watch will remain topside to keep an eye on the Africans quartered on deck and pay special attention to the king and his companions. I'll take care of getting this order to the guards."

The ship's bell signaled a watch change, the skipper waved his hand in a gesture that ended the talk. Walter Greenleaf stayed with the captain while Fritz Cheny and Tungee climbed the stern ladder to the deck. Fritz walked purposefully to the binnacle.

There had been an afternoon shower and the air was clean and fresh. The wind was holding steady and there was little to do as far as tack changes were concerned. All sails were working and the MFC was scooting over a short chop at close to fifteen knots.

Tungee jogged forward and signaled Jeff to follow him up the foremast. They climbed the pole and settled on the upper yard of the foretop gallant.

Jeff asked, "What did you make of the meeting?"

"Not much. But I have a notion you know something I don't."

"Maybe and maybe not." Then Jeff chuckled. "Funny thing. When they were talking to each other in their own language, knowing I couldn't understand, I got this feeling that they were playing games."

"I expect they are, Jeff. And by the way, after you left the meeting, Foster gave orders to restrict the movement of the African men and especially at night."

"He may be right," Jeff said as he turned to Tungee. "Remember, Kumi said he couldn't vouch for what some individuals may or may not do."

"Yeah, and he's also said he was no witch doctor, but there are a hell of a lot of things those people do that has nothing to do with witchcraft."

The MFC had plowed into the lower Caribbean and was within forty-eight hours of their destination. The bell struck midnight. King Kumi and his inner circle were all sitting near the forecastle. Kumi looked up at the stars and sucked in a deep breath of the cool night air and sat in silent meditation. He was well aware that as a political and religious leader, he had to walk a fine line between his people's old traditions and the ways taught by the missionaries.

Kulando came awake from a nap and began to wipe the sleep from his eyes. He sat across from Kumi, between Sasika and Isbele. The boy stretched and yawned. "I have just returned from a long journey."

"Where have you been, my son?" Kumi asked.

"I know not where, but I do know it was with the gone befores. The spirits of my ancestors."

"Your mind is receptive and much of what we have told you may be firing your imagination," Ekoi said as a wry grin played across his face. "Perhaps they are expanding your dream world."

"I heard them talk. I saw them take the evil mask and exchange it for the good."

Isbele gripped the boy's hand.

Kumi sighed. "You have been somewhere and that somewhere is your own private place, a part of the world that you will share with no one. You may tell of it, but you will not truly share it with anyone."

Kulando was no longer a child. His face bathed in the moonlight had grown far beyond his age. Maturity and wisdom had knocked and the messenger had opened the door and welcomed them in.

Kumi prayed. "May my Lord be tolerant and forgiving in a way that will allow some contact with our spirit world. May we ask our gone befores to mark the path? God, please allow the spirits of our ancestors to guide me and my people across the river."

Siepe cautioned. "Let us all remember this. We are Christians and I have no wish to disavow my Ebo heritage, but please be aware that when our Lord saved us, we turned away from many of our past beliefs. Are you, Kumi, asking us to go back to those ways just before the end?"

"No, my dear. My thinking is this, we should ask God to allow our gone befores spirits to shed some light on the most important act of our lives. It is God's help that we are all seeking." Kumi then looked toward the sky and chanted. "Vultures are the birds of death, scavengers who hover over the dying ready to claim their corpses silently, patiently waiting for the end. Those scavengers have made a pact with death and death has made war on my house. Queen Sarai and our firstborn have died at the hands of that war, where greed in the form of money hungry men of the trade plundered and pillaged mankind. They take one man's freedom, jail his spirit, extracting a profit for one on the back of another."

Ekoi put his hand on Kumi's and quietly said. "Amen."

Kumi looked into all their faces and said, "My children, I am not asking you to follow me like sheep, just for mine and Sarai's sake, but follow if you must for those of future generations. We must tell the world that no one has the right to sell his fellow man the way he would bargain away a sparrow."

The group held hands and completed the circle, each member looked up into the bright night and Ekoi said, "I shall follow you across the river, my king. And I will pray for the spirits of our gone befores to direct us to that life after death."

Siepe murmured, "I shall follow."

Isbele said, "I shall follow."

Sasika said, "I shall--- "

"No, no, no, Sasika!" Kumi admonished. "You must not go now. You have been chosen to assist Kulando, to witness and report our act. The only strength in our protest is our commitment to action. And if this telling part is not carried out, we will have been denied the results of our quest."

"Why me?" Sasika lamented. "I have looked forward to that crossing with the rest of you. To see Heaven's Gate before me is the ultimate dream fulfilled, please don't deny me this."

"Sasika, your dream will not be denied, but for now you have a far greater work here on earth. You must find the way to tell and retell the story of those few people who truly believed in something strong enough to die for. And that proposition is this -- that man who was cast in God's image must not go on buying, selling and trading that image."

Kulando spoke up and said, "The Great Book tells of Moses who was a slave."

"Yes, my son, and so were the children of Israel, they were all slaves held in bondage. But that does not make it right." Kumi hesitated and then continued. "You see, Kulando, the children of Israel escaped across the Red Sea, led by Moses and the hand of God."

"Please tell me what you mean by crossing the river?"

Kulando was eager to know more as the thirst for knowledge gripped him. "I have heard it before but I don't understand what it means."

"To cross the river is to go beyond and walk beneath the limbs and leaves of the dark forest."

"Is that death?"

"Perhaps."

"You mean you don't know."

"No one, my son knows what death is. Not in this life anyway. We who believe in God with all our hearts will not fully understand until we have quit this life. You see, we are still guessing. Until we are ambushed by death and he smothers out that last breath of life. Then and only then does our soul move out to joust with spirits and with other souls who have been left for a time to spin their earthly tales in limbo...Perhaps at that time we will begin to understand."

Kulando pleaded, "Tell us about the fire. You haven't talked about the fire."

"If you have lived your life as the Great Book teaches, you will never have to see the fire."

— TWENTY TWO —

It was late on a January day when the MFC slipped into the channel between Saint Simons Island and the Georgia coast. The ship was just settling into anchorage as the early evening breeze quit and a cold damp fog crawled in and across the waters.

It was an hour later when Gideon Foster acknowledged contact with Jeb Turner, the man who represented the company's trade activities in the Carolina's and Georgia. The slave trader rowed himself out to the MFC in a small boat and climbed up the aft ladder to the deck. Turner was a tall barrel chested man with a square jaw and black eyes. He wore a long gray coat and a wide brimmed hat to match.

Anxiety gripped Gideon Foster as he watched the man lumbering toward the quarterdeck.

Turner saw the look on Foster's face and laughed. "Gideon, you look nervous as a whore in church."

Foster grumbled, "I just want to get these folks off my ship and get to hell out of here."

The deck was alive with activity. All able-bodied seamen had been called on deck and Hank Jensen was passing out work assignments.

Fritz Cheny called Tungee to one side and asked him to go up the foremast to be a general observer and lookout during the unloading and ferrying operation. The first mate's parting comment to Tungee was, "Take Randolph along with you."

Tungee nodded and smiled, knowing Foster was concerned about Jeff's personal relationship with the Africans.

The captain made a defensive move; he decided to separate Kumi and Ekoi from the others. He put them in double chains and locked them inside the chart room. Foster figured if there was a secret plan of escape, separating the leader might be enough to disrupt it.

There was no moon and the ground fog seemed to have a mind of its own, sometimes swirling and stacking up without reason had dulled the stars. And there was a chilly bite to the air. The ship's regular running lights were augmented with four extra sea lanterns in an effort to make the ferry operation a more efficient process.

Jensen had assigned some of the crew members to work beside the guards who had boarded at Bonny and the whole operation of disembarking the Africans was under the direction of Turner.

Four longboats were engaged in the process and they would move back and forth from the ship to a tiny dock inside a reed-covered inlet that was located on the southwest side of Saint Simons Island.

Two separate crews, one working fore and the other aft on the starboard side of the MFC quickly loaded sixteen African's to the boat and sent them on their way.

All of the ship's sails were furled affording Tungee and Jeff a good overview of the whole operation. However, the fog made it difficult to see very far. From their high perch people were not people so much as forms and shadows. That murky view was accented by the clink and clatter of chains and shackles hanging from wrists and ankles of the African men. Tungee strained to hear and tried to separate those discordant metallic noises as each individual made his way up the ladder and out of their crowded quarters. And one by one those manacled figures climbed out of the stuffy hold and sucked in the fresh night air. The guards then directed them to their places and they rattled into a kneeling position inside the longboat.

The boat would then cast off and you could hear the muffled sound of the boat crews rhythmic chorus of, "Pull, pull, pull," until the sound diminished and then disappeared into the foggy night.

"You're being awfully quiet, Tungee, what are you thinking?" Jeff asked.

Tungee shook his head. "Aw, I've been trying to put it out of my mind, Jeff. But those folks down there remind me of the way my Indian ancestors were treated back in thirty six."

"Are you kidding me, Tungee."

"No, Jeff, I'm dead serious." Tungee told him in a matter -of-fact way. "Forced off their land, the men were chained and shackled. Then they put them on the trail and drove them West, like cattle"

"How did you escape the round up?"

"A fast horse." Then Tungee hesitated. "And like you, Jeff, I didn't look back either."

King Kumi and Ekoi had spoken little as the hours passed slowly in their chart house jail. They sat cross-legged in the darkened room sensing each other's emotions and gained inner strength from their long relationship and common bond.

"What did we call him, Ekoi? The one with the evil mask."

"Pipu."

"Yes, of course, Pipu and he died when we were about Kulando's age." Kumi chuckled. "He was a complete failure as a witch doctor. Oh, how Pipu wanted to be wicked, but he just couldn't."

Ekoi smiled as he remembered a good lesson. "Matthew writes in the Great Book that a good tree cannot bring forth evil fruit."

"The grownups didn't see through him as well as we did. But of course he saw through himself. My father had a clear picture of the fraud that surrounded witch doctors. How they played with the lives of others, everything from sex to assassination."

"Kumi, do you think this thing we are about to embark on will displease God?"

"It may, but I believe our only hope for salvation will come with God's forgiving nature. If it pleases our Father in Heaven that my soul should remain in limbo, then I must have the will to accept His judgement. It will be a small price to pay if our action has the desired effect on future generations." Kumi looked at his old friend and smiled. "I sense that you are fully resigned to follow me."

"Yes, my friend. I am anxious to hurry the moment when we join our gone befores. Then we shall see the truth and have all our questions answered. Will we join the spirit world or remain in limbo?"

"It all depends on God's will, my old friend."

Captain Foster and Jeb Turner stood on the quarterdeck observing and chewing over the makeup of the people debarking the MFC. Turner had accepted the fact that Ebo was what he was getting. And his only experience with Ebo was during the past year when Al Bonner came in with about two hundred and fifty people from that stubborn tribe. Captain Foster had grown almost giddy with anticipation. The last boatload of Africans would be away from his ship in less than an hour. Then he would try and put the whole slave business behind him.

Foster was giving a tongue in cheek quote from Henry Becker, "'Captain, you just tell Turner that Henry Becker said that Ebo was what was available and Ebo is what he gets. And one more thing, you can tell him this too, these people are quite intelligent."

"'And that a kind word will get a whole lot more than a switch of the cat,'" Jeb Turner said disdainfully. "Al Bonner repeated that same crap on his last trip."

Both men laughed at the joke as they monitored the progress of the unloading process. Turner asked Foster, "Have you heard tell of one of these Ebo's by the name of Kumi, sometimes called king Kumi?"

"I sure have, Jeb," Foster said jovially. "It's king Kumi all right and if he was a snake, he'd a bit you."

"Now what the hell is that suppose to mean, Gideon?"

"Just what I said, he's within spitting distance of you right now. I got him trust up like a turkey over there in the chart room."

"Oh shit, Gideon. Now why did they go and do a damn fool thing like that."

"Like what?"

"They should have left him back there. He'll be trouble here. Bad trouble, Gideon."

"You may be right. That's the reason I've got him locked up." Foster took a long drag on his cigar. "But what do you know about king Kumi?"

"That earlier bunch of Ebo. Some of them said if anyone could save them from living their lives in slavery, it would be king Kumi."

"The people who said that, are they still here on Saint Simons Island?"

"There may be a few."

Captain Foster paced the quarterdeck. "Where are they located, the Ebo's from that Al Bonner shipment?"

"They're up on the north end of the island."

"Could any of them be here in this gang, working these boats, or the dock?"

"No, Gideon, these are all my hands. But if what I heard is true, they wouldn't need to be here to make something happen." Jeb Turner shuddered. "That black magic Voodoo scares the hell out of me."

"Well, it gives me the willies too. From what I've heard back in Africa, the people on this ship came mainly from one tribe and they were captured less than two weeks before we made the pickup."

"I see what you're getting at. But from what's been told here, they don't need to be no direct contact for that stuff to work. Them that's already here know these are coming and now you tell me he's among 'em. It's spooky. Make's me nervous." Turner looked toward the chart room and said, "What do we do with him, Gideon?"

"Leave him in chains and take him ashore last."

"Couldn't you just keep him onboard and see that he's dropped over the side when you get to sea."

"Hell no. I want all these people off my ship right now. If I'm caught with one, it's the same as a full load." Foster then looked at Turner and said passionately, "Something else, I may go to hell, but if I do it won't be for slave killing."

"Aw, for crying out loud, Gideon. They do it all the time."

"Maybe some do, but not Gideon Foster. And that's all I'm going to say about it."

Jensen went inside the chart house and led Kumi and Ekoi onto the quarterdeck.

Jeff nudged Tungee. "I'd like to go down and say goodbye to the king."

"The captain won't like it," Tungee said wryly, "but let's go anyway."

They shinnied down the foremast and got to Kumi and Ekoi just before they entered the longboat. Jeff extended his hand to the king and said, "I wish you and your people well, king Kumi."

The king looked up and smiled. "Worry not for me, Mr. Randolph, praise God, I'm going home. I do accept your good wishes for my people." The king looked down at the longboat and then back at Jeff. "I have a request, if you would be so kind. Please to see that the young Kulando gets safely ashore with the others."

Jeff nodded. "Be glad to."

Then Hank Jensen stepped in and urged King Kumi and Ekoi onto the ladder and into the aft boat. Women and children who had earlier boarded made room as the two men climbed down to the boat and kneeled into their places.

Fritz Cheny walked from the forward position to amidships and alerted Captain Foster that the last of the male Africans were on board the forward longboat.

Captain Foster looked around and said, "Fritz, you take Jensen, Cahill and Randolph and make a clean sweep of the ship. I want you to search for any stowaways or contraband. Make sure all the guards and cooks from Bonny go ashore and I mean to the last man."

Fritz Cheny commanded, "Tungee you and Randolph go forward, search the deck, forecastle crew quarters and then double back through the hold. Jensen and I will begin back here with the aft cabins, meet you in the hold."

Tungee and Jeff worked their way past the coils of rope, then they pulled down the makeshift tents Walter Greenleaf had constructed to protect the deck people. And as they continued their inspection, Tungee thought about the short conversation Jeff had with Kumi. And he had a gut feeling that something was terribly wrong. But he couldn't put his finger on just what it was.

Satisfied that the upper deck was clear they moved to the forecastle door and descended the ladder into the crew quarters. The place was empty, not even a slacker in his bunk. Next they proceeded to the aft bulkhead and opened the hatch to the hold. And as they crawled through the hatch, Tungee was struck by something Kumi said. 'If you would be so kind, please to see that the young Kulando gets safely ashore with the others.' Good Lord! They are in the same boat. The youngster was already aboard and Kumi knew it when he made that statement. How could I have been so blind, Tungee stopped in his tracks, "Jeff, something's going to happen to the longboat that's taking the king and the others to the landing."

"What, Tungee?"

"I wish I knew."

Fritz Cheny and Hank Jensen came down the ladder at the aft end of the hold.

Tungee yelled, "Hey, Cheny. Has that stern boat pushed off yet?"

"I don't know."

Tungee ran through the hold followed by Jeff. "I think we'd better stop it if we can."

"How come, Tungee?"

"I'm not sure, Fritz. But I've got this gut feeling, something bad is going to happen on that boat."

Fritz Cheny moved aside. "Go ahead and check it out."

Tungee ran for the ladder and hurdled up the rungs. The other three followed hard on his heels. As he hurried along, he was trying to assemble in his own mind everything that Kumi and the Africans had said either to him or Jeff. What seemed to worry Kulando was that word action. But deliverance, he now thought, was the key word. Damn, why hadn't I put this thing together sooner. He scrambled onto the quarterdeck and looked around for the aft longboat. The boat had cast off and had already disappeared into the night. The captain stood with several men, all looking toward the fog shrouded landing. Tungee's first instinct was to yell at the skipper for letting the boat go. But as he stifled the impulse he looked toward the forward boat. It was not yet full and was still standing by.

There was an overwhelming silence on the deck as all men looked out toward the muffled sounds of the longboat oars, out there in the fog, pulling toward the landing.

Tungee turned to Foster. "Could we unload that forward boat, Captain?"

"What are you talking about, Tungee?"

"I just hope we can stop a tragedy from happening out there." Every fiber in his being told him it was too late.

The sound of the oars stopped and those sounds were replaced by the rattle of shackles and chains. Then there was a cry like some long lost bird coming from out of the past. But it was not a bird it was a chorus of voices made up of men, women and children. The sound began with a stolid scream and then blended into a wailing wordless ballad. Splash, swoosh, slosh of the channel waters covering some sounds and magnifying others.

He took no more than eight or ten running steps toward the forward boat when the puzzling conclusion he had just arrived at turned into horrific fact, right before his eyes. Every African in that forward boat threw himself or was pulled by his chained partner over the side and into the dark waters.

Then a more distant sound, coming from the landing area, seemed to be repeating and echoing what had happened just moments before on the king's boat. "They're drowning themselves, Captain!" Tungee yelled. Then he barked the order himself, "Go in after them, and pull them out." as he took off his jacket and boots and joined the others in the rescue effort. The noises of chains and shackles could be heard as the men thrashed about. Some called out to God for help while others seemed resigned to go. Those of the latter persuasion must have found their own quiet salvation, going down without a whimper. One by one the voices stilled and all that could be heard were gurgles and bubbles rising from the deep.

The crew managed to save eight of the men in the forward boat while seven survived from the king's boat. Kulando was among those survivors. The whole truth of what had happened jolted Tungee when he recalled those few words Kumi had said to Jeff. 'I may be a prisoner now but I will never become a slave.' In the king's mind the only way he knew how to back his words was to martyr himself along with some of his people, at least enough in numbers to draw attention to their cause. King Kumi, joined by more than a score of his people made their point about slavery and the moneymaking greed that was the driving force behind that insidious trade in black gold.

That little known African king had figured his plan and defied conventional wisdom by giving his life in an attempt to put an end to slavery. The elusive answer to which had evaded even the greatest minds of the day.

— TWENTY THREE —

Tungee stood on the landing and looked vacantly at the flames. He shook with indignation at his own worthless efforts. King Kumi had given him all the signs, but he didn't or couldn't read them.

The morning was just dawning as the group stood and watched the MFC burn to the waterline. No one knew how the fire started, but the Voodoo rumor had already surfaced. His face took on a pensive look and the corners of his mouth lifted slightly, as he watched the last smoldering embers turn into vapor, he thought, what a fitting memorial to last night's tragedy. And he personally felt a little taller that morning, having seen close up, a man with such courage, strength and character. King Kumi, the man, saw a world crazed with greed when some of his own tribe took large payments in exchange for turning over members of their own families to the trade. And he took it upon himself to do something about it.

The young Kulando looked up and said, "It is fitting."

"What do you mean by that?" Tungee asked.

"Someone said we may not see the fire," the young African smiled, "but it is fitting that we have. My memory will be better served for it."

"Now that just may be all right for your memory," Dobbs moaned, "but it plays hell with my well bein'. I wager we'll never see a bloody nickel out of this here voyage, we won't."

Dobbs had a point, Tungee thought. The group shivered in the chill of the January morning. Some of the crew had no shoes and others no shirts. Many of the Africans had lost their garments and were completely naked.

Kulando muttered something, half under his breath. "Better to swim with the fishes than wait in chains for the vultures."

Tungee knelt down beside the boy. "Where did you hear that, Kulando?"

"King Kumi said those words before he went into the water."

"Did he say why he wished to die, or as he put it, swim with the fishes."

"He told of a voice calling from somewhere beyond the river."

From the way the boy described the happenings of last night, it seemed the most natural thing in the world. Tungee was troubled by it though, for he simply didn't believe that suicide was an acceptable way out of life. He looked around at the African faces and then said to the boy, "None of you seem disturbed by the drowning of so many of your people. Why?"

"It is our way," Kulando said forthrightly. "The gone befores call out from their world for some to follow and others to wait and come later."

"Then you were not called?"

"No, I have much work to do here."

Dobbs leaned in close to the boy. "You ain't no witch doctor or some such thing, are you, little mate?"

"My work has nothing to do with witchcraft. I remain here to tell the story of my people."

Jeb Turner had a sloop waiting on the windward side of Saint Simons Island just in case of an emergency.

Gideon Foster and Turner laid out the proposition for the crew. Come along with us to Charleston and you'll get your regular pay. The offer was reasonable and to the man the MFC crew crowded aboard the Honey Belle and sailed up the coast toward South Carolina.

Tungee, Jeff and Dobbs sat near the bow and talked.

"What do you think they'll do about our promised bonus now that the MFC burned?" Jeff asked the others.

"Hard to say." Then Tungee pondered for a moment and then

speculated. "The company will likely double their profits on the voyage."

"How do you figure that, mate?" Dobbs asked.

"Well, they may collect insurance on the hull and grain cargo." Then he shook his head disdainfully. "And they'll also collect on the sale of the slaves, with the exception of those who chose to follow king Kumi."

"And you think they'll collect on the insurance as well as the slaves." Then Dobbs doubled his fists and gritted his teeth. "Those dirty bastards."

"Yeah, that's my sentiment too, Dobbs." Then Tungee looked up worriedly, "And the fact is, they'll likely get away with it. But ... If I had to make a bet I'd say they will pay the bonus just to keep everyone's mouth shut."

It was an easy sail up the coast and at sunrise the following morning the sloop nudged into the channel passed Sullivan's Island and into Charleston Harbor.

As soon as the Honey Belle tied up at the Broad Street Dock, Tungee hit the ground running. He inquired as to where the nearest telegraph office was? Rivers and Calhoun was the answer. Then he slowed his pace as he walked through Charleston's storied residential area that overlooked the harbor. He was impressed with what he saw. Grand one and two story houses with column porticos' and others with large porches, walled gardens, giant oak trees with their Spanish moss all producing a quite elegance. Tungee breathed a sigh of relief, glad to have his feet planted on solid ground and overall feeling of how lucky he was just to be alive.

When he got to the office he wrote out two messages, one to his uncle in Augusta, Georgia and another to his friend, Morgan Stern in Baltimore, Maryland. He asked a question in each of the telegrams and also indicated that he wasn't sure about his immediate plans.

The company secured temporary lodging for the crew and on the second day in port, Captain Foster passed the word for the men to stop by Jeb Turner's office and pick up their pay. Foster gave each man his wages and as another way to keep the crew in line, gave them the opportunity to go along to Boston where they would collect the company bonus.

Most of the old MFC crew spent that afternoon replacing personal property they had lost when the ship burned. And their first evening was spent like any sailing crew in any port, as soon as they got their pay, they would find a bar and engage in their own favorite kind of debauchery.

Tungee Jeff and Dobbs found a small bar that didn't seem to notice Jeff's skin color. During the earlier part of that evening the three of them had been engaged in defending Jeff's rights and then on two occasions fighting their way out of establishments that were not so color blind.

Nursing a shiner and dabbing at his bloody nose with a handkerchief Dobbs said, "I'm not sure I can stand much more of this here character building, mates."

"You'll mend, Dobbs," Tungee drawled.

"Just to keep the table straight, Mr. Randolph, you owe me one," Dobbs declared.

Jeff touched his glass to Dobbs' and grinned. "Put it on my tab."

Tungee smiled at the banter as he gazed out the window and mused, maybe the bar fights are a warm up for what I can expect in San Francisco.

The next morning suffering from headaches and empty wallets, most of the old MFC crew trooped into Turner's office and signed up for the trip to Boston. Tungee hung around the office and talked to most of the crew members. Blakely decided not to go along with the others, he was eager to get back to San Francisco and join his parents. Jeff and Dobbs had not made a decision and Tungee moved into their undecided camp for the time being. Dobbs made it clear that he would tag along with Tungee, whatever he decided to do.

Gabe Toombs came out of the office and called out, "Hey, Tungee you going to Boston?"

"Haven't made up my mind yet, Gabe."

"Well, Jensen, Greenleaf and a bunch of us will be onboard, why don't you join us."

"I'm working on it, Gabe. Did you manage to hang on to your hundred dollar gold piece?"

Gabe reached into his pocket and produced the coin, smiled and flipped it into the air as he ambled down the street.

For two solid weeks rain and heavy weather along the coast had disrupted travel to the north and the rains in Charleston had done nothing to calm the nerves of the men waiting to go to Boston.

Tungee hadn't committed either way, but he was leaning toward San Francisco. He had thought a lot about the slave trade and was almost as disturbed about it as Jeff, but what could they actually do about it? Maybe with some legal advice from Morgan Stern they could launch a court action against Lindsay Arthur Griffin. That wouldn't stop the trade, but it might be a start. On the other hand, you could make an argument against that immediate action with a question -- how do we finance the lawsuit?

The tugboat Charleston towed Southern Star into an anchorage just off East Bay Street. The ship got the attention of everyone in the harbor area, not because she was a sleek looking clipper, but because she was flying a distress signal flag. Tungee and Jeff saw the activity and walked to a position as near the Southern Star as they could get. They noticed Captain Foster talking to a man. Foster looked over his shoulder and gestured toward Tungee and Jeff, then he continued to talk for sometime. Foster finally turned away from the man and walked toward his former crew members.

"What's the problem, Captain?" Tungee asked.

"They hit a squall off Cape Hatteras, caught some of the men in the rigging. Lightening killed one man outright. Two others fell to the deck and were knocked unconscious and both got some broken bones." Then Foster gestured. "The fellow I was talking to is Luke Spencer, Skipper of the Southern Star."

"Will the injured men live?" Tungee asked.

"One is out of immediate danger and they can't tell about the other. But Captain Spencer decided they both needed hospital care."

"Where are they bound for?" Tungee asked.

"San Francisco and then to China," Captain Foster said. "Which reminds me, aren't you fellows thinking about going back to San Francisco?"

"Thinking about it, Captain," Tungee said. He had already heard some bad news regarding commercial travel to San Francisco. The short route, by way of Panama, was rife with problems. Outrageous fares and no booking agent would guarantee, dates certain, passage on the West Coast leg of the trip from Panama to San Francisco.

Captain Foster saw some doubt in Tungee's eyes. "Luke just told me that he needed three top men to replace the people he lost. He asked me if I had any recommendations. I didn't give him any names because I wasn't sure about your plans."

Tungee looked at Jeff and got a negative nod. "Then you've decided to go to Boston?"

"Yeah, I need the cash," Jeff told him.

Tungee thought for a moment and made a quick decision. "Then, Captain Foster, I'd appreciate it if you would pass my name along and I believe I can also speak for Dobbs and Blakely for the top men replacements." Then Tungee asked, "How much time does he plan to spend in Charleston?"

"He didn't give me all the particulars, but I got the impression he'd haul anchor just as soon as he got those men in hospital and the harbor master cleared his papers."

Tungee and Jeff sat in the little bar and looked out the window at Charleston Harbor. "I wish you'd give some more thought to coming back to San Francisco with us, Jeff."

Jeff sighed. "Thanks for the invite, Tungee, but I've got to tell you something. Since the other night at Saint Simons Island something's been gnawing at my gut."

Tungee nodded. "I can understand that."

"I don't know why, but those people made me begin to think about my folks."

"Homesick?"

"I guess that's part of it." Then Jeff took a sip of his bourbon. "But it's more than that, Tungee. My people have been going through the same hell we have since we were shanghaied -- except it's been all their lives. I got my papers and ran. But it finally caught up to me the other night and I can't live with that anymore."

"What do you plan to do?"

Jeff took his time. "I'm not sure, but I can't just stand by and do nothing."

"I understand, Jeff." Then Tungee grinned. "Be careful in Boston and make sure you don't find yourself going to sea again."

Jeff smiled and nodded.

"Something else, if for any reason you decide to come back to California, look me up."

They sat sipping their drinks and enjoying the silence. Then Tungee picked up the bottle and filled each of their glasses. "I'd like to propose a toast." They held their glasses. "Here's to our friend who swims with the fishes. The king is dead -- long live the king."

Tungee went back to the telegraph office and asked if he had any messages. There were two, which he immediately opened and read. His uncle responded that he did have some information regarding the present ownership and was working on a title search for the old Cahill family property on the river. Morgan Stern simply gave the name of a law firm in San Francisco and asked when he could expect to see him.

Cahill, Dobbs and Blakely said so long to Jeff and were escorted to a longboat by the Southern Star's boatswain, Sam Clover. He was a tall affable man with light brown hair. His first comment to his new men was, "I hear you fellows were shanghaied out of San Francisco."

The three shrugged in agreement with the boatswains' statement and Tungee gestured to Dobbs who opened up and told Sam Clover the short version of their story.

When their boat arrived at their new ship's anchorage they all scrambled aboard, were taken below and assigned bunks in the forecastle. Tungee spent the balance of the evening making the rounds getting acquainted with the Southern Star and her crew and listening to general scuttlebutt.

It was near to midnight when Tungee was told to report to the captain's cabin. He knocked on the door and heard a, "Come on in," from the other side.

He was immediately struck by the similarity between Foster's cabin on the MFC and the one he was presently in.

The captain was standing over the chart table and looking down at the maps, smoking a long stemmed briar pipe. Luke Spencer was a lean man that stood just over six feet, had a handsome face and intelligent blue eyes. The captain wore a dress shirt with the sleeves rolled up, collar open and dark trousers.

Tungee got an idea from the captain's dress and demeanor that he was from society's upper class. The talkative Sam Clover had mentioned as much saying that the captain's father was a banker and they lived in a mansion just off Union Square in Manhattan.

Luke Spencer looked up and said, "Come on in, Mr. Cahill and have a seat." Then he shook his head and grinned. "I just had supper with Foster. He gave me chapter and verse of what you fellows have just gone through."

"Bad timing, Captain, wrong place at the wrong time, just about sums it up. And speaking for the three of us, your new hands, we appreciate this opportunity to work our way back to San Francisco."

"Well, I expect it may be of mutual benefit to all of us." The skipper gave a wry grin. "But from what I've heard, you could pay first class and never miss it. I was told you are a wealthy man, Mr. Cahill."

Tungee shook his head. "I don't know about that. I had some gold holdings before I left California, but it remains to be seen whether I can reclaim them or not."

"Captain Foster tells me that you're a first rate top man and I hope the other fellows you've brought along are capable."

"You can count on that, skipper. Now it's true they don't have a lot of experience, but they worked around the Horn, then to Africa and back to the states. We've been through hell together. I don't think you'll be disappointed."

"This is my first voyage on the Southern Star, but I discovered the first day out of New York that we had a real sailer. I'm sorry as hell to lose three good men, but if you fellows can take up the slack, I plan to make this a foot race to San Francisco. This horse that we've got under us is capable of setting some records. And I'd like to set a mark of sailing through the Golden Gate inside of a hundred days. Now, what do you think of that, Mr. Cahill?"

"Sounds good to me, Captain."

"You will replace Thornton, the man that was killed, as port side watch mate. Now, Mr. Cahill, you may be in for some hard work, are you up to the challenge?"

Tungee grinned, "Let's get under way and then you be the judge, Captain Spencer."

"Get yourself a catnap. I'm having all hands turn out at the end of the mid watch. The tug will tow us through the channel and into position to sail on the morning tide."

— TWENTY FOUR —

At exactly 0400 hours the watch bell tolled eight times and the quiet was broken on board the Southern Star. Boatswains mate, Sam Clover made the rounds crowing his wake up call and the ship began to come alive.

One hour after sunrise a Charleston Harbor tug towed the Southern Star through the channel and into the Atlantic. A gentle breeze increased to moderate and the outgoing tide was running and producing four-foot swells.

Tungee stood beside Captain Spencer on the quarterdeck and they watched first mate, Tom Murphy, move along the deck shouting orders to loose the jibs, stays and spanker. A light rain swept in from the southeast just as the tug cut loose and made her wide circle to starboard as she headed back to port.

Captain Spencer called out. "All hands make sail. Cast off the gaskets from t'gallant's down. You will brace for close reach sailing on the port tack. Stay on your tack helmsman and keep her close to the wind."

Seasoned top men scrambled up the shrouds and into the rigging, loosing gaskets from the sails while others on deck separated bunt lines from halyards and then began to lower each sail into position.

Twenty days out of Charleston the Southern Star neared the equator and was making good time. The ship skirted the shoulder of Brazil and from there Captain Spencer took a course south by southwest on a line that passed the eastern edge of St. Katharine Island. And from that point he almost duplicated in reverse the route of the MFC.

The ship's log showed the elapsed time from the equator to longitude fifty south, a position northeast of the Falkland Islands was recorded as twenty-three days and seven hours.

Then the captain steered a more southerly course and so far to the east that the crow's nest never reported land sightings of either Staten Island or Tierra del Fuego.

Four days later the ship was sailing a parallel course to the Drake Passage and not far north of South Shetland Island. The weather was frigid and a keening wind screamed up from Antarctica. A treacherous sea boiled every minute of the day and constantly slashed over the deck. Jibs, stays and spanker were the sails employed during most of those sub freezing days. The cro'jik was blown out twice and had to be completely refitted. It was hell week for ship and crew and there was no doubt that, when they finally turned north, old timers as well as novice sailors knew they had taken about all that old Cape Stiff could dish out, and they had won.

Tungee had just arrived at the captain's cabin for a meeting, Luke Spencer finished making a log entry and looked up. "Have a seat, Mr. Cahill." Then the skipper smiled. "Congratulations to you and your mates that came aboard at Charleston."

"I appreciate the compliment, Captain Spencer."

"You fellows made a difference around the Horn."

"It was a rough one, I'll say that." Then Tungee frowned and said, "You have a good crew, what do you plan to do with them in San Francisco?"

The captain cocked his head. "I don't understand the question."

"How do you plan to keep the crew on board for the rest of your voyage?" Then Tungee shook his head. "The town is notorious for that one fact, ships sail into port and the crews flock off to the gold fields."

"We may have a few defections, but not many. You see, I've worked it out to where every man on this ship will share in the profits of the voyage." Spencer leaned back in his chair. "I'm part owner of the ship, and I arranged to set aside shares for the crew before we left New York."

Tungee nodded his agreement. "Good idea. Will you be in ballast to China?"

"No, not quite. We have a contract for furs, pelts and several tons of finished leather goods. We also have a standard booking of fifty passengers to Canton."

"Chinese?"

"I expect most of them will be." Captain Spencer took a moment and dropped the formality, broke out the cigars and poured them each a brandy. They held their glasses up, saluted and downed the drinks. Then as Spencer struck a match to light their cigars, he said, "Tungee, Foster told me a little about your problems. Is it true that someone back in San Francisco planned to have you killed?"

"That's what I was told." Then he nodded and said, "In hind sight, I guess my choice for a banks was lousy."

"What do you plan to do about it?"

"I'm not sure. I have a good idea about who gave the orders, but proving it may be difficult." Then Tungee frowned. "There's a banker involved with a group of criminals that are known as the Sydney Ducks and they are dangerous. One other thing, a dying man told me that the banker was also connected with some pretty big folks in San Francisco."

"Did he mean politicians?" Luke Spencer asked.

"I'm not sure, but that's a possibility."

The captain arched his brow. "Well, now. That's interesting, Tungee. I have a business connection with one of the top democrats in San Francisco. He's a fellow by the name of Harvey Prescott. I know him because my father had to do business with his crowd back in New York."

"Had to?" Tungee questioned.

"That's right. Prescott comes out of Tammany Hall, the most corrupt political machine in this country."

Tungee nodded. "Yeah, that's what I've heard. And I know for a fact they hold a tight rein on the port of New York."

The Southern Star crossed the equator sixteen days after leaving longitude fifty south. Tungee sat near the port bow and leaned back on a coil of rope, enjoying the salt spray kicking off a choppy sea. In less than forty eight hours they would sail through the Golden Gate and he had to give some serious thought about what kind of odds he faced in San Francisco. One thing was a given, once he showed up at the bank he would likely go onto a target-list. The question is how do you protect yourself against unknown assassins? How many people am I dealing with? And if Luke Spencer's guess is right and they turn out to be politicians, that could open a whole new can of worms.

Dobbs sauntered up the deck and flopped down next to Tungee. "What's up, mate?

"Aw, I was just thinking about what we'll be up against when we hit the streets of San Francisco."

"Maybe we should stick together for a while," Dobbs said cautiously, "watch each other's back."

"Not a bad idea, Dobbs." Then Tungee sat bolt upright. "In fact it's a hell of an idea."

"Common sense, mate."

"I just thought of something else. If things work out, I'll be in need of some help. How would you like to come and work with me in the mining business?"

"Best offer I've had in months, mate."

"One more thing, if we manage to stay alive long enough to get to a lawyer, I'll make you my partner."

"Then I suggest we give some serious thought to the staying alive part of that there proposition."

The Southern Star was just ninety-four days out of Charleston when the lookout reported land. San Francisco's Telegraph Hill was spotted five points off the starboard bow.

All sails had been furled and the tug Juniper had tied onto the stem and was belching smoke and clawing her way toward the Front Street Dock.

Tungee and Dobbs stood near the bow and watched the tug angle toward the quay.

"Dobbs, who was Alf Talbot's immediate boss?"

"If I'm not mistaken it was Freddy Peterson, the crimp."

"Any other Duck bosses?"

Dobbs scratched his head. "A couple more come to mind, Biggs Barker and Cal Long. I suppose you'd call them enforcers."

Captain Spencer stood on the quarterdeck chatting as he passed out pay envelopes to Tungee, Dobbs and Blakely.

"I wish there was some way I could talk you fellows into staying on board. But I guess this is home port to you. Glad we hooked up at Charleston."

"Captain Spencer, sir," Dobbs said in a serious tone, "You might make it plain to your men to be careful in this here town, nights most of all."

"Thank you, Mr. Dobbs, I understand what you're saying. I'll pass the word along."

Dobbs looked directly at the skipper and with a sly grin said, "Any more of this polite conversation and I'm tempted to sign on for another tour."

Tungee tipped his cap to the skipper and looked at Dobbs and Blakely. "Well, gentlemen, like it or not, we're back. What do you say we hit the gangplank and try out our land legs."

— TWENTY FIVE —

Tungee, Dobbs and Blakely walked across the dock and up to the street. They stopped at the corner of Front and Filbert put their duffel bags down and Tungee began doing a series of deep knee bends in an effort to get acclimated to solid ground. Dobbs nervously looked up and down the quay, edgy about his standing with the Sydney Ducks. Gene Blakely was calm, but concerned about his parents and where they were.

Tungee finished his short workout, picked up his duffel bag and said, "Dobbs, try not to be obvious, but take a look up Filbert, third doorway on your left. See if you recognize the man standing there. He's been giving us an awful lot of attention."

Dobbs barely got a glimpse as the fellow turned and hurried up the street. "It's Tommy Perkins, a bloomin' Duck's informer. I'll wager he's off to tell Freddy I'm back."

"Then let's get out of here. There are a half dozen hotels within a couple of blocks."

They turned and walked down Front Street. Tungee knew the hotels in the area his brother Davy had used one or two of them in the past. "You two check in at the Battery and I'll take the Union across the street. And by the way, don't use your right names when you sign in."

The Duck's informer, Tommy Perkins, spotted by Dobbs stood no more than five feet five inches tall, had dark hair, green eyes and a long nose. He had stooped shoulders and walked with a quick gate along a blighted section of Sansome Street. By the time he got to his destination, a pool hall at the corner of Chestnut, he was almost out of breath. He shuffled past the pool players to the back room and went into the crimp's stuffy little office.

Freddy Peterson looked up from his desk, a large man wearing a green visor above his spectacles. He had a puffy face, squinty gray eyes and bulbous lips. "Tommy, you look like you've seen a ghost."

"Dobbsy's back."

The big man smiled. "Well, now, maybe you have seen a ghost at that."

"You told me to look out for him," pointing out his diligence. "A ship named Southern Star just tied up to the Front Street Dock."

"And Dobbs was onboard?"

"Walked off as big as you please."

"I was beginning to think that bunch had just dropped off the face of the earth." Freddy Peterson took a long drag on his cigar. "Was he alone?"

"No. No, sir. He was with two other blokes."

"Recognize the other two?"

"One I think was the youngest in that crowd that went along with Alfie and the rest. He was paid for. Don't know his name, thin build and he wore spectacles."

The crimp reached into his desk, pulled out a piece of paper and studied it for a moment. "I think that's the kid named Blakely. What about the other one, what did he look like?"

"Tall. Six feet or more, slender and muscular build and he had light reddish hair."

"Shit! That sounds like Cahill."

"Is that bad, chief?"

"Well, it depends. You hang around for a minute while I write a note and I'll have you run it over for me."

"Be right here."

The big man scribbled a note on a piece of paper, put it in an envelope and wrote on the outside. Mr. Mason Albreght, President, The Mining and Merchant Bank. "Now, Tommy, you take this note to the bank. Give it to the teller and let him know that you would like to wait for an answer."

Mason Albreght sat in his office nervously reading the contents of Freddy's note. He stared for a moment, then slammed his fist down on the desk. "Damn it!" Then he breathed heavily, got up in an agitated state and began to walk around the room. Finally he sat on the edge of his desk and reread the note. 'The informer saw three men in a group; he was only sure about one, a fellow named Dobbs. Another one he thought was a youngster named Blakely. The third one is sort of a guess, but from the description, it might be Cahill.'

The banker lit a cigarette and after taking a few puffs he stubbed it out in the ashtray and began scribbling a note to Freddy. 'Find and hold main subject. I'll make positive identification and give further instructions at that time.'

Tungee checked in at the Union Hotel under the assumed name of Robert Harbin, using his first name and Davy's middle.

Dobbs and Blakely made it look routine as they took their new names and checked into the Battery Hotel. Dobbs called himself Philip Hanson, a neighbor he had known down in Sydney. Young Blakely took the name of a cousin from Philadelphia, Eddie Farr.

Tommy Perkins walked through the pool hall with a smile of satisfaction on his face. He eased through the door, crossed to the crimp's desk and handed him a plain white envelope.

Freddie looked up and grinned at Tommy. Then he opened the envelope and read the note. The crimp sat back in his chair and took a long breath. Then he struck a match and put it to the paper he had just read from and threw it in the fireplace. He turned and said, "Tommy. I have another errand for you. Find Barker and Long, if you don't mind. And tell them to ... No don't tell them a thing, just tell them to report to me as soon as possible."

Tommy stood near the desk and fidgeted, obviously waiting around for something.

Freddy had seen the act before and smiled. "Oh, excuse me, Tommy." Then he reached in the drawer, took out a silver dollar and flipped it to his informant.

Tommy immediately shoved the coin into his pocket and turned to leave the room.

"Tommy," Freddy Peterson called out. "Remember those fellows you saw at the dock?"

"Of course I do, Freddy."

"If you see any one or all of them. Try and find out where they're staying or where they're going. Don't get too close. Just watch and report what you see."

The three men huddled in Tungee's hotel room to decide their next move.

Tungee laughed when he heard the aliases taken by Dobbs and Blakely, not because they sounded phony, the fact is there was a ring of truth in them, Phil Hanson and Eddie Farr.

"Perkins, the informer. How well did you know him, Dobbs?" Tungee asked.

"I didn't know him well at all, mate. I did know that he worked for Freddy Peterson. I've been present in Freddy's office when he came in and passed news along to the crimp."

Tungee pressed, "Like what?"

"Oh, things like, we got two more for some ship or other. Once I recall him saying, Barker had taken care of something or maybe it was someone, likely as not it was someone, if you get the gist."

Gene Blakely sat near the window, looking down on the intersection of Battery and Union. He gestured to Dobbs and pointed out two men standing on the corner, lighting up cigarettes.

"That there is Barker and Long, gents. Them two Ducks could give you nightmares" Dobbs touched Blakely on the shoulder. "What have they been up to?"

The kid, resting his chin on the back of the chair said, "Walking in and out of hotels."

"The search is on, mates. You can bet your arse on it."

Tungee crossed the room and looked out the window to identify the two. Then he turned back to the others. "It's me they're really after, so a word of caution. You fellows don't know me if we happen to see each other on the street."

"That may be good advice, mate, but I'm damned if I plan to be intimidated by them bloody rogues."

"Just a precaution, Dobbs."

"Well, it all comes down to the gold you put in that bank, ain't that so."

"I suppose."

"Can't you just take it out and move it to another bank."

"I don't know that it's still there." Tungee began to pace. "I have one big problem in regards to the bank. I don't have a receipt for the gold. And if they wanted to play dirty, they could just say they had never heard of me or my account."

Blakely said, "Isn't it worth a try, to ask for your money. Maybe they won't need a receipt."

"Too iffy. I think I'll try something else first." Then Tungee turned to Dobbs. "I want you to go over to my old hotel, the Kinsey House, at Clay and Montgomery. That's where I was staying before I was shanghaied."

"What do I do, mate?"

"First, I want you to go to the desk and ask for Tungee Cahill. Then observe the reaction of the clerk when you mention my name. Does the name ring a bell? Insist that you know I was there. Then if you're quite sure they don't know anything about me. Ask for Bob Sloan, he was the only clerk I knew by name. Sloan is a man in his thirties, high forehead, wears gold rimmed glasses and he was clean shaven when I saw him last."

"What if I'm talking to Bob Sloan? What do I ask him?"

Tungee thought for a moment. "If you're talking to him and he doesn't want to recognize my name, we may be in trouble. If it's not Sloan you're talking to, ask when Sloan comes on duty or where you might find him. Nothing more."

Dobbs grinned. "Does this here detective agency have a name, mate?"

Tungee laughed. "No, but we might give it some thought."

Dobbs cleaned up and put on his best clothes, dungarees, a clean white cotton shirt and a fitted cutoff jacket. He walked to the Kinsey House, entered and crossed the lobby to the desk. He knew immediately that the clerk was not Bob Sloan. "Hello there, mate. I'm looking for a friend of mine, his name is Cahill, Tungee Cahill."

The clerk, an older bald headed gentleman hesitated, but gave nothing away. "No. He's not registered here."

Dobbs said, "Perhaps I was misinformed as to his whereabouts. But listen, there's a fellow that works here by the name of Bob Sloan, is he around?"

The clerk gave an affable smile. "Bob Sloan's moved up in the world. He is now manager over at the Windsor Hotel, classy place up near the foot of Telegraph Hill. I believe it's on Kearney Street."

Dobbs said, "Thank you, mate." Then turned and walked briskly out of the hotel.

After listening to Dobbs report, Tungee knew there were two errands he had to run himself. And the only safe way he could move about the streets of San Francisco was to take on another identity. He sent Dobbs out to purchase some used clothing and to make sure that everything except the shoes was a little oversized. Dobbs did the shopping and brought back a dull gray set of overalls, a brown cotton shirt and a pair of gawky looking box shoes. By the time Tungee put on the slouch hat and affected a limp, not even Dobbs or Blakely would recognize him on the street.

The man wore a dark rain slicker and a floppy hat, was hunched over and struggled to keep his footing. Wind whipped the rain into his face and waters cascaded off of Telegraph Hill and ran down the middle of Kearny Street. He spat a huge slug of tobacco juice into the free flowing stream.

When he arrived at the door of the Windsor Hotel, he struggled against the wind, but finally slipped inside the lobby. The man shook the water off his rain slicker and crossed to the desk. "I'd like to speak to Mr. Sloan, please."

The clerk politely asked, "Who might I say is calling?"

There was a slight pause before he said, "Cahill, he'll likely remember me from the Kinsey House."

The clerk returned just moments later and said, "Go right on in, Mr. Cahill. Mr. Sloan will see you."

Tungee walked with his affected limp into the office. He took off the slouch hat and stood looking across the room at the desk clerk he had done business with at the Kinsey House.

The manager's office was impressive. It had dark oak paneling below the wainscoting and plaster above. A brass chandelier and several ornate lamps provided the lighting. The place had a masculine look, leather and wooden chairs and a small sofa. Sloan got up from behind a polished mahogany desk, walked to the middle of the room and extended his hand. "Mr. Cahill. What happened to you? You just disappeared."

"That's exactly what some folks wanted." Tungee frowned and shook his head. "I was kidnapped."

"Good God. I didn't know," Mr. Sloan said painfully.

"They put me onboard a ship and tried to make it look like I'd been shanghaied."

"I figured something was wrong." Bob Sloan pursed his lips, "And what happened two or three days after your disappearance added to my concern."

"What was that?"

"Two marshals came to the hotel with a court order and demanded to search your room. They also wanted to confiscate anything you had left in the safe."

"What did they give as a reason?"

"They said it was to be used as evidence in a court hearing."

Tungee gave a fixed smile. "I see. Tell me, did they say what I had been charged with or what the hearing was about?"

"No," Sloan looked puzzled, "and I guess I should have asked, but I didn't."

"What were they looking for?"

"I took them to your room and kept an eye on them. They looked at everything, opened drawers, bags and your footlocker. Two long guns and a pistol were found and they rifled through the pages of all your books. But when they finished it was obvious they hadn't found what they were looking for. And as a matter of fact, they didn't take anything from the room." Mr. Sloan looked thoughtfully at Tungee. "Then we went down to the safe. They wanted to look at the log of items you had left with us. They looked it over and took everything that was listed on the log."

"What did that include?" Tungee asked nervously.

"There were three small pouches of gold. They didn't amount to much, eight or nine ounces I believe."

"That sounds about right," Tungee said. Then he cleared his throat. "Mr. Sloan, there should have been an envelope on that log. I left it with you the last afternoon I was at the hotel."

Bob Sloan smiled and crossed to a wall safe. He opened it, took out an envelope and handed it to Tungee. "Is that what you're referring to."

Tungee opened the envelope and removed two pieces of paper. He took a long look at the deposit receipts, breathed a sigh of relief and a broad grin crossed his face.

"I didn't open the envelope, but something told me it was very important. Maybe a bank receipt or some other kind of legal paper."

"How did you figure that out?"

"Well, when you came in the hotel that afternoon, I believe you asked for an envelope and maybe some stationary. Don't know why I remember so clearly, but I do. You took something out of your coat pocket, a piece of paper that had been wrapped around a cigar. You took that and another paper from your pocket and put them into an envelope and handed it to me for safe keeping."

"Why didn't you log it in?"

Mr. Sloan seemed a little embarrassed. "You know something, Mr. Cahill. It was a mistake on my part. I simply put it in the safe with your gold pouches and forgot to enter it into the log. I didn't think a thing about it until the marshals came. Then I remembered that scene and my thoughts at the time and since it wasn't on the log, I just set it aside. You see, by the time we got back from the room, I had become suspicious. There was something about those men that just didn't ring true, so I took the envelope home and eventually brought it here and put it in the safe."

Tungee could have hugged him, but he didn't, he just nodded and casually said, "I owe you one, Mr. Sloan."

— TWENTY SIX —

Tungee hung the lantern near the door of the Kinsey House storeroom. There was a musty smell to the place, but he grinned when he found his belongings, it was like seeing an old friend for the first time in a while. He picked up his shaving gear and several pieces of clothing, a dog-eared volume of Shakespeare's plays and Mama's Bible and shoved them into a carpetbag. Then he dug down into his travel trunk, opened the bottom panel and took out a box containing several pouches of gold and a pearl handled Navy Colt 44.

He put the gold into the carpetbag, shoved the pistol into his pocket and returned to the lobby, paid his storage fee and thanked the clerk for his cooperation. Then he hunched his shoulders forward and limped back to the Union Hotel.

Three days off the Southern Star and both Dobbs and Blakely were getting restless from inactivity. The kid looked down on the intersection and didn't see any of the Ducks, took a deep breath for courage and said, "Dobbs, I'm going out for a while."

"Don't think it's a good idea, mate."

"I'll be careful." He put his hand on the door handle and then turned back. "I'm gonna try and find my cousin. I think she lives in the 1600 block of Taylor Street."

"Good luck, mate." Then Dobbs frowned, "Now you may not see 'em, but they are out there."

The kid hurried up the long Green Street hill and stopped at the corner of Taylor to catch his breath. There was an old gentleman sitting in a rocking chair at 1600. Gene Blakely walked half way up the steps to the porch and called,

"Excuse me, sir?"

The old man responded, "What can I do for you?"

Gene Blakely scratched his head and said tentatively, "I think I have a cousin that lives on this street."

The old man grinned. "Does your cousin have a name?"

"Laura Dubek."

The old man came alive. "Well now, it just so happens the lady lives at 1650 Taylor." Then he pointed. "That big white house in the middle of the block. She runs a boarding house."

"Thank you, sir," said Blakely as he strode out in the direction of his cousin's place. He had taken only a few steps when a voice called from behind him. "You wouldn't be Gene Blakely, would ya?"

The kid turned and shuddered when he recognized the two enforcers Dobbs had pointed out earlier. "No, my name's Eddie Farr."

The second man said, "Well I hate to call a man a liar the first time I meet him, but I'm gonna call you a liar. We think you are Gene Blakely, but I'll call you Eddie Farr if it suits you better."

Cal Long grabbed one elbow and Biggs Barker took the other and they hustled young Blakely off toward the Barbary Coast.

The kid knew he was out manned, so he simply went along with the two. As they walked in the direction of the bay Barker said, "You was seen coming off that Southern Star a day or two ago along with two others. Dobbs was one and Cahill is likely to be the other."

"Don't know any Cahill," the kid said tightly.

"Listen here, Eddie Farr, we know that you and Dobbs along with a dozen or more of our associates shipped out of this here port aboard the Orient Leaf last September," Biggs Barker said calmly. "But, since we ain't had no word from them, we plan to ask you, and if we don't get some damn good answers you'll find yourself going to sea again."

"Now hold on just a minute," Gene Blakely blurted. "I didn't say I wouldn't talk to you." Then he shrugged nonchalantly, "I'll tell you anything you want to know." He figured if they wanted to know what happened on the voyage, why not tell them, after all he had more or less gone along with the mutineers up to the time of the fight. Better just tell them he had stuck with them all the way. "Go ahead, ask me anything you like," Gene Blakely said earnestly.

Biggs Barker asked, "Do you know who Alf Talbot is?"

"Yeah, I do now. When I first got on the ship I was too scared to say anything, but after a few days I got to know some of the crew and later on Alf Talbot asked me to join in with them on the gold scheme."

Blakely rattled on about the crew, the ship's name change and by the time they arrived at a warehouse, somewhere in the bowels of the Barbary Coast, he had about covered the whole voyage, mutiny and all. When they got inside the dark warehouse the kid became frightened because neither of the men seemed to give any kind of reaction to his story. But he took a deep breath and kept on talking, he ticked off the names of the men killed in the failed takeover and were buried at sea, from Willie Baxter to Thunder Parker. Then he said, "Of course, Alfie never got in on the burial service since he was blown over the side by the force of a cannon."

Knots formed in the kid's stomach as he began to sense some reaction. It wasn't good news for it appeared that Cal Long hadn't believed a word he said. But, on the other hand, Biggs Barker seemed to be a bit more interested.

Then Gene Blakely screwed up his nerves and said brashly, "Well, I guess I've been all the help I can be to you fellows. And if you don't mind I'd like to get on with my errands."

"No you don't get off that easy," Cal Long said brusquely.

"Come on, Cal. I think we ought to let him go." Then he winked at his cohort. "He's told us about everything we need to know."

Cal Long grumbled. "I think we ought ta slap him around a little, but you may be right, Biggs. So go on, get out of here kid, before I change my mind."

Gene Blakely guessed what they were up to, but didn't hesitate to follow his instructions. He hurried out the door of the warehouse and quickly strode down Lombard Street and made a right onto Sansome. Then he slowed to a normal pace and never looked back. He assumed he was being followed and moved along in the direction of his cousin's house. Suddenly he turned into a bar at the corner of Sansome and Filbert.

The kid ordered a beer and paid for it. Then he went to the free lunch counter, asked for and received a corned beef sandwich. Then he moved to the end of the counter next to the street window. He stood casually with one foot on the brass rail in plain sight of the street, munching on his sandwich.

Tungee slipped out of his hotel, walked to the livery and filled Mack in on his shanghai experience.

Mack grabbed Tungee's hand and just stood there shaking his head. "Now if that don't beat all. Then he settled down and said, "Your friend, Charlie Boone's been worried about you." The old man spat a slug of tobacco juice into the street. "Charlie stop's by every now and again to check on your team. Somethin' else, we've both used 'em from time to time. I figured they ought to get some work now and again."

"That's very thoughtful of you, Mack. Tell me, how are they doing?"

"They're all right, not so much as a cold. But you know something, Mr. Cahill. Don't ask me how I know, but I got this funny feelin' that them two black's miss you."

"Well, man and animal can develop a strong bond and to tell you the truth, I've missed them too. I'll take a look at the horses and then stop by and say hello to Charlie."

"Charlie's on a run to Oakland right now, but I'll tell him you're back."

"Thanks, I'd appreciate that." Tungee looked at Mack and said, "Tell him I'm back, but I'd appreciate it if you'd both keep it quiet. There are a few things I need to take care of before making my presence known."

Mack grinned. "Gotcha."

Tungee turned toward the back of the stables and when he arrived at their stall, both horses looked at their owner for a long moment and then moved away to the far corner of their individual stalls. Tungee chuckled, well I'll be damned, those characters are snubbing me. He stood and talked and called their names, but it didn't seem to do any good, they continued their snub. It's all right, he thought, I'll bring sugar next time. He shook his head and thought guess I've got some fence mending to do. He then turned and walked up the isle between

207

the stalls and before he'd reached the street, Big Sam whinnied. Tungee grinned and walked out the front door of the livery.

Gene Blakely had almost finished his lunch when he spotted Biggs Barker standing in the shadow of a building just across the intersection from the bar. He sat there gazing at the street and pondering his next move. He didn't want to lead them to his cousin's house; neither did he want them to find his and Dobbs' hotel or Tungee's. Just as he took the last bite of his sandwich and finished off the crisp dill pickle, he came up with the obvious answer. He turned to the fellow standing next to him at the counter, gave him a hearty slap on the back, and walked out to the street. The fellow gave the departing stranger a long curious look and felt his pocket to make sure his wallet was still in place – it was.

The kid made his exit, turned right and another quick right into Filbert. He walked at a reasonable pace in the direction of the bay. Then after passing battery he picked up the pace and moved toward Front Street. Then as he crossed that intersection, he began jogging toward the dock and ran up the gangplank of the Southern Star.

*   *   *

Tungee stopped in front of the tailor's shop, looked up and down the street to make sure he wasn't being followed, then he opened the door. The bell tinkled as he went inside the shop.

Willy looked startled. "Mr. Cahill," he said with a smile. "You know something, Mr. Cahill, now I've had customers late for their fittings, but seven months, now dot's a long time. Back to the gold fields, you went?"

"No. I went to sea, now I didn't sign on to any ship."

"Shanghaied, you voss?"

Tungee nodded. "I was here in the afternoon and that same night I was knocked in the head and hauled onboard a ship. When I woke up we were on our way to Panama. The Ducks gang was in on a scheme to take over the ship and pirate for gold that was heading for the States. Fortunately it didn't work out the way they planned."

"I didn't know dem Ducks voss in de shanghai business."

"I'm afraid they are, Willy."

"You got to talk to Jim Garrigan, he heads up de Vigilance

Committee." He stopped for a moment and a wry grin crossed his face. "One thing is a fact, Mr. Cahill."

"What's that, Willy?"

"Dem gallows down at de wharf."

"Yeah, what about it?"

"We gott to use it more often."

Tungee walked directly from the tailor shop to The Pacific Building on Montgomery Street. Morgan Stern's friend had an office there. He went into the building, climbed the stairs to the second floor and located the office, tapped lightly and opened the door a crack. A tall stately gentleman with a long face and hawk nose stood behind the desk, he wore a charcoal-single breasted suit. "Come on in."

Tungee entered the large bright office furnished with two massive desks. There was a whitewashed fireplace and mantle, dark wooden chairs, three small tables and several landscape paintings hanging on the walls. He removed his hat, crossed to the desk and handed the man his copy of Morgan Stern's telegram.

The gentleman read it and looked up. "I'm Eric Grishom and you must be Tungee Cahill?"

"That's right, Mr. Grishom."

"Then you are acquainted with Morg."

"Yes and I consider him one of my best friends," Tungee told him.

"I went to school with Morg, he's a person you can always count on. Have a seat, Mr. Cahill." Then the lawyer sat down and looked at Tungee, "What can I do for you?"

Tungee took a deep breath and launched into the story, beginning with the bank deposit and bringing the lawyer up to the present.

Eric Grishom finally said judiciously, "Then you believe the bank president was implicated in the plot to have you shanghaied and assassinated."

"That's what I was told by the man that was supposed to do it." Tungee leaned forward. "And I believe it to be a fact."

"Have you been in contact with the bank since your return to San Francisco?"

"No I haven't. Maybe it's my own insecurity, not wanting to face bad news." Then Tungee squirmed in his chair. "I also have this feeling that as soon as I contact the bank, they'll try and gun me down," then he chuckled, "or put me on another ship."

"About the bank deposit. Do you have any paperwork on the weight of the gold and exchange rates you agreed to."

"Yes I have those receipts."

"Well, Mr. Cahill, I don't know at this point whether it will turn out to be a legal matter or not. Of course the part regarding the assassination would be something for the police to look into."

"What do you suggest I do about the bank account?"

"You have the right to transfer your money to another bank and if the original bank is not forthcoming, you can sue for the amount on your receipt."

"Mr. Grishom, if we sue the bank, that would mean going to court." Then Tungee looked directly at the lawyer and said, "Now, I'm not apologizing for my heritage, but you see I'm part Creek Indian. And you must know what odds I'd be up against in front of some judges."

Eric Grishom didn't say a word, but slowly nodded his head and drummed his fingers on his desk.

— TWENTY SEVEN —

Tungee looked out his hotel window and watched the late afternoon fog roll in from the bay. He needed to see Dobbs and Blakely. Give it another hour, he thought and between the darkness and the fog I should be able to walk to their hotel without being spotted.

Gene Blakely hid out on the Southern Star all afternoon and passed the time talking to his shipmates. All the while, he worried, knowing Tungee and Dobbs had to be told about his encounter with Long and Barker. He knew some of the Ducks would be watching the ship, so he decided to wait until dark before making his move. He went to the chow table along with the others and pretended to eat, but his stomach was tied up in knots.

The ship's bell rang four times and the first dogwatch was handed over to the second as Gene Blakely climbed the ladder and went on deck. He smiled at what he saw. The fog had cut visibility down to almost zero, couldn't ask for better cover. He screwed up his nerve took a deep breath and tiptoed down the gangplank. Then he moved cautiously up the dock and onto the street. The fog was so dense that he stumbled twice before recognizing that part of his problem was condensed moisture on his glasses. He stood for a moment and cleaned the lenses. He chuckled as he slipped the glasses back into place, didn't help much. The visibility was not more than two or three yards. He shivered and got the sense that he was being watched, but shook it off and shuffled up the street. He got to the hotel, hurried up the stairs to his room and tapped lightly on the door. Dobbs called from inside, "Who's there?"

"Eddie Farr."

"Well, well, Eddie Farr is it?" Dobbs said as he opened the door.

The kid heard a rustle behind him and looked over his shoulder just as Barker, Long and two of their goons shoved him into the room with guns in their hands. Tungee, Dobbs and Blakely were caught flat-footed.

The thugs didn't give the room a glance, they simply jerked the three into the hall, manhandled them down the stairs and into the darkened street.

The Sydney Ducks apparently knew the area like the back of their hand. They shoved the three along Battery and in less than five minutes they made a left turn into another street. A hundred yards from there, they stopped in front of a building.

Biggs Barker opened a latched door and the Ducks escorted their prisoners toward the center of an almost empty warehouse and quickly tied their hands behind their backs. The Ducks then searched through all their pockets looking for identification, but without success. They forced the three to sit down then they tied them with their backs against a supporting post.

Cal Long commented with an air of approval, "That ought to hold you for a while."

Biggs Barker looked at the few papers they had taken from the men's pockets and snarled, "We know you, Dobbsy and you too, Eddie Farr... Blakely." Then he circled the three and kicked Tungee's boot. "But who are you, governor?"

"Harbin, Robert Harbin," was Tungee's terse reply.

"Harbin, my arse," Biggs Barker chortled. "I wager it's more likely to be a Cahill."

Cal Long shook his head. "Never mind the guess work, the boss e'll put a finger on him right enough."

Then the Ducks moved across the dusty warehouse, entered a dimly lighted office and closed the door.

"Home away from home," Blakely said facetiously.

"What was that?" Tungee asked.

"I was here this afternoon."

"They caught you when you went searching for you cousin. Bloody shit," Dobbs said irately. "I told you to be careful."

"Get off my case, Dobbs."

"They questioned you this afternoon?" Tungee said.

"Yeah. They leaned on me pretty good and I told them about some of the voyage and what happened to Alf Talbot and the killing."

"Nothing wrong with that," Tungee told him.

"It's you they're really after, Tungee. They asked about Cahill. I said I didn't know any Cahill. They let me go and followed me. I ran to the Southern Star and waited till dark before going to the hotel. I thought I could get by 'em, but it looks like they see pretty good in the dark."

"You did the best you could," Tungee said. "They mentioned a boss. Any idea who they mean, Dobbs?"

"Not really, mate. The only ones I knew for sure that were on the top was Alf Talbot and these blokes, Barker and Long. Of course it could be Freddy Peterson, the crimp, but I doubt that."

Gene Blakely struggled against the tight rope that chafed his wrists. "We might do better trying to get loose from these ropes and get out of here. I don't think it'll be healthy for any of us if they find out that you're Tungee Cahill."

"You've got something there, kid, but let's keep our voices down."

Dobbs chuckled. "Seems to me we've been in this same fix before, gents. We got out of that jam, what say we go for a double."

Barker, Long and the third man, named Smith, were having drinks inside the warehouse office. The fourth man had gone to bring the boss in to identify the man thought to be Cahill.

"Freddy said he'd heard that Southern Star needed three seamen. Said they've been scouring the dock area since they've been in port," Cal Long drawled. "Give 'em another day and we may get an order."

Biggs Barker giggled. "Why, I believe we can supply their needs from our present stock."

Cal Long rolled himself another cigarette. "Best just count on two. If that third one is Cahill, I doubt he'll qualify as an able bodied seaman when we're finished with him." He laughed hysterically as he leaned in to light his cigarette on the lamp chimney.

"The boss told Freddy Peterson in no uncertain terms that he wants no second rising of Lazarus," Biggs Barker said cryptically. "If that fellow out there is Cahill the boss wants it done right this time."

The door to the office opened and Smith came into the dimly lit warehouse checking on the prisoners. He took a look and mumbled. "Yep, we still got company," then he turned sharply and went back into the office.

Gene Blakely had stretched his long arms as far as he could in the direction of Dobbs. And the Aussie was having some success loosening the ropes.

"What do we do when we get out of these here ties that bind, mates?" Dobbs said quietly.

Gene Blakely whispered, "Captain Spencer said we could count on him. How about heading for the Southern Star."

Tungee fumed at his own indifference. He had been thinking about it since they got inside the warehouse. How passive he had been since arriving back in San Francisco. It finally boiled over and he rebelled harshly. "No, dammit!"

I'm sick and tired of running. We get these ropes off and take over. Two can play their game. We'll tie them up and wait for their boss to show."

Dobbs said warily, "I hope you know what we're dealing with, mates. These blokes are brutal, they'll kill you for a ha penny."

"We've got to make a stand somewhere, Dobbs. So let's get out of these damned ropes and do it now," Tungee said testily. "You guys making any headway?"

"Not yet, mate."

Gene Blakely hadn't said a word, but was first to spring loose. "My left hand's free." Then he grunted. "Now, my right."

"Untie the outside ropes," Tungee muttered softly, "then get my hands loose."

"What about me, mates?"

"Don't worry, Dobbs, we're not going to leave you. But it's close to time for one of them to make another check. I'd like to take him out and get his weapon."

The kid finished his work on the outside ropes and just seconds later he had Tungee's hands free.

In a hoarse whisper, Tungee said, "Blakely take Dobbs ropes off and then get around here in my position. Take your glasses off and slouch down. I'll move over next to the office and when their man comes out, one of you call him over, tell him you want a drink of water. Anything to get his attention, I'll take it from there."

Then Tungee eased across the warehouse and picked up a good size chunk of two by four. Then he got into position and waited.

Smith came out of the office and walked toward the prisoners. He stopped, leaned forward and squinted into the darkness.

Tungee held the club with both hands and took a full swing. An immediate dull thud was heard and the Duck collapsed to the floor. Dobbs rushed over and dragged the unconscious man to the post where they quickly tied him up and stuffed a handkerchief into his mouth.

The three then eased over near the office door. Tungee motioned the others to stand aside and he banged the door open with his foot. Cal Long stared unbelieving from his position behind the desk.

"Get your hands in the air, gentlemen!" Tungee yelled.

Biggs Barker, standing to his left, fired a round and missed. The bullet lodged in the top of the doorframe.

Dobbs dove across the room and flattened the shooter.

"What the hell! How did you get out of them ropes?" Cal Long blubbered.

"Never mind that, me maties," Dobbs said jovially, "it's a trick we perfected at sea."

Dobbs gathered up the guns and they shoved the Ducks into the warehouse.

Tungee checked the street while Dobbs and Blakely tied up and secured Long and Barker to the post next to Smith.

Dobbs was posted outside while Tungee and the kid waited inside the office for the boss to show up.

Less than a half had past when Dobbs ran into the office and closed the office door behind him and signaled company was on the way. In less than a minute there was a solid rap on the door. Dobbs pulled the door open and stood behind it. Tungee and Blakely trained their weapons on the men who were about to enter.

"What the hell?" Mason Albreght blinked helplessly at what he saw.

Tungee calmly said, "Come right in, gentlemen and, Mr. Dobbs, close the door behind them please."

Mason Albreght's face paled and he gasped for breath. It was unreal, Cahill standing behind the desk. The bank president scanned the room and croaked. "What are you doing here?"

"I suppose you're looking for Barker and company," Tungee said sarcastically. "Well, we've changed all that. They decided to wait out there in the warehouse."

Mason Albreght could barley speak. "Cahill, you're not ---"

"Of course I'm not supposed to be here, am I," Tungee said reproachfully. "By all rights I'm a dead man, is that correct, Mr. Albreght?"

Mason Albreght muttered incoherently and his legs apparently turned to jelly.

Tungee made the observation. "Sit down in that chair, Mr. Albreght, before you faint and embarrass yourself. Tie him to the chair Dobbs and put the other fellow behind him."

Tungee began to pace. Albreght looked up pleadingly and as he was about to speak Tungee cut him off. "I suggest you keep your mouth shut, Mr. Albreght ... I may just lose my temper. Blakely, check on our detainees, and then go out front and stand guard. If you see a Vigilance Committee patrol, get their attention, I'd like a word with them."

He walked behind the desk and looked into Albreght's eyes. "Now I don't expect to get all the answers I'm looking for, but I'll ask a few questions. "Is your bank solvent, Mr. bank president?"

Albreght gave an affirmative nod, but didn't utter a word.

"Second question. What is the standing of my personal account?"

Sweat poured down the banker's forehead. "Why, I don't know. I don't look at customer's daily accounts. I'd have to check the books."

"Well, Mr. Albreght, when was the last time you looked at the books?"

"I don't know, but my recollection is that it was sometime ago."

"My account balance should read something over three hundred thousand dollars. Does that square with your memory?"

Albreght was lily white. "I can't remember, I don't recall."

Gene Blakely rapped on the door and immediately stuck his head inside. "Tungee, there's a fellow here says he's been following one of these men that just arrived and he wants a word with you."

Before Tungee could answer, a broad shouldered man brushed past Blakely and into the office. The man had a handlebar mustache, wore a dark suit and a wide brimmed hat. "Sorry to intrude, gentlemen, but I got a little peek through that window and when I saw you tie him to the chair, I could wait no longer."

"Who are you and which man are you talking about?" Tungee asked.

"I am Inspector Benjamin Tossi of the Sydney, Australia Police Constabulary." He took out a wallet and badge and then looked directly at Mason Albreght. "That's the man I'm looking for." Then he said decisively, "That's my quarry right enough, Mr. Henry Blair."

"That's not Henry Blair, this is Mason Albreght," Tungee said with a look that left an opening for some doubt. "I know him to be Mason Albreght, a local bank president."

"He may be president of a bank here and you may call him Albreght. But, back in Sydney he's called Henry Blair."

Tungee looked at Dobbs. "Do you know anything about this?"

"I don't know Albreght or Blair, but I do know the Duck's change their names more often than their socks."

The inspector was exasperated. "Henry here and his brother Edward have led me a merry chase. I've got murder warrants for their arrests. But it'll take time to go to court and work out an extradition hearing."

"You say you've got a murder warrant?"

"To be more precise, they are charged with three murders, all mine owners. When word got out we were on to them they struck out for England. I was eventually put on the case and they've been leading me one merry chase." He gestured toward Henry, "Caught up to this one through the mails and had him under surveillance. I followed him tonight in hopes he'd lead me to his brother."

Tungee looked at Blakely. "Has the fog cleared any?"

"It's clearing."

"Then you go and find some of the Vigilance Committee and tell them we've got some Ducks they may be interested in."

"Where do I find them, Tungee?" Blakely asked.

"Go down Battery and just past Clay you'll see their headquarters on the west side of the street."

Ben Tossi growled, "I aim to find this man's brother. Now I doubt that Henry here is going to divulge the whereabouts of his sibling. But I'll tell you something, gentlemen, there's more than one way to skin a cat."

* * *

Twenty minutes after Blakely left the warehouse he returned with Jim Garrigan a strong intelligent looking man, with bright brown eyes tucked underneath heavy eyebrows and a large forehead. Tungee and Inspector Tossi told their stories. The Vigilance Committee leader made a quick decision and announced, "We'll take 'em to my place."

— TWENTY EIGHT —

Jim Garrigan's warehouse office was filled with Vigilance Committee members and they listened in stunned silence as Tungee told his shanghai story. By the time he finished, every man in the room wanted to see Albreght hanged. But, in good conscience, they couldn't do a thing without a lot more evidence than Tungee could provide. He knew as well as they that the courts would consider the only proof he could provide as hearsay and probably not strong enough to get an indictment, much less a conviction.

Maybe they didn't have enough evidence for the courts, but Tungee felt better about his situation. He had found a new ally in Ben Tossi and he also felt good about Jim Garrigan and his people.

The committee examined Inspector Tossi's warrants and they concluded that while the documents were impressive, without extradition papers, they didn't have any authority to act on them. They did, however, add enough legal weight for them to take a vote to hold Albreght. But they also voted to set Long, Barker and the other two Duck underlings free. Tungee and Tossi both disagreed with the latter vote, but couldn't persuade them to change it.

Following that meeting, Tungee and Ben Tossi went out to breakfast. Both men realized they were on shaky legal ground, but neither of them was about to quit. As a practical matter though, Tungee was in need of cash and during their meal the Inspector let it be known that he was also short on funds. Tungee knew that the status of his bank account could make the difference, but he was still nervous about making the actual inquiry at the bank. He wiped a spot of egg off his lip and stood up at the table. "Inspector, if you'll take a short walk with me we might just solve our financial problems."

"Sounds good to me."

At precisely ten am. the Mining and Merchant Bank opened its doors for business. Tungee walked inside and moved directly to the teller's cage. Inspector Ben Tossi followed close behind and casually stood to one side.

From Tungee's recollection, the teller was the same young man who had taken his original deposit and if his memory served him right he was wearing the same suit. "Good morning," the teller enthused.

"Morning," Tungee said and then added tentatively, "I'd like to, ah, withdraw some money from my account."

"Name please."

"Robert T. Cahill."

"Of course, Mr. Cahill. How much would you like to withdraw?"

"A thousand will do, thanks."

"All right, just sign this draft for me and I'll take care of it right away."

"Excuse me, young man. While you're about it, would you give me an account balance?"

The teller nodded and walked past a glass partition where he handed Simon Estes the draft and said a few words. Estes looked toward the customer, then turned and pulled out a file, wrote down some figures and handed the paperwork back to the teller. Then the young man went inside the large safe and soon came out with money in his hands. He walked briskly to the front and counted out a thousand dollars. Nine one hundred dollar bills and five twenties,

"That's one thousand in cash, Mr. Cahill," then he pushed the paper over. "And there's your account balance, sir. I think you will find everything in order."

Tungee smiled. "Thank you." He stuffed the bills into his pocket and studied the figures on the paper. Then a wry grin played over his face as he turned to Ben Tossi. "They haven't taken a nickel out of my account." Then he shook his head and added warily, "I suppose I ought to be relieved by that, but I'm not."

They turned and walked out the front door to the street and Tungee said, "Well, Inspector we have funds and I'll bow to your experience as an investigator for direction."

Ben Tossi twirled the end of his mustache and they didn't say a word for a long moment. "Then I suggest we take a walk up to your bank president's house."

Tungee looked up alertly. "You know where he lives?"

"Of course I do, I've had him under surveillance for some time. He lives alone in a fancy two story Queen Anne style house on Nob Hill."

Tungee put his shoulder in place ready to shove the back door in when Ben Tossi produced a skeleton key. He inserted it into the keyhole, turned it and opened the door.

The small mansion's interior was impressive and it was decorated with taste. A polished oak staircase curved in a grand sweep to the second floor, French provincial furniture and red velvet wallpaper. Even so, there was emptiness about the place. No pictures on the walls and all the breakfronts and sideboards were empty. There were boxes stacked on the floor. A quick inspection revealed that several cartons were filled with paper work. Bank papers, exchange rates of various countries and their currencies.

Ben Tossi, the professional, went to work opening drawers and going through cupboards. When he finished that task he joined Tungee looking through the paperwork from the boxes. They discovered correspondence with banks in Buenos Aires, Argentina, Valparaiso, Chili, as well as New York and Boston.

Ben Tossi went up stairs to take a look at the bedrooms.

Tungee continued to inspect the boxes. When he got to the last carton and looked inside he found a large envelope. A smile spread over his face and he quickly turned to go upstairs.

Two tickets for passage on the mail packet to Panama this coming Saturday. Then they had made land arrangements across the Isthmus and first class Clipper service to Boston. In bold script at the bottom of the tickets were the passenger's names, Henry Blair and Edward Blair.

If Tungee ever had any doubt about Ben Tossi, those tickets dispelled that notion. He thought about his last conversation with Thunder Parker. The old man said the orders to kill me had come from Mason Albreght and some pretty big folks in San Francisco. How does the other brother, Edward, fit into the puzzle and where? Police? City hall? The courts?

He walked into the upstairs bedroom and handed the ticket envelope to the inspector. Ben Tossi's expression didn't change until he took a long look at the tickets. All the information began to come together, the bank correspondence they had seen downstairs and then the tickets. Tungee and Tossi both began to laugh as they looked around the room. Their timing had been crucial. A half packed valise rested on the tall oak double bed, an open footlocker and a large trunk filled with clothing.

"Yep," Tungee said tightly, "I'm not an accountant, but from what I can tell they planned to raid at least a half dozen bank accounts on Friday afternoon and sail on Saturday."

Ben Tossi wiped his brow and grinned. "We didn't get here a minute too soon."

"Well, I guess we have Luke Spencer to thank for that," Tungee said.

"Who is Luke Spencer?"

"Skipper of the Southern Star. Tungee looked at the inspector and said, "If we hadn't hooked up with him back in Charleston and if he hadn't wanted to break some speed records, I wouldn't be here."

Ben Tossi paced the room. "What's that they say about luck and talent? Well, from my experience, I expect we could use a little of both." Then he screwed up his face and said, "Tungee, my friend, I have handwriting samples on both of the Blair brothers from sources in Sydney. Now I suggest we take another look into those boxes downstairs and see if we can match up some of these handwriting samples. And one more thing, from what I've learned about the Duck's organization here in San Francisco, we need someone with an inside connection to that scurrilous group. Somebody that can help us ferret out this second brother. I can't go back to Sydney with half a loaf. We've got to clean this thing up."

* * *

"Aw, mate, what does the inspector want to talk to me about?" Dobbs said with more than a touch of insecurity.

"Now, you told me you have never been a part to murder."

"I'd swear on my mother's grave," Dobbs said as he mopped his brow, "that is if she was dead, I'd ---"

"Stop babbling, Dobbs. For God's sake, all the inspector wants to do is ask you a few questions about the Duck's organization." Tungee laughed. "He's not trying to arrest you or pin anything on you."

Dobbs took in a deep breath. "All right, mate, if you say so."

Inspector Tossi, Tungee, Dobbs and Blakely gathered in Jim Garrigan's warehouse office.

Ben Tossi looked at Dobbs and said; "I understand you were once a member of the Sydney Ducks."

Dobbs looked up sheepishly. "I'm afraid I'm guilty as charged, Inspector."

"My thinking is that you may know a thing or two about the Ducks organization," Tossi said easily, "something you might think unimportant in regards to connecting Henry Blair to his brother."

Dobbs said innocently, "I don't know. All this stuff about the Blair brothers is new to me."

"Do you know anyone inside the Duck's group that might know the upper workings of the organization?" Ben Tossi asked.

"I'd have to say that Long and Barker, the two gents the Vigilance Committee let go would be on the list," Dobbs hesitated and furrowed his brow. "And there's Freddy Peterson, of course, the main crimp in San Francisco."

Gene Blakely quietly reminded, "Captain Spencer said to call on him if we needed a hand. Maybe he could do something with the crimp."

"Good thinking, kid," Tungee said. It also gave him an idea. Something Luke Spencer had mentioned about a political connection he had in San Francisco.

Inspector Ben Tossi pursed his lips and looked into the eyes of Tungee Cahill. "We've got Jim Garrigan's word that he'll hold Henry Blair for another forty eight hours." Then he said in a less than optimistic tone,

"Of course my police authority here in California may be worthless, but I believe there are still old laws on the books regarding citizens arrests." He held up his hands and smiled. "So, gentlemen, keeping that in mind, I believe if we join forces in this investigation, we'll find a way to smoke the elusive Mr. Edward Blair out of hiding."

Gene Blakely walked out of Garrigan's warehouse and turned left on Bush. He was determined to find his cousin and from her, try and locate his family. The kid had walked a block and a half when he heard someone running up behind him. And before he had time to turn, a fist slammed into his neck just at his right shoulder. He turned and saw three men. One of them kicked him in the right knee while another ripped his spectacles off his face and as he fell to the ground, he heard his lenses being smashed into the hard dirt sidewalk. He reached out desperately trying to save his spectacles only to be met by a kick in the face. The kid drew up into a fetal position, trying to protect himself as one of the Duck's snarled. "Keep your bloody nose out of Duck business, or the next time you'll find yourself outward bound on a bloomin' ship to nowhere."

The three bullies turned and walked toward Montgomery Street. They talked as they neared the street intersection and Gene Blakely's keen ears picked up a fragment of their conversation. One of the three men said, "We've got to tell Big Bart about his brother." And that was all the kid heard before he passed out.

Two committee members returning from foot patrol along Bush Street recognized Blakely, dragged him back to the warehouse and called for a doctor.

Inspector Tossi was pacing the hall when the young man was brought in. Already frustrated by the soft approach the Vigilance Committee had taken in the questioning of the Ducks. He exploded when Blakely mumbled that he had been attacked and warned off by some of the Duck's thugs.

Tungee entered the hall and heard the inspector lash out at the situation. He laid his hand on Ben Tossi's shoulder and said softly, "Easy, Inspector."

Ben Tossi was red with fury. "That's the trouble, Mr. Cahill. Just look at what they've done to your young friend." He took Tungee's elbow and guided him into the small room where they had taken the patient. Gene Blakely's face was like raw meat, bruised and bloody."

"What the hell happened to you?" Tungee spat.

"Some of the Ducks beat him up. And the way I see it, we've been too damned easy on those fellows. Now I think it's time to take off the gloves." The inspector paced the room, shaking his head, and then he stopped abruptly. "Mr. Cahill, I'd like to borrow Mr. Dobbs for a short expedition I've got in mind."

Tungee felt a personal responsibility for young Blakely's well being and the way things were going; he hadn't done a very good job of protecting the boy. He went into Blakely's room. The kid was awake. "Didn't you say you had a cousin in San Francisco?"

The patient turned his head and grimaced. "Yeah Laura Dubek. She lives up on Taylor Street, 1650 Taylor Street, I think she runs a boardinghouse."

"Have you seen her since we got back to San Francisco?"

"No, but I started out two different times and never made it to her place." He forced a smile. "That's where I was going when they knocked me in the head."

"When's the last time you saw your cousin?"

"I don't know, Tungee. Gosh I must have been ten years old at the time. She was attractive, looked a little like Ma's family. She was married to a Frenchman. I seem to recall he was killed in an accident of some kind."

"Was your mother and your cousin close?"

"Yeah, they use to write each other."

"I'll take a walk up there and see if she knows how to contact your family. I think your folks ought to know that you're here in San Francisco." Tungee looked warmly at the boy, "Maybe a little the worse for ware, but you're alive."

The boy struggled to sit up in the bunk. "Thanks, Mr. Cahill."

"Tungee is still just fine, young fellow," then he turned and walked out the door.

Laura Dubek was casually sweeping the front porch of her boardinghouse. Her dark chestnut hair was tied up in a bun. She had sparkling blue eyes and a beautiful face that displayed a gentle maturity. She wore a frown that day, worried about the situation in San Francisco. Laura came to California in 1849 with her husband, Christian Dubek, a mining engineer who worked for a large Eastern conglomerate. He was inspecting the deep shaft of a mine north of Sutters Creek, there was an accidental cave in, Dubek and two other mineworkers were killed instantly.

Mrs. Dubek had her husband's body taken into Sacramento and buried in a quiet cemetery. She went directly from the funeral to San Francisco with her mind set on returning to Philadelphia. But during the weeks it took for her to work out travel arrangements she heard horror stories about brutal things happening to women traveling alone to or from the states.

During that period, Laura read an ad in the newspaper that intrigued her. It was the sale of a boardinghouse by a Mrs. Addie McCandless. Laura followed up on the ad and after one meeting with Mrs. McCandless, decided to buy the house on Taylor Street.

Laura Dubek stood motionless, still holding the broom and in deep thought when Tungee walked up the pathway to the house. He was almost out of breath when he reached the front steps. He cleared his throat and the lady looked in his direction. "Excuse me, mam. I'm looking for a Mrs. Dubek."

Laura said almost reluctantly, "I'm Mrs. Dubek."

Tungee seemed confused. "Maybe I'm looking for the elder, Mrs. Laura Dubek."

"I am the only Laura Dubek living here."

Tungee looked at the gorgeous lady and was almost speechless. "I'm afraid I'm a little out of breath. Steep grade leading up here."

"Takes a while to get use to these San Francisco hills," Laura Dubek said with a smile.

"Excuse me, Mam, my name is Tungee Cahill and I need to ask you a question." Then he hesitated for a long moment. "Do you have a cousin by the name of Eugene Blakely?"

"I certainly do," she stammered, "at least I did. He disappeared soon after arriving in San Francisco. My Aunt Mary and Uncle Paul had just arrived from Philadelphia when Eugene disappeared. The police looked into it and everyone believes he met with foul play. They are worried sick about the boy."

Tungee smiled. "Well then, I have good news for you and the family. He's alive."

"Thank, God." She put down her broom and asked, "Would you come up on the porch and take a seat. Please, tell me what happened to Eugene?"

Tungee walked up the steps and sat down in one of the several porch rockers.

"Would you like a cup of coffee, Mr. Cahill?"

"Yes, thanks."

Laura Dubek opened the front screen door and called, "Marie, would you please bring coffee for two to the front porch."

A half-hour later and the remains of a second cup of coffee that had grown cold, Laura Dubek shook her head in disbelief. "That terrible group called the Sydney Ducks scare me to death, Mr. Cahill."

"The Vigilance Committee people are doing what they can."

"I suppose that should be some comfort." Laura Dubek shuddered. "Please, Mr. Cahill, bring Eugene here. We'll take care of him."

— TWENTY NINE —

Freddy Peterson sat behind his desk, studying the face of Ben Tossi, and mulling over the inspector's words. The crimp pushed his green visor high up on his head and began to clean his thick glasses. "I'm afraid I can't do that, Inspector. I don't know any Edward Blair, but even if I did, I'm not sure I'd tell you. You see, I don't know what you might do if I don't talk." Then Freddy swallowed hard and his face paled. "But I know what they'd do if I did."

Ben Tossi accepted a cigar and a light from the crimp. Then he brashly put both feet on Freddy's desk and leaned back in his chair. There was fear in the eyes of Freddy Peterson and the inspector knew he was talking to a middle man in the Duck's organization. But then he decided to try one more tact.

Ben Tossi took his feet off the desk, looked the crimp in the eye and added a sinister smile. "We want Edward Blair and we're perfectly willing to pay for him. But if you continue to play your little game, let me warn you that some of my sea faring friends described a guaranteed way of getting at the truth, it's known as keel hauling, Freddy. You might do well to give that some thought."

Beads of sweat formed on the crimps brow and his face flushed as he sputtered, "Give me a bit of time to work something out."

"Now, that sounds more reasonable, but just for your information, we do have certain time constraints."

Freddy Peterson squinted through his thick lenses and took a long breath. The look on his face was that of a man who had just been granted a last minute reprieve.

The inspector turned and walked out through the pool hall, knowing the crimp would never divulge Edward Blair's identity. But maybe he had squeezed hard enough to make Freddy Peterson do something foolish.

Dobbs stood across the street from the pool hall and watched Ben Tossi walk out of the place. The inspector smiled and gave a signal to Dobbs as he walked along the quay and headed back toward Jim Garrigan's warehouse.

Tungee filled Luke Spencer in while the captain assembled his charts and prepared his log for the Southern Star's run to Canton. The skipper looked toward Tungee and puffed on his pipe. "My offer is still open, but we sail on tomorrow's outgoing tide."

Tungee frowned. "That's cutting it mighty close," then he hesitated for a long moment. "You realize we're skirting the law and you'll have to look the other way. Inspector Tossi has warrants, but no extradition papers."

"I'm aware of that," Captain Spencer said knowingly.

"All right, Captain, then you can count on Henry Blair and Inspector Tossi as definite full paying passengers. And with a little luck we'll add Edward Blair to that list." Then Tungee began to pace about the cabin. "Now that doesn't answer the full transportation problem to Australia, but it will get them out of San Francisco and that's the important thing right now."

Luke Spencer glanced out the porthole and turned back to Tungee and said, "Why don't we forget about Canton, I may have a better idea. One of the ships I have an interest in is in port. Matt Craven, skipper of the Sunrise plans to haul anchor tomorrow bound for Australia."

"Do you think he'll go along with the deal?"

"He'll manage," Luke Spencer said deliberately.

Dobbs didn't have to wait long. Less than five minutes after Ben Tossi walked away from the area Tommy Perkins hurried out of the crimp's office and led Dobbs on a merry chase. The crimp's messenger walked with a quick gate in and out of small streets and cut through alleys. It was apparently a pattern he had developed in case he was ever followed.

Dobbs had to hustle to keep his quarry in sight, he knew well what the messenger was up to, he had used the same ruse himself. He figured Perkins must be carrying an important message or he wouldn't be in such a hurry.

In less than ten minutes after leaving the crimp's office, Tommy Perkins arrived at the doorsteps of city hall.

He walked into the building, turned right down the hall and entered Harvey Prescott's office.

Dobbs backed off, not wanting to be spotted. He knew the office because he had made those same kinds of deliveries when he was a part of the Duck's organization.

Tungee went to the interrogation room provided by Jim Garrigan. The furnishings consisted of three chairs, a table in the middle of the room and a lamp and stand in one corner.

Henry Blair sat at the table, rolled a cigarette and nervously lit it. His hands were shaking all the while.

Tungee said judiciously, "I'm going to say this right up front. I know for certain that you or someone in your organization ordered my assassination."

"I didn't order anything of a kind," Henry Blair babbled.

Tungee sat down slowly in a chair and glared at the man he was questioning. "If not you, then who did?"

The banker said nothing, but he sat with a stoic look on his face and both corners of his mouth twitched.

"Now then, Mr. Henry Blair, you may have just been following orders, but I know for a fact that you personally gave the order to have me shanghaied." Tungee looked into Henry Blair's eyes. "Was it someone up the line, possibly Edward, that told you to have me shanghaied and killed?"

The mention of Edward's name brought stark terror to the eyes of Henry Blair and he clammed up.

Tungee got out of his chair and prowled the room, like a big cat and considered his options. The committee won't hang the man on his hearsay proof. And even the paperwork they found in the house didn't prove that Henry gave orders to have him killed. The Blair brothers were accomplished criminals, no doubt about that. The bank transfers wouldn't take place until the day before they left for Panama. And Tungee knew, at this point in time, he couldn't prove a thing against the Blair's. So far, it was a robbery that was still in the planning, so there was no crime. A killing that never took place and for all but a few who knew the facts, there was no crime, but there had been a crime and Tungee knew it.

Then he stopped abruptly in front of Henry Blair, pulled his Navy Colt 44 from his waistband and holding the weapon in plain sight, he opened it and removed all but one cartridge. Then he closed the weapon and walked behind his prisoner, spinning the cylinder and snapping the heavy hammer onto an empty chamber. He knew what he was doing and how far he would go. He had no intentions of killing the man in cold blood. He was no assassin, but he figured there were other ways to extract a measure of revenge and perhaps even see a little justice thrown in for good measure.

Henry Blair was terrified and retched as if he were about to vomit.

"Do you know what that little game is called, Mr. Blair?"

Sweat poured off Henry Blair's forehead. "No, I don't."

"It's called Russian roulette."

Henry Blair vomited into the spittoon.

"Now, now, Mr. Blair. You're getting a break. I've seen the game played with only one chamber empty."

"I don't like your games, Mr. Cahill."

"That's fairly evident, Mr. Blair." Tungee eased the pistol into his belt and put a piece of paper in front of the bank president. Then he handed him a pen. "Now you write what I tell you to write and I'll stop the game. It's not a confession, Mr. Blair, I simply want you to take down my words."

Tungee, Tossi and Dobbs were all in Blakely's room. The kid was bandaged and beat up, but was conscious. He told the others about the attack. Then he said, "I heard something as they walked away. 'We've got to tell Big Bart about his brother.'"

The name didn't mean a thing to anyone in the room so Tungee

231

went out to the hall and collared Jim Garrigan. "Do you know anyone in San Francisco politics named Big Bart?"

"There's a road agent called Black Bart." Then Garrigan paused and wrinkled his brow. "Um. There's a fellow named Barton McCord down at city hall. He's supposed to be the hatchet man for the Democratic Party's Harvey Prescott."

Tungee nodded. "Thank you Mr. Garrigan." He was struck by the sequences of names and events. Something Luke Spencer had said about a politician named Harvey Prescott. He finally looked toward the kid's room and said, "Mr. Garrigan I'd like to get our young friend out of the line of fire."

"What have you got in mind?"

"If two or three of your men could transport him up to 1650 Taylor Street, I'd be much obliged."

"Sure thing."

"And if you don't mind have them take a round about route and be careful that they are not followed."

"I understand, Mr. Cahill, I'll handle it myself."

*   *   *

Tungee and Ben Tossi stood in front of the warehouse talking. The Inspector continued his thought, "That doesn't give us a whole lot of time and I'm still determined to collar Edward before our departure."

"I'd like that too, Inspector, so why don't I go along with you to City Hall."

"I think not. I believe in the burglary business, one is better." Then he shot Tungee a wide grin. "Another thing, I happen to be quite good at it, if I do say so myself."

Tungee's mind drifted off to another part of their operation, but he automatically smiled an agreement with the Inspector's comments.

Ben Tossi could see that Tungee's mind was somewhere else. "Did you hear what I said?"

"Yes, yes, but I was just thinking of something. We have a problem we haven't talked about and that's getting our prisoner or prisoners on board the ship."

Ben Tossi said, "Well, we may just have to run the gauntlet."

Dobbs hurried around the corner from Battery and announced, "Gents. Got a piece of news for you. Now, you may not like it, but I went back to some of my old haunts. And while I didn't uncover a thing that might lead us to this here Edward Blair," then Dobbs grinned, "they took the bait, Inspector. The Ducks plan to keep a close watch on that ship bound for Sydney."

Ben Tossi rubbed his day old whiskers and said worriedly, "From what you just told me, Tungee that adds to our boarding problem, but it does tie up some of their men."

Tungee looked at Ben Tossi and said thoughtfully, "I'm not too keen on your idea about running the gauntlet. Why don't you go ahead and take care of that piece of business at City Hall and Dobbs, you stay here and keep an eye on our prisoner. I've got an idea that needs some work, I'll see you gentlemen later."

The streets were almost dark as Tungee rushed from the warehouse to Charlie Boone's dock.

"Tungee Cahill!" Charlie Boone enthused, "If you ain't a sight for sore eyes. I heard you was back."

"Good to be back, Charlie, glad I caught you here." Tungee said as he stopped to catch his breath.

Charlie shook his head. "Mack told me you'd been shanghaied. Damn nation, I might believe that about some folks ---"

"I'll tell you about it later, Charlie. But I'm in a helluva hurry and I need to charter your boat."

"That's my business. You need it right now?"

"No, it'll take a while, but I do want you to be on standby starting now. We should be back in port sometime tomorrow afternoon. Figure your pay for twenty four hours and then double that."

"You know somethin'," Charlie Boone squinted, "if it was anybody but you, I'd ask a whole lot of questions."

"Don't ask any. The less you know for now, the better." Then Tungee turned and ran up the quay to the Southern Star. He found Luke Spencer at the foot of the gangplank took his arm and led him toward the end of the dock. "Are you and the Sunrise still sailing on tomorrow's tide?"

"That's the idea," Luke Spencer said, "and something else, Tungee, I've got some news that might interest you."

"About what?"

"A politician we've discussed, Harvey Prescott. I just had an early supper with him and one of his associates, a big fellow named Barton McCord."

Tungee took a deep breath. "Interesting. Did they say anything we could use?"

"Not in so many words. But I was struck by Prescott's political take on things. He's apparently associated with the Ducks, but now he seems to be doing his best to distance himself from them. Says he's afraid of the Vigilance Committee. They've done too much hanging to suit him."

Tungee grinned. "Sounds like a smart fellow."

"Listen to this. During our talk at the table, I brought up the fact that I had spent some time in Sydney and this fellow McCord seemed awfully interested."

"Did he say he'd been there?"

"No, in fact he said he hadn't been there, but by the time he said that, I'd already figured he had. Another thing I detected about Barton McCord, his speech slipped in and out of at least two different accents. One was as American as apple pie. But wedged into his jargon I heard a few lapses. There were times when his speech was either London Towne Cockney or Aussie, but I don't know which."

Tungee took a deep breath and grinned. "Well, I'll be damned. Where did you have supper and when did you last see that party?"

"Ernie Maxwell's place and it hasn't been more than half an hour. They walked into the game room just as I left."

"Skipper, come with me to the chart room. I need to see what you think of an idea I've just hatched."

Inspector Tossi wearing a double-breasted suit and a derby hat walked quickly over Kearny Street toward city hall. He held a hooded lantern in his hand. When he got to the intersection of Kearny and Pacific, he looked around and then quickly walked to the back of the municipal building.

His skeleton key didn't fit the lock in the back door, but he picked the lock within a few seconds and eased into the building. He followed his light down the hallway to the third door on the left that had a sign reading Harvey Prescott. He entered the office and moved to the large file cabinet on the other side of the room. There were more than a dozen file drawers, but it took him less than ten minutes to sort through the materials and find the writing specimens he was interested in. He put those letters into his coat pocket and left the office. Then he quietly moved down the hallway, made a clean exit and walked down the back steps.

A uniformed police officer rounded the corner of the building just as Ben Tossi's foot touched the ground.

The inspector turned and fumbled with the fly of his trousers and gave the officer an embarrassed look and a cough. "Excuse me, sir. I had to relieve myself."

After a long studied look, the policeman said, "Yes, well next time you need to take a leak, we would appreciate it if you'd use the facilities around the corner."

"Sorry, sir," Ben Tossi said nervously as he buttoned his fly and quickly moved across the darkened street.

— THIRTY —

Tungee and Dobbs went to the livery stable, hitched up the team and drove over Clay Street toward the base of Nob Hill.

Tungee held the reins and called to Dobbs, "When you told the Inspector to meet us at Ernie Maxwell's Place, did he say anything?"

"Said he knew where it was and he seemed in awfully good spirits."

"All right, Dobbs, when we get to Ernie's, I want you to stand by the wagon and wait."

"Aw, mate, can't we eat first."

"That'll have to wait. Eddie Blair may be at Ernie's place right now and if it all works out we'll have to hustle him down to the warehouse where he can join his brother."

"Sounds to me like you've got it all worked out."

Tungee said, "I hope so," as they pulled into an alley near Mason Street and parked the rig. Dobbs immediately jumped down to the ground and began to pace back and forth nervously while Tungee crossed the street and went into Ernie Maxwell's place.

Tungee looked around the busy saloon and saw that Ben Tossi had already arrived and was waiting at the bar.

Ernie Maxwell came out of the restaurant and was headed for the game room when he spotted a familiar face. The congenial host went to Tungee's side and put his hand on his shoulder. "Where in hell have you been, Tungee Cahill?"

Tungee gave Ernie a long look and said, "I've been on an unexpected voyage, Ernie. In a word, shanghaied."

"Well, I'll be damned."

Tungee gestured and said, "Ernie I'd like to introduce you to Inspector Ben Tossi of the Sydney, Australia Police Constabulary."

"Good to meet you, Inspector," Ernie Maxwell said affably.

The inspector said, "Mr. Maxwell," and smiled.

Tungee spoke quietly and directly to the saloon owner. "The inspector is investigating a triple murder and in a round about way it relates to my shanghai experience."

"Good God," the saloon owner sputtered.

Then Tungee told him, "The inspector has warrants for two brothers suspected of those killings that took place back in Sydney. He's located one of the brothers, but the other one is proving a bit more difficult. We've got an idea who he is, but there are a few loose ends we need to tie up."

"Which reminds me, Tungee," an energized Ben Tossi said, "do you have that letter on you, the one we picked up at the house?"

"Yes and I also have a comparison note I watched Henry write."

"Mr. Maxwell, I wonder if we might impose on you for the use of your office." Ben Tossi said judiciously," I need to examine several documents."

"Be my guest."

The men walked into Ernie's office and the host lighted an extra lamp.

The inspector spread the material out on Ernie's desk, removed a small magnifying glass from his pocket and studied the letters he had just picked up at city hall, the samples they got from Henry's house and the one just furnished by Tungee.

Ben Tossi compared the writing in great detail and after what seemed an eternity of silence he looked up and smiled.

"Gentlemen, we've got a match. McCord is our prime suspect and if I'm not mistaken he is presently in the game room." The inspector turned to Tungee, "Do we have transportation?"

"Waiting outside."

"Then, Mr. Maxwell. Could you arrange for Mr. Barton McCord to come into the office?" he coughed, "alone, if you don't mind."

Ernie Maxwell mopped his brow. "Are you sure of your facts, Inspector?"

"I'm sure, Mr. Maxwell. But if I'm wrong, you won't be implicated." Then with a wry grin, Ben Tossi said, "And our Mr. McCord will be in line for a first class apology."

Ernie looked hard at Tungee for verification.

"That's right, Ernie. His actual name is Blair and we know his brother as Mason Albreght. They had me shanghaied and ordered my assassination."

Ernie's jaw dropped. "For your gold?"

"That's the way it looks, Ernie."

"Good God, Tungee. I'll get him, and I sure hope you fellows are right."

"You just tell him there's a gentleman in your office that has a message from his brother," Tungee said bluntly.

Henry Blair's face flushed as Tungee and Tossi escorted Edward into his cell. The brothers glared at one another, but said nothing.

The Inspector took the letters he used to match up their handwriting out of his pocket and waved them in front of the brothers. "It makes no difference whether you confess, dear boys, to being brothers. You see we've already identified the facts. Mason Albreght is Henry Blair and you, Mr. Barton McCord, you're Edward Blair. And if I recall correctly, down under, they called you Eddie B."

"You don't know what you're talking about," Edward Blair spat.

Ben Tossi smiled. "Roll up your left sleeve, Edward. I'd like to see your forearm."

"I'll do nothing of the kind," Edward Blair snapped.

"We've got ways. Now, you sit down and show me your forearm or I'll knock you down and rip your sleeve off. Take your choice."

The prisoner reluctantly rolled up his left sleeve and on the inner side of his forearm there was a bright red and blue tattoo scrawled in an archaic script. The large letters that spelled out MOTHER were inside a bed of daisies.

Ben Tossi took a small drawing from his pocket, which matched Edward's tattoo perfectly. He handed it to Tungee, just to have him verify that fact. Tungee and Tossi looked at each other and grinned satisfied they had the right men in custody.

Tungee looked toward the Inspector and said, "Wait here for one minute. Then he immediately walked down the hall and found the Citizens Committee Master at Arms and informed him that they would be taking the prisoners away and would it be all right if they used the back door. It was.

Tungee said, "Thanks," and called out to Jim Garrigan who had just entered the building. "Yo there, Mr. Garrigan."

"Mr. Cahill," and as he walked toward him asked, "any luck?"

"Yup and Tungee nodded. "Something else, it's important to us that two ships, the Southern Star and Sunrise, sail on time tomorrow. The Ducks may try and hassle the boarding process and delay their departures. I'll pay for the extra help to make sure those ships leave on time."

"That's part of our patrol duties," then he directed a dubious look toward Tungee, "but we'll put some extra men along the quay in the morning."

"I'd appreciate that, Mr. Garrigan."

Ben Tossi and Tungee gagged the brothers and handcuffed them together. The Blair's made it as difficult as possible, but by using brute force Tungee and the inspector wrestled their prisoners out the back door of the warehouse. They spotted Dobbs hunkered down near the front seat of the wagon. He gestured and pointed across the street. "There's some of the Ducks over there in the shadows."

"That figures," Tungee said as they loaded the prisoners onto the back of the wagon.

Suddenly the Ducks made their presence known as they laid down a barrage of rifle and pistol fire several feet above the wagon an obvious scare tactic since they had no intention of hitting the Blair's.

Tungee and Tossi crouched behind the tailgate and returned the Ducks fire.

Biggs Barker called to his men. "Get back to the dock and head 'em off. They'll be goin' for that Southern Star or that ship docked at the foot of Lombard that's bound for Sydney."

Dobbs popped the reins and the horses raced down Market Street, careened around the corner onto the quay and pulled up in front of

Charlie Boone's boat. Dobbs and Tossi dragged the prisoners onto the Molly B and stowed them below.

Tungee hustled the wagon away from the wharf area to the livery and called, "Mack, take care of the horses for me. See you tomorrow afternoon."

"Right enough, Mr. Cahill."

Tungee raced back to the boat and got there just as Charlie Boone cast off the last line. As soon as they cleared the dock, Tungee had the skipper steer a southerly course. There was some light fog, but to make sure their actual course could not be determined by the Ducks, they steered the Molly B in a wide circle that eventually took them to a little cove on the far side of Alcatraz Island.

Patchy ground fog hugged the low areas around the bay. Freddy Peterson rubbed his eyes just as a dull glimmer of daylight began to appear in the east. The crimp had assembled all the Ducks they could round up and positioned them in and around the buildings fronting on the quay and across from the Sunrise and extending down to the Southern Star.

Cal Long stammered. "We chased 'em up this way, they must have boarded the Sunrise."

"They ain't boarded and that's the last I'll say about it," Freddy Peterson insisted.

Two blocks away Biggs Barker had positioned his men near the Southern Star. The Ducks hassled and intimidated every passenger attempting to board the ship that was bound for Canton.

Biggs Barker said to his men, "You know who we're looking for. Anybody wearing scarves or wigs snatch 'em off and take a good look."

The search continued to the discomfort of the Chinese passengers. The thugs were patting them down and body searching both men and women. And not to miss an opportunity, the Ducks went through their bags and picked their pockets in the bargain.

A uniformed Committee patrol arrived none too soon at Filbert and Front Streets. "Leave those people alone," the patrol leader demanded.

Biggs Barker quickly realized he was out gunned and signaled his goons to back off.

The fog was beginning to break up as Tungee, Charlie Boone and Inspector Tossi watched the wharf area from the highest point on Alcatraz Island.

Tungee used a Long glass and from their position he could see every move the Ducks made. "The skipper of Sunrise is talking to Cal Long and several of his men," he reported. Then he laughed. "Was talking. Jim Garrigan just walked up and said something ... Long and his men backed off."

Charlie looked at his pocket watch and said, "Let's get out of here."

Tungee closed the long glass and they returned to the Molly B. Charlie Boone immediately stoked the fire, built up a head of steam and maneuvered his boat out of the small cove. Then he set a course just south of Point Bonita and toward the open sea.

By late morning a bright sun broke through the overcast and the harbor seemed to come alive. A steam driven tug approached the Sunrise and in a short time began to work the tall ship away from the dock. And at the same time a second tug was tying on and preparing to pull the Southern Star away from her berth. The tugs gently moved their respective ships, stern first, away from the dock and then tied onto the stem. Once they got the bows pointed west it became a routine operation for the tugs to tow the clippers toward the Golden Gate.

Captain Luke Spencer had worked it out with Matt Craven to follow his lead. And if his timing was right, the Southern Star as well as the Sunrise would be in position to ride the outgoing tide through the breakwater and into the Pacific.

At 1300 hours the Sunrise was running in a flotilla formation three hundred yards broad on the port quarter of Southern Star. They were on a two hundred and sixty-degree compass heading which would put them in position to pass one mile south of the southern most Farallon Island.

Charlie Boone had the Molly B in position and everyone on board was in a jovial mood with the exception of the brothers Blair. The prisoners were sullen and antagonistic as they huddled near the stern. Edward directed a venomous glare at his brother. Then he focused his attention on Inspector Tossi, "You've got no right to do this. You've got no extradition papers," he growled, "this is not lawful. Why, it's just bloody kidnapping, that's what it is."

Ben Tossi winked at Tungee and laughed uproariously. "Sounds like the pot calling the kettle black."

"You think you're dealing with lightweights, don't you, Inspector?" Edward glared at Ben Tossi. "Well, you'll see we've still got muscle back in Sydney Towne."

"Keep talking, Mr. Blair, it'll be good for you to get it off your chest," Ben Tossi told him.

"Inspector, it sounds to me like you are in for a difficult crossing." Tungee commented with a note of satire in his voice, "We could feed them to the sharks and be done with it. Same execution order they gave for me." Then he directed a piercing look at Henry and Edward. "Wasn't that the plan gentlemen?"

"It's not true," Henry Blair whined, "I never gave any such order."

"Shut up, you sniveling idiot," Edward Blair blurted.

"Good God, Tungee," Ben Tossi shook his head and said sadly, "what ever happened to brotherly love." Then he laughed. "Can't wait to see these two go at each other inside the court room. But that will be just part of the fun." Then the inspector said in a cold cynical tone, "The good part comes when you two do your dance at the end of a rope."

"Sail ho," Charlie Boone called as he took the long glass down and squinted toward the east. "Hoist the signal flag, Tungee."

"Aye, Skipper," Tungee said as he reached into a locker, selected the green pennant and ran it up the mast.

The Sunrise approached from the leeward side and the Southern Star the windward. And fifteen minutes after contact was made the two clipper ships had pulled their canvas and stood almost still in the afternoon sun.

Charlie Boone pushed the throttle forward and eased the Molly B to port and in the direction of Sunrise.

Tungee called above the noise of the steam engine. "Sorry about your luggage, Inspector Tossi. Be glad to ship it down to you if you'll tell me where you were staying."

"Windsor Hotel."

"Manager's a friend of mine. I'll send it down on the next ship bound for Sydney."

"Send it C.O.D., Tungee, the state will pick up the tab."

"It'll be prepaid, Inspector. Believe me, I owe you that much. Something else, I'll see if Jim Garrigan and some of his boys will go with me up to take a longer look at Henry's paperwork at the house. There may be some evidence you might use for your prosecution."

"We'll appreciate that, Mr. Cahill."

Henry and Edward Blair were steely eyed, but silent on the current subject.

Charlie Boone steered the Molly B along side the Sunrise and Dobbs threw a line from the bow to the deck of the clipper.

The Blair's were none too happy as they made their way up the rope ladder, but climb they did. Inspector Ben Tossi followed his prisoners onto the deck and the boatswain tossed the line back to Dobbs. The separation of the two vessels was almost immediate.

Captain Matt Craven called out orders to prepare to make sail. "Set the jibs, stays and main sails and brace for close haul sailing on the port tack."

Charlie Boone put the Molly B into a wide sweeping half circle to starboard beginning at Sunrise and ending near the stern of the Southern Star. A kind of thank you gesture and salute to the captains who were both mentally preparing for their long voyages across the Pacific.

Luke Spencer stood on the bridge of Southern Star and bellowed to his crew. "Shape up, men and prepare to make sail."

As the Molly B neared the Southern Star, Tungee noticed the Chinese passengers lined up along the rail, smiling, waving and some light applause could be heard from those sedate folks. He mused at his own assumption. Those passengers likely assumed the three men tat had just boarded the Sunrise had somehow found a way to catch up to the clipper they had apparently missed at the San Francisco dock. Of course they had no way of knowing that two of those men were destined for the gallows.

After a round of congratulations on their successful rendezvous, Charlie took hold of the wheel and pointed the bow of the Molly B toward San Francisco.

Tungee and Dobbs had just settled into seats near the prow. Dobbs leaned back, pulled his cap down over his eyes and relaxed. Tungee looked up at the white wispy clouds and could almost hear Mama Sue, 'Don't forget to give thanks to your Father in Heaven.' And he said a short silent prayer. Thank you, Lord. The nightmare is over.

As he looked past the whitecaps toward San Francisco, a fuzzy image began to form in his mind. He recalled the day he was shanghaied and watched the little tug Juniper bobbing her way toward the Golden Gate. He had seen his freedom slipping away over the horizon. And as he thought about that moment, he realized that at that point in his life, he had not know the true meaning of freedom. He would learn that later from an ex slave and a king called Kumi.

— THIRTY ONE —

The Molly B was passing Point Lobos and nearing the Golden Gate when Dobbs rose up from his seat and stretched. "What have you got in mind for the afternoon, mate?"

Tungee thought for a moment and began to tick off his plans. "Pick up the team at Mack's Livery, then stop by Jim Garrigan's warehouse, borrow a couple of men to ride shotgun and —"

"Ride shotgun! What for, mate?"

"The Ducks are still out there, Dobbs. Their heads have been chopped off, but they don't know it yet." Then Tungee said reflectively, "If I recall, you told me how deadly Biggs Barker and Cal Long could be. It'll take a day or two to get the word out that their bosses are on their way to Australia. That's when I expect them to back off. They'll look around and realize what they're stuck with -- a bunch of petty thieves and pickpockets."

Dobbs drew a deep breath. "I suppose you're right. Now, you were announcing our routine for this P.M."

"Yeah, right. We pick up our stuff from the hotels and check out." Then he turned to Dobbs. "Throw the kid's things in with yours and bring them along. Then we stop by our lawyer's office and sign a partnership agreement."

"Oh, mate. We don't need to sign no papers between you and me. A hand shake will do."

"We'll do both, Dobbs, and after the lawyer's office we go to the

Windsor Hotel where I plan to arrange for a suite of rooms and also take care of Inspector Tossi's luggage."

From there we go to Nob Hill and pack up Henry Blair's paperwork. Then we look in on Gene Blakely and see if he'll be able to travel. If he's well enough I suggest we plan to leave for the gold fields tomorrow morning."

"Ain't that rushing it a bit, mate. Jees, I'm almost out of breath just trying to keep up with your announcements of this afternoons schedule."

"Well, you'll have to catch your breath on the wagon. We've got mining business to take care of. We need to file new papers on the old claims reflecting our partnership. And that means we should be in Marysville as soon as possible."

"Guess I was thinkin' of sleepin' in tomorrow." Then with a mischievous grin, Dobbs said, "But I suppose you're right. And one other thought occurred to me."

"What's that, Dobbs?"

"Business or no, we need to get Studs Blakely out of town. We don't really need the competition, do we, mate?"

It was sundown when Tungee tossed the last box of Henry Blair's papers onto the wagon and climbed into the seat next to Dobbs. The men riding shotgun crouched in the back of the wagon.

"Get a move on, Dobbs," Tungee called, "make a right into Green and then a left on Taylor."

Tungee jumped down from the wagon just as the horses came to a halt. He strode into the walk and went up the steps two at a time. Before he had a chance to knock, Laura Dubek opened the door, smiled and stepped onto the porch. "Mr. Cahill."

He was seldom at a loss for words, but the lady's personality was absolutely disarming. "Mam. Ah. I. That is, I stopped by to see if Blakely, that is if Eugene will be ready to travel tomorrow morning?"

"He may be, but I believe another day of rest would help."

"Well, mam. We've got two problems. One, we need to get to Marysville and settle some claim business and the other is there are still some fellows out there that are trying to gun us down."

"Some of the Ducks?"

Yes, mam." Tungee looked at the lady and smiled. "That gang is just about out of business, but a few of them don't know it yet."

Laura looked into Tungee's soft brown eyes and saw someone she could trust. "He'll be ready to go in the morning." Then the corners of her lips curled up, and she spoke softly. "Eugene told me some of his experiences. He said he owes his life to you."

Tungee was embarrassed by the praise. "I appreciate the boys confidence, but I'm not sure it's deserved." He tipped his hat. "See you bright and early in the morning, mam."

"I'll be looking forward to that, Mr. Cahill," Laura Dubek said as she tilted her head and flashed a coquettish smile.

Mid afternoon on the third day out of San Francisco, Tungee, Dobbs and young Blakely pulled into Placerville, California. They asked around the Tent City and soon determined that Gene Blakely's family was working a claim three miles out on the road to Marysville. They drove out and found the Blakely's working their claim. And from the reception the boy got it was obvious the family had given up all hope of ever finding their son.

Tungee and Dobbs spent several hours talking to the Blakely's before they continued on to Marysville with the promise that they would come back for a longer visit before returning to San Francisco.

The town of Marysville was not much to look at, but it did afford a decent hotel for the night. The next morning after breakfast they went directly to the recorders office. Tungee made changes on eight existing claims that were in his and Davy's names. He changed them to the Cahill and Dobbs partnership and paid new filing fees. When the paperwork was finished they hurried out of the office and took an old mining road to the southwest and headed out to locate the first stash. During that ride Tungee talked about his experience in the gold fields. "During those years we worked long hard hours and at one time or another we had a score of claims, half of which were dry holes." Then he laughed, "But even those worthless claims were important because when salted properly they kept claim jumpers busy and away from our productive mines."

"What do you mean by salted, mate?"

"You'd scatter a few small nuggets around, just enough to keep them busy for a while."

"I see."

"We worked hard and some days up to twenty hours. And at one time we had three mines working full crews. Eventually though, it became difficult for us to hide our wealth and my brother Davy and I began to argue about how much success was enough. Davy wanted to back off, get some rest and have some fun. Well a favorable time came in the spring of 1851. There wasn't much snow the winter before and the creek beds dried up early. So we passed the word to our miners that the last assay was no good, the vein was running out and the mine would have to shut down. The men took layoff with a so-be-it-attitude, picked up their pay and drifted off to Sacramento."

"And that's when you fellows headed for San Francisco," Dobbs said.

"No. Davy wanted to do just that, but I guess I was a little more ambitious and thought it wasn't quite time to cash it in. I argued that we should open up the rich vein at Lost Mountain, work it ourselves until mid November and celebrate Thanksgiving in San Francisco. Well, beginning that spring I argued badgered and prodded my brother to do it my way. And he grudgingly went along until the middle of August when he finally gave me an ultimatum. 'I quit, T,' Davy declared. 'Dammit I'm dog tired.' Well I was tired to, but didn't want to quit. We stood toe-to-toe and glared at one another. I guess we were both too tired to fight or even make a good case for an argument. Then after a long minute we both began to laugh like a couple of fools. Once we stopped laughing we had to figure a way to secure our gold. Not many folks trusted the local banks, so we took two large stashes into the mountains and buried them. Then we sealed off the rich vein at Lost Mountain, covered the entrance, blended it into the terrain and headed back toward civilization."

"And that's when you ran into the ambush."

"Yeah, that's right, Dobbs."

Tungee located the general area he was looking for, marked it off and took two shovels out of the wagon.

About an hour later and with sweat pouring down his back, Dobbs grumbled. "I knew I was bein' lulled into thinkin' the easy life was at hand."

"Quit bellyaching, Dobbs. You'll survive."

Then Tungee began poking around an area Dobbs had just given up on and struck the tip of a wooden crate. It took them less than half an hour to haul the boxes up to ground level where they removed the top off the first crate. Then Tungee opened the goatskin bags and Dobbs eyes bulged. "Oh, mate. This is like a bloomin' fairy tale, it is. And this here gold is legitimate, right, mate."

"It sure is."

"The sole property of Cahill and Dobbs?"

Tungee grinned. "Yep."

The next morning they located the second stash and immediately drove back and deposited half the gold in the Bank of Marysville and took the other half to Sacramento for deposit there. Tungee had learned his lesson in San Francisco and decided that in the future he would never rely solely on one bank.

Following their banking business the partners walked out to the street and boarded the rig. Tungee rifled through the paperwork and advised. "Today's deposit was a hundred and three thousand dollars." Then he grinned and slapped Dobbs on the back. "That makes our total bank deposits add up to almost a half million dollars and your share of that is nearly one hundred thousand."

"Good Lord, Tungee," Dobbs wailed in utter disbelief. "You know what I'd like to do. I'd like to send me mum enough to buy that house she's always wanted. Could I do that?"

"Of course you can, it's your money."

They rented the best hotel rooms available in Sacramento and for the next week they lived the good life, as far as that went in mining country. Their days were spent tromping around town looking for a mining company they could engage to open up and mine their claims. It took almost a week of searching before they found a company they were satisfied with. Then after getting a nod from their bank, Tungee and Dobbs decided to go with the Rialto Mining Company.

Company engineers took random samples for assay out of all eight claims. And Tungee's original assessment had been correct, three of the claims looked like good producers. The Lost Mountain mine southwest of Marysville could turn out to be one of the best claims in California.

During contract negotiations, Tungee demanded and won the right to have an on site liaison man of his own choosing.

The sign read "Placerville 10 miles. Tungee suddenly had the urge to get back to San Francisco and he didn't want to admit the real reason, even to himself.

"You got a helluva serious look on your face, partner," Dobbs chided.

"Oh. I was just thinking about getting back to San Francisco."

Dobbs laughed. "San Francisco, my foot. Odds are you got Cousin Laura on your mind."

Tungee's face flushed. "I'm afraid you guessed it, partner."

"It was easy, I saw you two on the porch, lookin' at each other, the day we left for Placerville."

Tungee just smiled and nodded.

A short time later when they neared the Blakely's campsite, Dobbs asked, "Just what does a liaison man do?"

"He'll be our go-between. Keep an eye on the mining company for us."

"You mean a spy?"

"No. He'll be out in the open; the company will know he's our representative. He'll take his own ore samples and keep books on production." Tungee turned to Dobbs and said, "We didn't spend much time with the family, but what did you think of Mr. Blakely?"

Dobbs laughed, "He seemed more like a professor to me than a prospector."

"That's the way he struck me too." Then Tungee looked at Dobbs and said, "Think Mr. Blakely could do that liaison job for us."

Dobbs declared. "Well, I expect if you could take the kid as a chip off the old block, we've likely got our man."

Vigilance Committee Headquarters was their first stop in San Francisco.

Jim Garrigan stuck his hand out and enthused, "Tungee Cahill and Mr. Dobbs, good to see you fellows back in town."

"Good to be back."

Garrigan moved to his desk and sat down, gesturing the others to take a seat. "We're winning the war."

"With the Ducks?" Tungee asked neutrally.

"Yeah. We put the fear of God into Biggs Barker and Cal Long."

"Oh, did you now," Dobbs said dubiously."

"Deporting the Blair brothers turned the trick." Then a cynical smile came over Jim Garrigan's face. "And we added an old fashioned method to finish it off."

"What was that?" Tungee asked.

"Took them down to the dock, showed them the gallows and gave them an ultimatum." Then Garrigan said soberly, "Live by the law or we'll hang you right here. Now you take a long look. We'll play it any way you like."

"What did they say?" Tungee drawled.

"Nothin'. They both swallowed kinda hard and looked up at the noose."

"And you think they got the message," said Tungee.

"They got it, in spades. Less than two week after we had that little talk Biggs Barker, Cal Long and a flock of the others bought passage and shipped out to Sydney."

Tungee stood, reached across the desk and shook Jim Garrigan's hand.

*   *   *

Dobbs checked in at the Kinsey House and Tungee moved to his suite at the Windsor Hotel. He drove the rig to the livery and then walked to the post office. There he picked up three letters, one from his Uncle Mitchell another from Morgan Stern and the third was an unexpected letter from Gideon Foster. His uncle acknowledged the telegram and said he had looked into the property ownership and deeds of the river property near Hawkinsville. And from what he could tell, the person who bought that property at the tax sale still owned the place, but his information was sketchy. Tungee's stomach knotted up when he considered the possibility that the same person who murdered his mother might live on their old property. Damn, I hate that.

Morgan Stern mentioned to be sure and call on his old friend, Eric Grishom. 'And tell me about that shanghai thing.'

Gideon Foster told Tungee that he had decided to try and take some kind of court action that might tie Lindsay Arthur Griffin and his company to the trade. The captain said he wasn't sure how to proceed and he was presently looking around for legal advice. After reading Foster's letter for the third time he muttered, "Good -- it's about time he showed some backbone."

Tungee mopped the sweat off his brow as he neared Laura's house, not because of the uphill walk, his mind was on something else. He wanted to see Laura and was excited at the prospect of seeing her. He had thought about her and even dreamed about her while he was away. But he didn't know what to expect from a relationship, even if the lady was amenable. I don't know if I'm capable of a long-term relationship. Never had a steady girl in my life, he mused. Lots of one night stands in ports all over the world, but never a steady. Then he stopped for a moment to catch his breath and thought heck I don't have time for a long-term relationship anyway. Something else, Dobbs and I will likely be going back to Boston for the trial. And then I've got to look into the property situation in Georgia. But I guess I could at least ask her to go with me to the theater and it'll give me a good reason to wear one of my new suits. Then he was suddenly struck by another thought. If Dobbs recognized what I was thinking on the porch the other day, then Laura must have too.

Without realizing it, he had knocked on the door and was suddenly looking into the smiling face of Laura Dubek. She held the door open.

He hesitated a long moment, then stammered. "Ah, Mam. Mrs. Dubek. Laura. I ah, thought you ought to know about Eugene's reunion with his folks."

"Why don't you come on into the parlor and tell me about your trip," Laura Dubek said as she did a slight curtsy and took his arm. "Coffee or tea, Mr. Cahill?"

"Tungee, mam. And tea will do just fine."

— THIRTY TWO —

Tungee moved into his five-room suite atop the Windsor Hotel and immediately set up an office in the alcove just off the living room. His plan was to work on an investment strategy that would diversify his gold holdings. He sent Dobbs back to Marysville to take a look at their mining operation. Then on his way back he would stop by Sacramento and take a look at a parcel of land.

While Dobbs was away Tungee got busy and searched the San Francisco waterfront for available open land and Market Street for commercial property. As soon as he got a handle on the real estate situation, he took time off and stopped by Laura's boarding house to say hello. While he was there he asked if she would give him some pointers on interior decoration. He told her that Bob Sloan's people had done a good job on his suite, but he wanted the place to look a little more like home and not so much like a hotel. During those discussions that lasted through several cups of tea the subject of theater came up. Tungee told her that he had read a lot of Shakespeare, but had never seen a play. Laura was stunned that this man of the world had never been to the theater. She grew up in Philadelphia and had gone to plays all of her life. It was probably her enthusiasm for the theater that gave Tungee the courage to ask her out. A touring company was in town doing a series of plays and Hamlet was among them. He said he was familiar with Hamlet and that he would like to see the play. Would she be interested in going along? Laura was delighted and immediately accepted his invitation.

As it turned out, the touring company was a second rate outfit and their production of Hamlet was not very good, but their evening out was. They capped their first night off by having a late supper at Ernie Maxwell's place. Then once the ice was broken they began seeing each other almost every night.

Dobbs returned from gold country with glowing news. The first monthly mining reports surpassed all expectations and he got all the information they needed on the Sacramento land deal.

Tungee was so pleased with the good news and turn of events he figured it called for a celebration. Maybe it was a good time to invite his friends to his new place for dinner.

Chatter and laughter filled the living room with a party atmosphere. A fine crystal chandelier hung from a vaulted ceiling, two large leather couches, a grand fireplace and a black marble mantle. Tables and chairs were all in the French provincial style. There was a click of china and the rattle of silver as the waiters cleared the dining room table. Ernie Maxwell's chef had prepared a delicious four-course dinner and the saloon owner also provided some of his best champagne for the party.

Tungee and Laura stood at a large bay window just off the living room looking into a dull darkness that was broken only by a few city lights, several ships in the harbor and a scattering of stars.

Laura wore a black velvet ball gown with an open collar and diamond necklace. Her hair fell in loose curls past her shoulders. Tungee held her close and looked around the room at his friends chatting and enjoying themselves. Charlie Boone had had a few drinks and was talking loud. He was explaining his new idea for a fishing fleet and how he was going to augment that with charter boats for excursions and sports fishing. Bob Sloan, Willy Hurtz, Eric Grishom and Ernie Maxwell listened to Charlie's plans. Their wives, Sally, Olga, Mary and Harriet stood near the fireplace mantle and chatted.

Everett Dobbs was telling about the MFC crew's debauchery at St. Katharine Island. His audience, Jim Garrigan and three Vigilance Committee members doubled over with laughter.

Tungee smiled, turned to Laura and said easily, "I must be about the luckiest man in San Francisco. I'm standing beside the most beautiful woman in the world." Then he looked into the darkness and shook his head. "Less than a year ago and only a few blocks from here, I was shanghaied and taken into what I can only describe as one hellish nightmare."

Laura kissed him on the cheek, smiled, stood back and took his hand. "Now that you've brought up the subject, I think this may be a good time to tell them."

"Tell them what?"

"About the voyage, darling. Why the ladies have been hinting all evening that they wanted to hear the story." She squeezed his hand and escorted him to the center of the room. "Mr. Dobbs, come over here please. Now we want you two to tell us what happened on that awful ship after you were shanghaied."

Tungee and Dobbs obliged and spent a good part of the evening recounting the details of the voyage. As the events of the story unfolded Tungee was reminded of the tragedy of Kumi and his people, and the effect it had on his friend Jeff Randolph. 'I got my papers and ran,' he said, 'but it caught up with me the other night when I saw those brave folks stand up to slavery like they did. I saw myself running all those years and I felt like a coward.' Tungee winced at his own thoughts, aware that, like Jeff, he had done some running too.

Tungee and Dobbs finished their story and answered a number of questions. Then after several minutes of reflection, a party atmosphere returned to the room. Tungee and Laura mingled among the guests for a long while before they wandered into the shadows of the bay window.

Laura noticed a frown on Tungee's face. "What's the matter, darling? Tired?"

"Maybe a little, but I've got a feeling that some folks in this room didn't take the tragedy at St. Simons Island seriously." Then he shook his head and furrowed his brow. "They didn't seem to care what happened to Kumi and his people."

"Darling, I sensed that some were embarrassed and others were just indifferent, after all slavery is an issue that has the whole country divided."

"I guess you're right. And there are two sides to the argument, but damn I hate the idea of slavery."

The clock on the mantle struck one just as the last of the guests were leaving. Tungee stood at the door and watched Dobbs and Charlie Boone as they made their way down the hall.

"You're sure she'll be open when we get there?" Dobbs asked in a coarse whisper.

"You can count on it," Charlie Boone slurred as they staggered amiably toward the stairs.

Tungee grinned and figured they were on their way to Belle Mundy's place. Then he closed the door and turned into an empty living room. He put a small log on the fire just to keep the chill out of the air. Then he removed his dinner jacket and tie, tossed them onto a chair and walked down the hallway to the master bedroom.

The room was almost dark until the bathroom door opened and Laura came out wearing a beautiful fawn colored nightgown. Must be from Paris, he thought. It was short and the low lamp light from the bathroom filtered through the sheer garment showing off her exquisite figure.

"Maybe you should have asked Charlie and Dobbs to stay, they were awfully drunk," Laura suggested as she moved into Tungee's arms.

"I have an idea they've got other plans--" His words trailed off as they embraced into a passionate kiss. Moment's later Laura fumbled with the buttons on his shirt and while he finished undressing Laura threw off her nightgown and they both stood naked. It was the first time he had seen her voluptuous body. She had firm sensuous breasts, a narrow waist and long beautiful legs. They held each other close as he combed his fingers through her hair and felt the light curls that was as soft as spun silk. Following another long passionate kiss they moved onto the bed. They fondled and explored each other's bodies both filled with longing and desire. Soon Tungee rose up onto his elbow lowered his head and nibbled her firm breasts. She stroked his hair and moments later their bodies yielded to a natural impulse and blended into perfect harmony and lustful pleasure. Tungee was captivated by Laura's wild sensual moves as their passions ebbed and flowed like a storm that would break over the horizon, move in, unleash its fury and pass on leaving in it's wake a sudden stillness. Then there came an eventual calm and they both relaxed onto their pillows.

They snuggled close and Tungee chuckled softly.

"What was that, darling?"

"Aw, I was worried earlier about our first time."

"Worried about what?"

"Well," then he hesitated, too embarrassed to say. "I guess it had to do with your experience and being married and all. And to a Frenchman to boot."

Laura whispered softly into his ear. "Not to worry darling -- I have never in my life been so fulfilled." Then she closed her eyes and murmured, "I love you Tungee Cahill."

They were both happily exhausted and soon drifted off into a deep sleep.

Tungee woke up before dawn, rolled over and kissed Laura on the cheek. Then he slid out of bed, put on a robe and walked into the living room. Hot embers remained in the fireplace and he added a log. Then he sat on the couch and as the fire began to take hold, memories of the past filled the room. And while he had never believed in ghosts, he somehow sensed the presence of Mama and Papa and Davy. He sat still racked with conflicting emotions and he thought about the miserable treatment his Creek Indian ancestors got at the hands of white settlers. Memories flooded the room. Papas horse being led up the hill and into the yard with their father's body draped over the saddle. Killed in West Georgia as he fought to defend Creek Indians rights. Tungee had relived the day of Mama Sue's murder a thousand times. That same day a terrified thirteen-year-old and his brother rode away from their home and went to sea. Then as the years passed the dream of running had mixed with a sense of guilt. And that guilt had loomed even larger since the day Davy died in the ambush. But that morning it all seemed different. The faces were all there Mama, Papa and Davy and they were all smiling. And when Tungee smiled back and gave a salute to his father that sense of guilt suddenly disappeared.

He woke up with a start. Then rubbed his eyes and looked sleepily around the room. He shuddered as he recalled parts of the dream. The fire had burned itself out and crimson streaks of the morning light began to filter into the room. He took a deep breath and stretched, stood up and crossed to the window. Then he looked out past the Golden Gate and watched the dawn spread over the Pacific. Then as his earlier thoughts dimmed and reality came back, he wondered if Laura was still asleep. Moments later his answer came when he smelled the coffee and heard bacon sizzling in the pan. He gazed into the distance and murmured softly, "No fog. Looks like it's going to be another fine day."

— EPILOGUE —

Tungee, Laura and Dobbs departed San Francisco July 7, 852 and traveled by way of Panama to Laura's home town, Philadelphia.

Robert T. Cahill and Laura Ellington Dubek were married in the Arch Street Methodist Church on September 4th and Everett Dobbs was Tungee's best man.

The newlyweds honeymooned at Saratoga Springs, New York. They later joined Dobbs in Boston the first week in October.

Gideon Foster's charges against the L.A.G. Spice and Tea Company for slave trading were heard in the U.S. District Court in Boston. The witnesses were deposed at a long drawn out hearing. But since there was no contraband brought in as evidence the court, using old precedent law with its strict rules failed to indict Lindsay Arthur Griffin on the slave trading charges. However, lawyers for the insurance cartel paid close attention during the hearing. Then using the earlier evidence and depositions, they pressed insurance fraud charges and won their case. The L.A.G. Company was then forced to return the fraudulent claim monies, plus penalty and court fines. Costs of the fraud trial and adverse publicity put Lindsay Arthur Griffin out of the shipping business.

Dobbs returned to California at the end of the trial to look after the mining business while Tungee and Laura sailed to Savannah. They traveled by coach to Augusta, Georgia for a visit with their Uncle Mitchell Cahill. The uncle joined them and they all traveled to Pulaski

County only to discover that the man who had bought the Cahill river property in 1837 was dead and other members of his family had abandoned the place. Tungee and Laura bought the land for taxes. Tungee located the graves of his parents and had headstones carved for Robert T. and Susanna Cahill. Then they landscaped the area and fenced in a small cemetery, overlooking the river.

Tungee asked questions regarding the death of his mother, but got no satisfactory answers. He determined that if the deceased property owner was not his mother's killer, he was likely the last person who could have shed any light on the subject. It was with great reluctance that he gave up on the idea of bringing her killer to justice. But in factual analysis, he decided that sixteen years after the murder took place was probably too late to pick up the threads of an investigation.

Tungee and Laura returned to San Francisco where Dobbs reported that all three mines were producing well.

Ben Tossi wrote and said the Blair Brothers had their day in court. They were found guilty and hanged the day after the verdict.

The Cahill and Dobbs Company gave Eugene Blakely its first college scholarship. He attended and graduated The College and Academy of Philadelphia. Young Blakely returned to San Francisco where he worked for and eventually became general manager of the mining division of Cahill and Dobbs.

Jeff Randolph took care of his family obligations in Virginia and returned to San Francisco in 1857. He was welcomed into the company and worked with Eugene Blakely in the mining division.

*   *   *

On Thanksgiving Day of 1859, Cahill and Dobbs gave their annual company party to honor all their employees, a traditional turkey and dressing affair at Ernie Maxwell's.

During a lull in the conversation, a large red faced man at a nearby table tapped his fork on a crystal wine goblet to get everyone's attention. The man declared in a voice that could carry to the cheap seats in a theater balcony.

"On my last trip to Savannah I heard a tragic and most disturbing story about an event that took place off the Georgia Coast. Saint Simons

Island, to be exact. It seems there was a group of Africans who were being sold into slavery. But rather than become slaves, they drowned themselves." There was a hush in the room as the man mopped his brow. "It's a story they tell all the time down in the islands off the Georgia coast and they call it "The Legend of Ebo Landing."

Tungee squeezed Laura's hand and looked around the table and into the faces of Jeff, Dobbs and Blakely. And after a somber moment of reflection they all held up their glasses as Tungee led the toast, "The king is dead. Long live the king."

Printed in the United States
By Bookmasters